the gravity

of missing

things

the gravity

of missing

things

marisa urgo

Entangled Publishing, LLC
10940 S Parker Road
Suite 327
Parker, CO 80134
rights@entangledpublishing.com

Entangled Teen is an imprint of Entangled Publishing, LLC.

Visit our website at www.entangledpublishing.com.

Edited by Jen Bouvier
Cover design by Elizabeth Turner Stokes
Cover images by
Maria Okolnichnikova/Shutterstock
Interior design by Toni Kerr

ISBN 978-1-64937-217-8
Ebook ISBN 978-1-64937-231-4

Manufactured in the United States of America
First Edition June 2022

10 9 8 7 6 5 4 3 2 1

*To my Grandma Nina, who would've shown this
book to everyone at Dunkin' Donuts
And my Grandma Annamarie, who was so proud.
I love them very much.*

At Entangled, we want our readers to be well-informed. If you would like to know if this book contains any elements that might be of concern for you, please check the back of the book for details.

CHAPTER ONE

DAY ZERO

Everything ends. I knew that, but it didn't make it easier. I clutched the dark curtain and poked my head out ever so slightly. If you could see the audience, they could see you, which was like, totally illegal in theater. You got thrown in stage-crew jail if that happened. But it was the last five minutes of the fall play, my last play ever. Okay, maybe not ever, but at least in high school.

My family sat in the middle row, center. My older sister, Savannah, thumbed through the pamphlet. Looking for my name, maybe. Next to her, my dad's eyes darted around the set, no doubt taking in the designs I'd made. It had taken me hours to paint the grand staircase they wanted for the backdrop, but I got to use fancy acrylic paint, which costs way more than what I earn working at the local pickle store after school. Yes, we have a local pickle store. Don't ask. And my mom—

Wait.

Where was Mom?

The seat next to Dad was empty.

Maybe they weren't sitting together. That was our new normal, after all.

Either way, she better get back soon. I didn't want her to miss when I took a bow. All our hard work had paid off. I wouldn't be up here without her.

"Violet?"

I whipped around to find Mr. Tariq, our director, peering at me curiously. His kind, dark-brown eyes twinkled with the ghost light behind us. He was a soft-spoken short guy and my favorite teacher here at Wakefield High.

I snatched the curtain shut and leapt back. "I'm sorry! I just wanted to see the audience react and—"

"No, no, it's fine," he said kindly. "I wanted to take a moment to personally compliment you on your work. The set is wonderful. This is something you like to do?"

"Um, yeah." By that, I meant that I'd already designed alternative set designs for *Rent*, *Wicked*, *Hamilton*, and my other favorite musicals, and they sat in frames on my bookshelf next to my prized space-shuttle replicas. Science and art were equally fun in my weirdo world.

But what I really wanted to do? Sometimes I imagined myself out there, actually on the stage under the warm lights, making people laugh or cry. Telling stories. My singing voice was awful yet enthusiastic, but I thought, deep down, I could act.

But I guessed I could do that from behind the curtain. That was my safe place.

"Great, because I'd like you to work with the set designer for the spring musical," he said. "Draw up some ideas, and we'll present them to her at the meeting. Okay?"

Okay? *Okay?* More than okay. More like, my heart

threatened to leap out of my mouth and I would've screamed with joy had we not been in the quiet haven that was backstage.

"Thank you so much, Mr. Tariq," I whispered. Then I couldn't help it—I flung my arms around him. "I already have a few sketches I made up once you announced the show. I did the math, and with a stage twenty-nine feet across, we could have a rotating piece in the middle. If it spins at a perfect 180 degrees, then—"

He chuckled and let go of me. "Violet, that's wonderful, but you're about to miss your special bow. Go!" Mr. Tariq gave me a light shove, and I walked to the middle of the stage to meet my fellow crew members.

Mom still hadn't come back yet. My pulse sped.

Could the bathroom lines really be that long?

She was going to flip. Mom had helped me measure the stage a few weeks ago, late at night after practice had ended. At first I'd been annoyed because I'd wanted to do it myself, but being a pilot, her measurements were way more precise.

"I'm so proud of you. You've put so much time into this." Mom had flipped her light-blond hair from her face. The same short pixie cut she'd had my whole life.

"Thanks."

"You've got such a gift, Violet," she'd said. "Promise me you'll use it."

"Of course."

After the play was over, I took my tech-crew bow with a big smile on my face, warm from the stage lights. Or from the excitement of it all.

By then, the audience was on its feet. I looked into the crowd to find my own family—parents, siblings, and friends clapped. An empty gap like the Grand Canyon sat between Savannah and the strangers two seats away from her. Not only was Mom missing, but Dad had left too.

He'd missed my bow.

A dark pit opened in my chest, and a wave of anxiety hit me like a tsunami.

I'd been at the theater all day, and my best friend Alex had given me a ride this morning, so I hadn't seen my dad and sister since last night.

Mom had already been in Brazil, ready to take the flight from Rio de Janeiro to JFK in the city, then home. She'd promised there would be enough time after landing to make it to the show, *at least* to the second act.

Had something happened? Maybe our Grandpa in Florida needed help? Or—oh God—if anything had happened to our dog, Onion, I would absolutely lose it. He was ten years old, old for a pug, and life would simply not be worth living without his horrible snores and bulged-out eyes.

The audience dispersed into the hall as the cast and crew went back into the wings. I had to get out there into the lobby to find out what was going on.

Alex joined me on the way back to the dressing room. She was dressed in an old 1920s gown and had applied her own makeup. The black lipstick wasn't right for the period, but Alex insisted it was what her character would've worn. AKA, she wanted to wear it. Either way, it complemented her short, dark hair and tan skin.

"Can you believe there's no budget for a play next year? I mean, the school has a new football field, but no fall play?" she asked.

"Yeah, it's ridiculous," I mumbled, still rushing toward the lobby.

"It's an insult to the arts. If it turns out we can't do a

musical in the spring next year and there's nothing, I'll lose my mind." Alex jogged to keep up. "Hey, are you okay?"

"I'm not sure," I said. "I need to find my parents."

"You want me to come?"

"No, it's cool, get changed. I'll meet you there."

Alex frowned and gently placed a hand on my shoulder. "I'm sure everything is fine. I can pull a tarot card if that will give you some peace of mind."

I didn't believe in them, but I usually went along with it to appease Alex. Not today though. I couldn't handle any bad fortunes. More importantly, though, I didn't want to slow down. "No thanks. I need to be in the lobby pronto."

"Okay. I'll change and be there as soon as I can."

"Thanks."

We parted ways as she went to ditch the costume for real clothes.

One thing that made me ineligible to be an actor: I couldn't get naked in front of people.

Okay, it was different if it were a cute guy or girl I was doing my thing with. I wasn't ashamed of my body. Who would be, with my adorable butt? But if anyone saw my scars, there'd be a lot of questions I didn't want to answer.

I power-walked toward the lobby. It was crowded with families eagerly awaiting actors, who were running down the hallway to greet them. My fellow stage crew were accepting flowers or explaining how the set worked. As I scanned the lobby for my own family, I heard snippets of conversations bouncing off each wall.

"You were so good!"

"I didn't really understand the part where…"

"How did you memorize all those lines?"

A woman rushed by me and ran to one of Alex's castmates, enveloping them in a huge hug.

I'd been in the theater club since I'd been a freshman, and after every performance, my family met by the snack bar. Mom usually brought me flowers, so I wondered if she'd have peonies or roses this time. I appreciated it, since tech crew usually got left in the dark. It was always all about the actors. So cliché.

But today, it was only Savannah.

The hair on my arms stood. Where the hell were my parents?

She leaned against the wall, her long Gigi Hadid legs extended in front of her with her ankles crossed. I knew that position. It meant she was nervous or she had to pee. Sometimes both. I was hoping for the latter, though.

Just tell me where Mom is.

When she saw me, she forced a smile.

"What's wrong?" I asked.

"Congrats!" Savannah said, totally ignoring what I'd said, as per usual. She was only a year older, but sometimes the space between us felt like decades. "The set looked amazing! The staircase looked so authentic. You even got the shine on the wood."

This time, her smile was real—and so was mine. I brought her in for a hug.

"Thanks! It took me precisely 20.3 hours." I surveyed the lobby. No sign of Mom, but Dad was talking on his cell phone outside. He was walking in circles with one hand over his ear. "Mr. Tariq asked me to help design the spring musical. We're doing *Beauty and the Beast*."

Her eyes widened, the pupils so black against the light blue. We didn't look much like sisters: Savannah, a tall, blue-eyed blonde with Dad's pert nose and strong jaw; and me, with dark hair, brown eyes, and Mom's hourglass shape. I used to be jealous of how beautiful Savannah was, how she looked like a Barbie straight out of the box, but now I was proud. Like, *yeah, my sister is a bombshell. We share approximately 50% of our DNA, so by nature, I'm half bombshell!*

"Are you serious? Violet, that's amazing!" she said. "I... I'm proud."

I couldn't remember the last time Savannah had said she was proud of me. If ever.

"Wow, thanks."

"So you're serious about this theater designer career, huh?" she asked.

"Set design. But yes, very." I frowned. "Tell me what's going on, though. Where's Mom?"

"Dad didn't want me to say anything." Savannah glanced to the floor. "He was afraid it would mess with your artistic groove or whatever."

"Well, the play is over. So spill." I crossed my arms.

Savannah toyed with the edges of her hair. A nervous habit. I wanted to shake her until she told me the truth.

"*Spill,*" I said.

"Mom didn't come home tonight," she blurted out.

I blinked. No way I'd heard that correctly.

I'd been thinking I was facing a level 2 threat. Maybe 5, if it was Onion. Mom not coming home? That was a Level 10 threat. 12, even. My blood went cold.

"What do you mean?" I asked.

"Mom left Brazil this morning at eight, and was supposed to land in the city at six, but she isn't home yet," Savannah said carefully. "Don't get nervous, though! Dad says there's bad weather in the distance, so she could've landed to wait it out."

My mom had been a commercial pilot since before I'd been born. Delays happened all the time—but never without her contacting us.

"She didn't call? I talked to her last night. I texted her. She responded." It was only then that I realized she hadn't texted me telling me to break a leg, as she did each performance.

This felt wrong. Like, horribly, insurmountably, Scar-pushing-Mufasa-off-a-cliff wrong.

Savannah placed her hand on mine. "Dad is on the phone now with the airline. I'm sure they'll tell us everything is okay."

"Right. Of course," I said.

She had to be right. There was no other option. The airline had to know exactly where she was, what had caused the delay.

I'd see her soon. I had to.

The sound of the school's entrance door clicking shut soared over the cacophony of voices in the lobby. Dad headed toward Savannah and me, and my stomach dropped. He'd gone pale, dark circles under his wide eyes. The air became too thin to breathe. By the look on his face, I knew. I knew.

He approached us and ran a hand through his shaggy dark hair.

"They can't find the plane," he said. "It vanished off the radar."

CHAPTER TWO

DAY 1 – EARLY MORNING

Aircraft didn't simply disappear.

Not in the United States, where our tracking and radar systems claimed to be the best in the world, in the universe. But this morning, a commercial Boeing 747 had vanished into thin air.

149 passengers aboard, four crew members, one co-pilot, and one very important pilot.

My mother.

I'd been attached to the television ever since we'd gotten home from the play, like my fingers had gotten sewn into the remote. In my other hand, I held my phone. I was waiting for a call from the pilot, assuring me she was safe.

I hadn't moved for four hours.

"Turn it off." Savannah trotted down the stairs, her long legs bumping up and down. Her face was so pale this morning, it could rival Casper the ghost. And I couldn't blame her. Neither of us had been able to sleep.

"I can't," I said. The news reporters might've known something I didn't.

I looked to my phone. It showed an empty screen with a background of Curiosity, NASA's rover that had gone to Mars, my favorite. No messages.

"Is your sound on?" Savannah sat on the rug beside me. Her knee poked mine. I guess neither of us found the couch appropriate. Too comfy for a time like this.

Our house felt eerily empty, like a major draft had wafted in. I'd been sitting in the dark by myself for hours now, but every few minutes, I glanced at the door, hoping it would creak open.

"That way you'll hear it if she calls," she said.

If.

Not even a full twenty-four hours yet, and Savannah was saying if.

There would be a call from Mom. There had to be.

There had already been a cornucopia of calls and texts from basically everyone else. Alex, all my aunts and uncles, even my manager at the pickle shop, who'd told me I could take as much time off as I needed. I guessed they could find another brining expert.

Even people I didn't talk to often; this nice guy in Savannah's grade, Landon Davis, had Instagram-messaged me. Not only had he said he was sorry, but he'd said how nice he'd always thought my mom was. No one else had mentioned her directly like that. Then, like everyone else, he'd said he was "here if we needed anything." I wasn't sure if people meant it, but it was nice to hear.

Or, maybe it had stood out because I'd always thought Landon was really dreamy. But, like, from a distance. I barely knew the guy.

The clock struck five a.m.

We were one of those bizarre families that still had a cuckoo clock, and ours was *Nightmare Before Christmas*–themed. It was already annoying as hell if I fell asleep on the couch, but now, Jack Skellington popping out on the hour seemed more than irritating. Offensive, actually.

How dare he remind me how long I've been waiting?

"I hate that thing." Savannah stood up, marched to the clock, and mashed Jack Skellington right back where he'd come from. The blue light of the news reflected on Savannah's body.

Mom loved that clock, though. Watching the news talk about her made me ache for her the way I used to when I would go to a slumber party. I would sneak off into the bathroom and use the special cell phone she'd let me have for sleepovers, and no matter what time I called, she'd pick up to tell me she missed me, too, and everything would be fine. Hearing the gentle alto of her voice for even a minute calmed my entire existence.

I would've given anything for that right now.

Anything.

The news reporter said, "New development in the search for the missing plane, Flight US133. Reports indicate that pilot Jennifer Ashby recently filed for divorce. Only a month ago, the pilot and her husband split…"

Savannah and I exchanged glances. Dad had been up all night talking on the phone with the airline company, the governor, and tons of other politicians or government officials. Around two a.m., he'd fallen asleep at the kitchen table before forcing himself to go sleep in the bed that used to belong to him and Mom. He'd said it would be a "real bummer", but we didn't have a guest room.

"What does the divorce have to do with anything?" I asked.

Savannah didn't answer. Instead, she glared at the television, like she knew what they were about to say.

"Could it be a reason to drive her plane into the mountain, into the sea? We invite a leading researcher in the psychology of suicide missions…" The reporter raised an eyebrow as if he was playing a guessing game.

"What?" I whispered. No, no. If they knew Mom, they'd know these accusations were wrong. In the twelve hours the plane had been missing, they'd thrown out mechanical failure, hijacking, and emergency landing—but this was the first time they'd talked about the "s" word.

That Mom would do something like this *on purpose*.

"That's ridiculous," I barked. "They don't know anything about her."

The screen split in two, and on the right, a man with white hair and a long beard appeared. He adjusted his tie, then his glasses, the motions of every mediocre man who thought he had something important to say.

"This is so unfair." Savannah sighed. "But it's not personal. This is what the media always does."

That didn't make it okay.

"You don't think last night has anything to do with this, do you?" Savannah asked. "The car she got into?"

How was I supposed to know? Yesterday, everything had felt normal. Today, it felt like I'd stepped into a twisted Brothers Grimm story.

"I doubt it," I said. "She said it was errands. I believe her."

Savannah and I hadn't talked about the weird black car that had pulled up into our driveway yesterday because it hadn't seemed important. Who cared? But now, I questioned everything.

I unlocked my phone and went online to find different

perspectives, but every Google search turned up articles where "experts" suggested Mom might not be innocent. I then made the mistake of reading the comments section. If you wanted a sure way to ruin your evening and fill you with dread about the state of America's intelligence, read the comments section on any article:

So sad. I say if the plane isn't found by tomorrow, they're all dead.

Probably a murder-suicide. Thoughts and prayers to the families.

she probably had her period and took everyone down lol

I bit my lip so hard I drew blood. The metallic taste pulled me back into the real world. I didn't know why I'd bothered with the comments section.

"Everyone is blaming her." I wanted to cry, but I could barely catch my breath.

Savannah's gaze bored into me, like she knew what I was thinking. She always did, somehow. "You're letting this stuff get to your head. I think you should try to sleep."

"Yeah, right." My fingers were acting with their own mind. They typed out a response under an anonymous name, elphaba243, my username since forever.

She is actually a fantastic pilot with over ten years of experience under her belt. She would never, ever hurt anyone.

It sounded childish, but I clicked send. It was like yelling into a void. I knew no one would listen, but still. I had to shout. Do something.

Savannah dropped to her knees beside me and gently took the phone from my hands. "It's time for bed. Even if you just lie down. School starts in like two hours—"

"School? Who the hell is going to school?"

Mom was missing, and Savannah thought she was going to jam a granola bar down her throat and sit in first period AP U.S. History?

I knew that my sister was a genius and that she was convinced her Stanford University future would be ruined if she missed even one day of school her senior year, but hell, I didn't realize that she'd also lost every single one of her marbles.

"I need a routine! I can't sit here and watch the news all night like you." She ran her hands down her face, pale as milk, contrasting against the dark circles under her eyes. "It's torture."

The "expert" psychologist on the TV said, "In many cases, suicidal thoughts can be triggered by emotional trauma, such as a recent divorce—"

"Oh please," I said.

"Technically, they haven't signed papers yet," Savannah said. "How are they even getting this info?"

I rubbed my temples. A dull roar started in the bottom of my head. I checked my post on the article. Already, tons of comments were telling me I was wrong and that a plane vanishing was no accident. Ugh.

Onion, our pug, curled up next to me. Maybe he didn't know exactly what was going on, but he was staring at us with confused, crossed eyes. He kept sniffing the door to Mom's bedroom.

I pulled him into my lap and kissed his fat rolls. "I know, my baby. This is so hard."

The expert leaned forward. "But most importantly, phone records indicate that the last text message sent was a simple, eerie message to her daughter. Can we get the text on screen?"

My heart thrashed against my rib cage.

The last conversation I'd had with my mother appeared on the TV.

How?

I said the words out loud from memory before the text appeared. "I'm sorry, I can't anymore. I love you." My throat dried out instantly. How did they get my private conversation? Why were they twisting it to make Mom seem like the bad guy?

Savannah's head whipped toward me. "What? She sent you that?"

"She was talking about the concert!" I scrambled to find our conversation in my phone. I'd read her texts six hundred times since the plane had been declared missing, but the message hadn't struck me like that. Because it couldn't have been a message in disguise, right?

ME: hey! When you drop us off for the Trixie Mattel concert next week, can you drive Alex too?

MOM: Sorry honey, I got scheduled to work next weekend.

ME: Oh, I thought you could?

MOM: I'm sorry, I can't anymore. I love you.

As she read the conversation, Savannah's eyes reddened. "They're taking it out of context."

"Hell yeah, they are." My blood was boiling. How dare they take my conversation with my mom and turn it into a suicide note? Of course they didn't show the earlier part of the conversation on TV. Of course. Whyever give the whole truth?

A tiny voice squeaked in my head, that maybe, just maybe, it really was a message in disguise. A warning about what she was trying to do—and a final goodbye.

Mom had been a wreck lately. The cost of the divorce, the proceedings. I'd caught her crying more times than I dared to remember.

No, no, no. I pushed the thought away. My mother would never kill herself and take over 150 innocent people with her.

"I need a minute," I whispered.

Savannah didn't look back as I walked up the steps to my bedroom.

Without her by my side, the house felt so…weird.

I'd been home alone plenty of times, and we were used to Mom not being here, since she was always out flying. But this felt empty, in a weird way. Like I was looking at a map, trying to figure out where to go, with the entire midsection torn out.

I wanted to lie down for a minute, eyes closed. As I crossed toward my bed, I tripped over a crumpled pile of my laundry. I seriously needed to clean my room.

But something caught my eye. A piece of folded paper, on top of my laptop on my desk. It was printer paper, crisp and white. I opened it slowly.

> *My Violet,*
>
> *Okay. I know that if you're reading this by now, you are probably upset with me. None of this was supposed to happen this way. I am just asking you to trust me. This wasn't my original plan, but I do have a plan. We get each other like no one else—not Dad, not Savannah, no one—so I'm hoping you will understand me here. Please don't tell anyone else about this for now. Let this stay between you and me. We will work this out together.*
>
> *P.S. I always tell you to "break a leg", and I don't want to ruin the tradition. So, break a leg! I am sorry I can't be there tonight.*
>
> *Love always,*

Mom
P.P.S. Next time, I think you should be on stage.

Um. What.

I put the letter back down on the desk, then quickly picked it back up to read it again.

What the heck was she talking about? A plan? If she'd known she was going to be gone, then this meant she was okay, right?

We will work this out together, she'd said. Future tense.

So she'd planned on coming back.

I fought the urge to scream and burst out the news, but she'd told me not to. I didn't get it. Why not tell Dad and Savannah?

I paced around in my room for a bit, the letter tightly in my hands.

Mom was right, though. She and I were more tightly wound together than me and Dad, or Mom and Savannah. We clicked. While my friends complained about their moms and tried to get out of the house, I was the one waiting for her to get home so we could hang out. The cord wasn't quite broken between us.

She was coming back.

That's what she'd meant, right?

It had to be. She really had a plan.

When I heard two knocks on my door, I quickly buried the letter underneath my laptop and school notebooks.

Savannah quietly opened the door. "You alright?"

"Me? Oh, yeah."

"I thought you might want to see what they're saying now," she said.

"Anything positive?"

"Um, no, but I figured you'd want to see," she said.

"And honestly… I don't want to be alone."

We descended the stairs together and sat on the living-room floor again. My head was swimming with what I'd just learned. I felt like I was underwater.

"They started talking about terrorism," Savannah said. "It's awful."

"The plane was declared missing several hours ago," the reporter said. "Yet, no terrorist groups have come forward. It leads me to believe this is an inside job."

"Now, that isn't necessarily true…" the other talking head said. Some cybersecurity expert with glasses too big for his face. "Cyberhijacking is extremely possible. My team has tested it."

Savannah was right. Watching this stuff was torture.
I refuse to let them ruin her.

Not when there was still a chance of finding her. I refused.

Maybe this was why she'd asked me not to tell anyone. I thought back to how the news had twisted her quote about the concert. Maybe she'd known how they'd twist this letter if I said anything.

"They're wrong," I said. "They have no idea."

"Of course they don't," Savannah said. "But… Neither do we, I guess."

I do, I wanted to tell her. *Mom knows what really happened.*

"Do you trust Mom?" I asked.

"What?" She raised an eyebrow. "Yeah, but that's not… That has nothing to do with this. Something happened. Some sort of accident."

"No," I said quickly. "I think there's something else going on. I think she's out there, waiting to be found."

Savannah stared at me incredulously, with tired eyes.

"Violet, I don't think you understand…"

Then, suddenly, there was a knock on the front door.

I froze and dropped my phone to the ground. Dad's footsteps scurried from upstairs.

My sister and I looked at each other, hesitant hope written on our faces.

"Wait," Savannah whispered. "It can't be Mom."

"What are you saying? Who else would be—"

"She wouldn't knock on her own door."

I blinked back tears. She was right.

Still, I turned the knob and opened the door. If hope alone could transform into something real, then Mom would be standing in front of me.

But she wasn't.

It was a different woman. Tall, wearing a black suit with a red tie. Serious, deep green eyes. And no smile.

"Good morning. I'm Agent Rosenfield with the FBI."

CHAPTER THREE

DAY 1 – MORNING

List of things I never wanted to happen again:
- Mom going missing
- Worrying about planes falling from the sky
- FBI agents coming to my door

"Can we help you?" Dad appeared at the top of the stairs. He obviously hadn't slept well, but at least he'd gotten a little rest. Unlike my sister and me. His hair was disheveled, his glasses askew, and he was wearing an old Jefferson Airplane T-shirt with copious stains.

Perhaps not the most ideal way to greet a government employee.

"Do you have information about Jennifer?" he asked.

"May I come in?" Agent Rosenfield asked. She had chestnut hair in a tight ponytail and tall cheekbones.

"Did you find her?" I asked.

Agent Rosenfield side-eyed me, then Dad led her into

our living room and toward the couch. She didn't sit. "We have not found your mother," Agent Rosenfield said. "Yet. But we're hoping the three of you can provide us with some more information that might help. I also have my Evidence Response Team with me, as we have some things to collect."

"Do the girls need to be present for this?" Dad asked. He stood directly in front of Savannah and me, as if blocking us would make Agent Rosenfield forget we were there.

"It would be best if they were," she said. "I want to get the most information I can to help Jennifer. But legally? No, I can't force them. Violet and Savannah can go upstairs."

My stomach churned. We'd never told her our names.

Dad pointed to the stairs. "Go."

Savannah turned on her heel, but I stayed put. "No."

Dad crossed his arms. "Violet."

"I'm staying." I looked into Dad's eyes and he peered into mine. Our first standoff.

I didn't want to be alone. Not now. I was afraid of what I might do. My mind was like static. Self-control felt eons away.

"Upstairs." He didn't get it. Dad didn't know what I did to myself when I was upset. No one did, except Mom. It was the biggest of our shared secrets.

"Please," I said.

"Upstairs, or I take away your cell phone," Dad said.

"Fine, take it," I spat out.

"We can't waste too much time," Agent Rosenfield said. "This is important."

I narrowed my eyes. "Oh! Well, pardon me, then. I didn't realize I wasn't able to be included in a conversation about my own mother."

Savannah linked her arm in mine and dragged me toward the steps. "Sorry about her. She hasn't slept yet."

"Stop!" I hissed, but Savannah's I-go-to-the-gym-daily-for-two-hours arms were too strong for me to resist.

She dragged me to the top of the stairs, then came to a halt.

From that angle, we could hear Dad and the agent, but we couldn't see them—and any good stagehand knew that meant they couldn't see you either. Two guys with "Evidence Response Team" patches on their uniforms rushed past us without even a glance.

Don't go through my stuff! I wanted to yell at them, but knew I wasn't supposed to. I hated the idea of strangers rummaging through our home, our personal belongings. This was my safe place.

"Don't get yourself into any more trouble than you need to," Savannah whispered.

"You're smarter than me." I smirked, and wrapped my arms around my legs.

"No, I'm just quieter."

"She's pretty," I said.

"Can you stop drooling over women with high cheekbones for like one minute? This is serious," she said. "I swear, you have such a type."

I ignored her comment. I totally do not.

Okay, maybe a little.

I focused on watching Dad and the agent through the spindles of the stairs. We used to do this as kids. When Dad and Mom would fight, Savannah and I would sit here and listen. Back then, we'd thought they were fighting about us. Like when I'd spilled my plate at dinner and they fought over who had to clean it up. Listening to them had felt like a way to punish myself. But only a few years ago, I'd realized nothing had been my fault after all.

They'd fight over anything.

Dad and Agent Rosenfield went back and forth. No, they weren't divorced. Yes, they were about to be. *Separated*, Dad said.

It still stung.

"Is there any new information on the plane?" Dad asked. "Anything at all?"

"Only what we know already. US133 took off from Rio de Janeiro at 8:05 a.m. and was scheduled to arrive at JFK a bit before six p.m. Eastern. Around three p.m., US Modern's air station lost contact with the flight," she said.

"And you're positive Jenn didn't send a message? Or a distress signal? What about the co-pilot?" Dad asked.

"No distress signal. Around three fifteen, the transponder came back on, but not long enough to send a location signal. It shut off instantly. It repeated that pattern one more time," she said.

I frowned. Maybe I should've paid more attention when Mom talked about the technical stuff. I didn't know any of these words, what these parts did.

"Only pilots can turn the transponder on and off," Savannah whispered. "It's done manually. It's this little transmitter that lets air traffic control see you."

Savannah had started preparing for flight school a few months ago. Her dream job was to be an astronaut, and she'd thought it would be helpful. Mom had been thrilled.

"What if there was, like, an electrical problem or something?" I whispered. "Something that made it shut off."

"Hmm… I'm not sure. I'll check my flight manual later," she said.

It could've been the wiring going faulty. Maybe that

was why she couldn't communicate. It must've been an issue Mom didn't know how to fix.

But she'd been a pilot for twenty years, ever since she got out of the army. Our walls were lined with tons of medals for her achievements. What couldn't she fix?

"The last recorded ping from the plane was at three fifteen, as the plane was near Puerto Rico, hovering over the Atlantic," Agent Rosenfield said.

"Three fifteen? Why didn't I hear anything about this until, like, seven?" Dad asked.

"At that time, the plane was still in South American airspace," she said. "We are still trying to get more information, but it looks as if the plane stopped communicating as it crossed over into American airspace, so it may not have been picked up."

"How do you not pick it up?" Dad barked. "A whole airliner, in this day and age? This is my *wife* on this plane."

"We're doing the best we can," she said.

Dad sighed and ran a hand through his unkempt hair. "Listen, man, is there any chance my wife is okay?"

"It's impossible to say, Mr. Ashby," she said. "We're gathering all the information we can to see what's going on. This case is unusual, to say the least."

Unusual. A missing commercial jet in the freaking United States sure was unusual.

The lack of information made me grind my teeth. I needed something more. Something to grab onto.

We'd gone to Mexico for a family trip a few years ago. I'd panicked because my phone had lost service. Mom had "accidentally" forgotten to switch things over, and I'd been cut off from the real world for an agonizing seven days.

Maybe it was like that.

I pictured Mom on a gorgeous tropical island with

clear blue waters after a risky but safe landing. All of her passengers were safe, but cell service wouldn't let them reach their families. In a day or so, a rescue plane was sure to find them.

I had to believe that.

Savannah's voice broke me out of my thinking spell. "I can't believe this is actually happening."

"Do you know how strong cell signals are in Puerto Rico?" I asked.

"Uh… What?" she asked.

"Never mind." If I told Savannah my theory, she'd roll her eyes. Savannah was all facts and physics, and I was made of nothing but hope—though I thought we were more alike than we wanted to admit.

The Evidence Response Team descended the stairs. They carried plastic bags out of the house. It stung to think that those were Mom's possessions they were taking away, like they were nothing.

"What's in those bags? What the hell?" Dad asked. "You can't just come and take our stuff!"

"We have a search warrant," Agent Rosenfield said. "They took your wife's laptop, among other electronics and items."

Dad sighed and dragged a hand down his face. "Okay. Fine. She has nothing to hide."

"Your wife's mental health," Agent Rosenfield said. "Would you say she was mentally healthy? Or was she depressed at all?"

"Of course she's depressed," Dad said. "The economy sucks, the ice caps are melting, and I moved out. So yeah, she's depressed, but so is every other person. If you're asking me if she'd ever hurt herself or anyone else? No. No way. Jenn has a big heart. She donates all this money to the American Heart Association because she's always goin' on and on about how we'll all die of heart disease. And I'm like, cancer sucks, too, right? Throw some dough there. But Jenn is like, no. She wants to donate to what can help the most people. And she sponsors some kid named Ben in an orphanage in Oregon or something! So sad; he's like eight with no parents — "

"All right, Mr. Ashby. So you're saying you think your wife was mentally sound."

"In short, yeah, she wasn't going to kill herself or 155 other folks."

I shook my head. "When Mom comes home, she's going to be so pissed people think she'd ever do that."

Silence passed between Savannah and me. The same kind of awkward silence that would sometimes happen when girls my age had princess parties and I came dressed as a frog, and they'd share *that look*. Where I got excluded. For being me.

"Right," she said quietly.

"Don't act like that," I snapped. "You have to believe she's coming home."

"Okay, okay," she said. "Trust me, I wish she was here right now."

Finally, one thing we could agree on.

"The search is extensive considering we don't have a specific GPS point." Agent Rosenfield's raspy voice traveled from downstairs. "Sixteen countries have sent their best. I'm certain we'll have more information soon."

More information soon. That did not mean "Mom will be home." It didn't even mean "We'll find the plane."

It meant nothing.

"May I speak to your girls, privately? Just for a moment. I want them to know that if they have any information, they can talk to me," she said.

"Uh…Yeah. That's fine."

Savannah and I exchanged glances. She darted into her bedroom, but I took a left and ran into Mom's room.

I hadn't been in there since before the play, before everything fell apart. On the surface, I was searching for an escape, but underneath, I was searching for more. For something to believe in.

The bed was unmade. I wasn't sure if it was from Dad or from the search team tossing things around. Mom *always* made the bed, nice and neat. They'd left a few drawers in the dresser and desk open. I closed them, then neatened out the lotions and perfumes that the team had knocked aside. Slobs.

I ran my finger across the cool wood of her dresser, then drifted toward the jewelry box. Maybe if I wore her necklace or bracelet, I'd feel her with me. That strength in me was fading. A keepsake could keep me going.

In front of the box was a little beige business card: Dr. Avery Madison, LSCW. Psychotherapist. 25 Vanderbilt Avenue.

Huh. Why did she see a therapist? Maybe the media did know something I didn't.

I heard three knocks on the door.

"Violet, you in there?" Dad asked.

I slipped the card into my pocket.

"Yeah," I said.

But instead of my dad, Agent Rosenfield opened the door and took only a few steps forward. She didn't enter the room completely, but scanned it as if the room itself would be a clue.

"Your team made a mess in here." I crossed my arms.

"I apologize." She glanced around the room. "I wanted

to speak to you."

"Okay…"

"I wanted to let you know that if you want to tell me
anything, you can. You won't get your mother in trouble,
or anyone else who might be involved. Like…your dad."

"My mom did nothing wrong, and my father has
nothing to hide. I'm sure your investigation will find that."
I thought of my note. I wanted to tell her that I had proof,
that Mom had a grand plan here. But I couldn't.

"I'm sure." She crossed her arms. "So, Violet. Eleventh
grade. Tough year. Any thoughts on college? Your grades
show you're a bright girl. Could do better in U.S. History,
though."

I'd been slacking in U.S. because it bored me to tears.
And I hated that she knew things about me. "I don't know
about college yet. And I despise history."

"I see," she said. "Your sister is going to Stanford,
though."

"She will if she gets accepted." Unless the FBI knew
something I didn't.

"Right. California is pretty far away," she said. "How
do you think your parents will cope with that?"

I noticed how she said parents, plural, in the future
tense. Like they'd both be there to pack up Savannah into
the car and drive across the country. Was it on purpose,
or a slip? "My mom is the one who helped her with the
applications, and Dad is from San Fran originally. So I
think they'll be fine with it."

"How do your parents typically handle stress?" she
asked. "It's been a difficult year for them. The separation,
figuring out how to pay for college…"

"What are you getting at?" I raised an eyebrow. I felt
like Aladdin talking to Iago. No matter what I said, she

was going to trick me. I didn't trust her emerald stare. There was something in her eyes I couldn't place.

"I'm asking if you have anything to tell me," she said.

"I don't."

"Absolutely nothing to tell me?"

"Nothing, ma'am."

"I have a feeling we'll be talking again." She turned on her heel and left the room.

My thumb traced the edges of the business card in my pocket.

Nothing to say. Nothing at all.

The truth was out there, but I guessed I'd have to find it on my own.

CHAPTER FOUR

DAY 1 – MORNING / AFTERNOON

The next time the doorbell rang that morning, I answered, and it was a mistake.

It was only Sarah Walsh, one of Mom's friends, with another casserole. Mom's friends had been bringing them by all morning.

"I wanted to drop this off real quick before I go pick up my kids," she said. "Do let me know if you and the fam need anything, okay? I'm keeping you all in my prayers."

I could barely hear her over the cluster of reporters outside our house. It looked like a protest.

"Thanks, Mrs. Walsh. Do you want to come in?" I asked.

"No, no, darling. I've got to be going. Give Dad and Savannah some love for me."

People came by, but no one ever wanted to come in. Like our house was some vortex. If they stepped across the welcome mat, they'd disappear on a plane too.

She ran off with her sweater covering her face against

the bright camera flashes. The reporters crowded in on me as her car drove away.

Their questions pounded in my ears like a thunderstorm.

"Did your mother do it on purpose?"

"Violet, what did that text mean?"

"Where do you think the plane is?"

"Leave her alone! She's just a kid!" Dad roared from the door. "Get off my lawn or I'll call the police!"

"Thanks, Dad."

"Anytime. I'm just surprised I became the 'get off my lawn' type this early in life."

I appreciated Dad making me laugh, but somehow, it only made me miss Mom more.

We went inside and headed to the kitchen. Dad hesitantly sat across from Savannah, in what used to be his old seat. Before…before he'd left.

I wondered how he felt, back in a place that had been his home for twenty years, then suddenly, wasn't anymore. Like trying on your favorite sweater only to find it didn't fit.

I was happy he was here, though.

My inner 1950s housewife took over, and I got out my brownie mix and baking trays.

Nothing was going to make me forget what was going on, or give us an appetite, but I'd never known a human being who said no to brownies.

And honestly, I had to do *something*. My hands had to be moving, my brain had to be going. If I just sat here, I'd combust.

"What did that agent say to you girls?" Dad asked.

"She said we can tell her anything," Savannah said.

"And you're not going to, right?" Dad asked.

I quirked an eyebrow. "What is there to say?" The

therapist's business card felt heavy in my pocket.

"I don't know. If you think it can help your mother, say it. But if it's going to send more guys in suits here, I'm gonna get one of those Ring doorbell thingies." Dad opened the newspaper. It had US133 on the cover with the headline: *VANISHED*. Dad tossed the paper into the recycling bin. It bounced off the rim and missed. "Freakin' feds, man," he said.

Dad got arrested at an environmental protest back in the nineties. Something about stealing a cop car. Not sure. Either way, he'd been skeptical of law enforcement ever since, yet they remained heroes in the crime books he'd been writing over the years.

"Eggs are okay in the brownies, right?" I asked Savannah.

"Yep. Thank you." When Savannah had been only seven, she'd had a mild form of leukemia. Luckily, she'd made it out okay, but uncooked animal products bugged her ever since. Weird side effect of the chemo.

"I hate eggs," Dad said.

"You hate everything," I said.

"Well, excuse me if things have been tough around here," Dad snapped.

"Can we stop? Please!" Savannah threw her hands in the air. "Mom is nowhere to be found and we're all sitting around, acting like—"

The house phone rang. Loudly.

Once. Twice.

I dropped the wooden spoon and sprang toward it. Savannah hopped up, and Dad lunged.

He got there first. "Jennifer?" he panted.

My entire being was still. Each molecule froze in place, daring to hope.

"Oh. Hi." Dad didn't hide the disappointment in his voice. "No, no. It's nice to hear from you. I just thought... I know it's impossible, but..."

Savannah sank back into her seat. I picked up the spoon from the tiled floor, where batter lay like blood at a crime scene.

That day, we got a ton of calls or visits from my grandparents, aunts, uncles, and cousins.

They all said the same thing: They hoped everyone was holding up, and they were keeping us in their thoughts. Half of them said they were sorry about Mom. The other half didn't mention her directly at all but that they were "sorry to hear the news."

As I set a timer on my phone for the brownies, I thought about how quickly time was getting away from me. I did research that morning. A lot of it. People could survive without water for three days. Maybe four. Without food, people could survive for two weeks, though it would be unpleasant, to say the least.

Plane crashes themselves were incredibly rare, but when they did happen, people could survive. I'd read dozens of stories where people had made it out. Even pilots. I had to believe there was hope.

I ran through my texts from mom again. I couldn't get over how the news reporters had twisted her words like that. All she'd been talking about had been a concert, not death.

Right?

I'm sorry, I can't anymore. I love you.

I tilted my head, wondering if the words would form an anagram, or if the first letter of every word meant something.

I thought of the note again and scrutinized it the same

way I had the text.

Maybe there had been a mistake in her plan. Shouldn't she have been home by now if this was something she had set up?

Trust me, she'd asked of me.

I could do that—right?

"Maybe take a technology break," Savannah said gently.

Dad circled from the kitchen to the living room as he spoke to Aunt Sue on the phone. The last time he'd circled like that had been when Savannah had been in chemo.

"I can't. Sav, I'm desperate," I admitted. "I don't know what to do."

"None of us do. But waiting by the phone isn't helping," she said.

It had only been about twenty hours. She'd gone missing officially around three p.m. yesterday, and it was now almost eleven a.m. here.

I tried to pretend I was someone else. Anyone else. Maybe someone who was a YouTube star, so I could send a message to all my followers and make them want to find Mom. Make them care the way I did. People like that had so much power, but here I was, helpless as a baby mouse.

"Mom didn't leave you anything, did she?" I asked. "Like a note or something?"

"No," she said. "You?" She was telling the truth. I could see it in her eyes—stormy and blue, just like Dad's. Even their eyebrows were the same shape.

"N-no," I lied.

There were two quick knocks on the door, followed by a third a beat later. This time, I didn't bother getting amped. That pattern was distinctly Alex.

When I opened the door, she threw her arms around me. Her big, curly dark hair tickled my nose. "I'm so sorry,"

Alex said. She'd texted me that, like, ninety times, but it still felt better to hear it from her lips.

I shut the door behind her. "Thanks for coming over."

"You kidding? Of course." Usually, Alex plopped herself on the couch and we played PlayStation. She's what even the biggest nerds would call an expert at video games, even with her glass eye. Her Twitch stream had a couple thousand followers.

But today, she hung around my staircase, like my house wasn't familiar to her anymore.

Savannah poked her head out from the kitchen. "Hi, Al."

Alex waved. "Hi. Did Violet tell you I'm sorry about your mom?"

"She did," Savannah said quickly. "Thank you."

"Let's go upstairs." I took Alex by the hand and led her to my bedroom. The door creaked shut behind us.

One tiny perk to Mom not being home was her not being here to get upset if I was alone in my room with someone. Dad didn't really know what to do about me being bisexual. He'd said, "Well. Okay. That's nice... No dating until you're married," when I'd come out, so he was more lenient with the door issue.

She gravitated to my shuttle statues, as she always did. A row of antique space shuttle figurines from the sixties, back when regular people had given a rat's behind about exploration, sat on my second shelf, and the only people I let touch them were Alex, Mom, and sometimes Savannah.

The only thing more prized than my shuttle collection was my bookshelf. The books were neatly organized by color, but most of the copies were worn with bent page tips. Reading was my escape. It was a chance to forget who

I was for a few hours, to get wrapped up in someone else's happy ending.

"So, are you really doing okay?" Alex fiddled with one of the figurines. "You don't have to pretend with me."

"Yes and no." It was the truth. One moment, I knew a phone call from Mom was around the corner. The next moment, like now, darkness ate at me like licking flames.

"Care to explain?" she asked.

"Mmm… Maybe."

"I get it if it's hard to talk about," she said. "But it might be good to get it off your chest."

"Yeah. But it's more than that. I miss her, obviously. But I'm desperate to know what happened. I can't stop thinking about it."

I thought about telling her what the letter said, but Mom had said not to tell anyone. That meant Alex too. The burden of keeping this secret weighed on my chest like the Adirondacks, but if it meant that Mom would come home soon, so be it.

A part of me worried, though. This plan didn't seem to be going smoothly, with all this media attention, not to mention scaring the ever-living daylights out of me and my family.

What if something had gone wrong with the plan?

I sat cross-legged on my bed, and Alex followed. Onion plopped himself in front of us. I would've given anything to be him—he was loved, well-fed, well-rested, and didn't have the capacity to worry. Well, even if he was a little stressed. I rubbed the back of his black ear, and he sighed with comfort.

"I have theories." I busted out a notebook I'd been keeping under my pillow to record my dreams. It felt odd, but doing something, like working toward finding the answer, made me feel more in control. "Okay, first. What if Mom had some sort of plan for all this? Like, we don't understand it, but she does."

"You seriously want to talk about *this*?" Alex's eyes widened. "I meant you should talk about it in terms of, like...feelings and whatnot."

"I have to talk about it." It wasn't like I had anyone else in the world who'd listen to this kind of stuff.

Yes, I thought speculation was a waste of time and conspiracy theories were foolish. But that didn't stop me from wondering what exactly had happened and how probable it was that I'd never see the woman who'd braided my hair and had taught me to tie my shoes again. I was *not* ready to go there.

"Okay, fine." Alex crossed her legs and sighed. "I don't know how likely a plan is, to be honest. What kind of plan? Like, she did this on purpose for some reason?"

"No! No," I said quickly. Maybe that was why she'd asked me not to say anything, because none of it would make any sense to anyone except us. "There was bad weather yesterday near Brazil. She could've moved to avoid a storm, and maybe had to land on a remote island or something."

"Unlikely, but I suppose it's possible. But then why didn't she send out a call for help?" she asked.

"Hm. Maybe lightning hit the plane or something?" That was no excuse. I knew lighting hit planes all the time, and it didn't cause issues. "Or it was a mechanical issue, so she couldn't signal for help."

"Does that happen?" Alex asked.

I grabbed my laptop and opened it. "It can. I've been reading up on some websites."

"Why do I have the feeling this won't be a website

ending in .gov or .edu?" She sighed.

My best friend knew me way too well.

I opened up Reddit and clicked on the forum for US133.

"This thread is, like, eighty-five pages long," she said.

"Good. The more info we have, the quicker we can solve this." And find Mom.

"You... You really think you can solve this yourself?" Alex asked. "Not saying you can't. I just think it's maybe, like, the police's responsibility?"

"They don't care like I do," I said.

And they didn't know what I knew. That Mom had told me to keep things secret meant I was on my own.

We scrolled through the first few pages, things I'd read already, and Alex scrunched her face.

There were tons of comments about all types of theories besides Mom doing this on purpose. One that got mentioned a few times was how a passenger named Ayesha Ahmad, who was American, but originally from Iran, had been on the flight. People were accusing her of terrorism with absolutely no evidence, simply based on her ethnicity. Alex and I made a post on my account to remind narrow-minded jerks to kindly to pull their heads out of their butts.

As we continued to read, Alex furrowed her brow. "I don't understand half of this. What the hell is a transponder? Can you translate any of this into English?"

"I'll try," I said. Before this, Mom and Savannah had been the only ones who knew anything about how planes actually worked. But for the past day, I'd read so much, I could probably fly one myself.

Well, at least a simulator.

The comments on the forum didn't totally make sense

to me, but I knew enough to get by. Savannah would know more than me, since flight training was part of her grand plan to become an astronaut, but I didn't dare ask. She wouldn't help me. Not with this.

I scrolled down to the discussion about the lack of distress signal.

moblinguts: The transponder is turned off manually. So turned off transponder = they didn't want anyone to know where they were.

BigLebowski: Exactly. The pilot turned it off, she crashed the plane, or its been hijacked somewhere remotely. Russians, maybe?

Banjokazooie64: Then why haven't any terrorists come forward

TallTrees889: This is going to be like the Titanic, watch. We don't have the right technology to find it now, but we will eventually.

"Um, how long passed between the time the Titanic sank and the time people found it?" I asked Alex.

"It was literally, like, a hundred years," she said.

A hundred years? I barely had a hundred minutes if it turned out she was trapped on a remote island without food or water or in any other kind of trouble. I couldn't let that kind of time elapse.

JeanTouissant: Click here. This article says an electrical fire could turn off the transponder. It's totally possible. It's ALSO possible the pilot turned it off to crash on purpose.

BigLebowski: Then why no mayday signal? I'm sick of the PC nonsense. The woman did it on purpose. It is what it is. Stupid bitch

ThunderRoad68: How about we don't call women bitches? I know the pilot personally so I please ask you to be respectful when discussing this. There is no way she would've done this.

BigLebowski: simp.

ThunderRoad68: Can we all agree to ignore the person with the screenname based on a boring movie everyone pretends to like? Great. Anyway, here's another article that says the transponder could short circuit. Same for mayday signal.

"That was really cool of you to post," Alex said. "When did you get a new screenname?"

I blinked. "I'm elphaba243. I thought ThunderRoad68 was you."

"What? No. I have an account, but I don't post," she said.

What the hell? Savannah would never join a site like this, and all of Mom's friends only used the internet to show pictures of their kids and/or dogs.

But Dad… He and I could talk for hours about Area 51 theories, and he did in-depth research a lot for his mystery books. I tried to imagine loving someone for over twenty years, breaking up, then them disappearing. It seemed unjust. If he was defending her, maybe he did still love her.

I clicked ThunderRoad68's profile. No picture, no "About me." They'd posted only a few replies, almost all of them defending Mom and telling people not to judge yet. They paid careful attention to grammar in all of them.

"Are you sure this isn't you, in like, some sleepwalking phase?" Alex asked.

"That would be a new development in my mental illness." I typed the username into a Google search. Sure enough, there were barely any hits.

One said they were a member of an anxiety and health forum, though I couldn't read the posts without being a member. I'd have to request membership, which okay, fine. But the website said they typically approved within a week. I didn't have that kind of time. Clearing Mom's name was a taller mountain to climb than I imagined, and with every minute that ticked by, public support dwindled. The sooner they could clear her of any wrongdoing, the quicker they could focus on what *really* happened.

The other post was a link to a dead page from our town's community website.

So they lived here.

"Do you think it's someone from our school?" Alex asked. "Or one of your family members?"

"They're defending my mom, so they're obviously not a douchebag," I said. "That narrows it down."

While I pondered who the hell this mystery person was, Alex scrolled down the page.

Every theory led to more and more questions, and I had no answers to even the easy ones. This was hell. If she had had no chance to call mayday, that meant someone had hurt my mom. Or worse, something had malfunctioned and she couldn't call for help.

I couldn't go down that rabbit hole.

I had to believe that she was coming home. Not that she had disappeared intentionally, or that some awful person had targeted her.

"If it helps any, I love your mom," Alex said. "I don't think she'd ever hurt anyone." She shrugged. "But all that stuff in the news about her texting you goodbye? What was that about?"

"Ugh. A misunderstanding." I hated that she even had to ask. It made me clench my jaw. That was exactly why I was doing what I did—I had to set the record straight.

If there was anyone I could tell about the note, it

would be Alex. She'd keep it quiet. Again, the thought crossed my mind, but no. Mom had asked me not to, and I didn't know the reason for that yet. I had to trust that this would unfold the way she'd thought it would.

"You have no idea how badly I want to hop on a plane and scan the Atlantic myself," I said.

"Let's do it, bro."

I opened a map. The plane had lost contact outside of Puerto Rico, in the open ocean. On the map, it didn't look that big, but it was unfathomable to think about how much ocean was there. Miles and miles of just…water.

I quickly Googled the storm forming by Puerto Rico. It was gaining strength—quickly.

I wasn't sure how that would affect search planes and boats, but it couldn't be helpful. It was over fifty miles away from the area where the plane had last pinged, but that was way too close for my comfort.

"We're running out of time," I whispered.

It felt like no one was working fast enough. I knew there were search crews, planes, boats. All those things. But it wasn't quick enough, not for me. Not when answers were so far out of my reach.

I was helpless.

Savannah kicked her foot against the door twice, then wedged it open. In her hands, she held a tray of brownies, black along the edges. Behind her, the hallway smelled vaguely of smoke. "Forget something?" She raised an eyebrow.

Oops. "Sorry." I sighed. That was so not like me. Not to brag or anything, but if I was on *The Great British Bake Off*, I'd at least make it to the finals. Okay, maybe halfway. Alright, fine, I wouldn't get kicked off first.

"It's okay, Violet," Alex said. "You're overwhelmed."

Savannah placed the brownies carefully on my desk. The shuttle statues rattled on the shelf above.

"Watch the shuttles," I mumbled. I'd only told her that a thousand times.

She rolled her eyes. "What are you guys doing?"

I hesitated, bringing the laptop closer to myself. "Nothing."

"Whatever it is, it must be interesting enough to make you almost burn our house down," she said.

Such a drama queen—though I wasn't one to talk, clearly. "We're researching what might've happened to the plane."

Savannah pressed her lips tightly together, like Mom did when she was about to make a speech about my lack of room cleaning. I hated how much they looked alike when they got annoyed. It was like double the punishment. "Do you think that's the best idea?" she asked, the way a first-grade teacher might when a child tried to glue themselves to a desk.

Alex shifted uncomfortably beside me on the bed and glanced at her Apple Watch like she had somewhere to be. I doubt she did.

"It's better than sitting around and doing nothing." I shrugged. "You can help if you want."

She clenched her jaw, Savannah's tell-tale sign she was pissed. "Help? There's nothing to do. We can't do anything except wait."

I gave a brisk, sarcastic laugh. "Yeah, I can't get on a plane and join a search and rescue, but I can at least talk to the people who are doing that. I can at least do my best to clear Mom's name—which I haven't seen you do, by the way."

"I...should go." Alex wiggled off my bed without so

much as a mattress creak. She slipped out the door with her head ducked down, rushing past Savannah.

"Text me!" I called after her.

"Only if you stop fighting!" she called back.

As soon as Alex was out of earshot, Savannah stepped forward. "It's not my job to go on the news or some strange website and stick up for Mom, and it's not yours, either. It's our job to grieve, which I wish I could do in peace, but *someone* keeps talking about conspiracy theories. You sound like you've lost it."

"It hasn't even been a full twenty-four hours. No one is grieving yet." I slammed my laptop shut and stood eye to eye with my sister.

Savannah's jaw loosened and her usually cold eyes softened. "You know she's not coming back."

"You don't know that," I said. "People can survive with no water or food for forty-eight hours. Even longer, sometimes."

"Violet, she's not coming back."

If she used that condescending, know-it-all voice on me one more time, I swear. *I swear.* She always did this. When we argued, she always leapt on her high horse.

Tears blurred my vision. "Shut up, Savannah."

"I'm trying to help you." She reached out to touch my arm, but I took a step back. I thought I saw a flicker of guilt in her face, but it was probably my mind playing tricks. "I wish she was here, too, but pretending she's not gone isn't—"

"She's not gone!" I panted from the anger coursing through me. "You're not even giving her a chance!"

"There is no chance!" Savannah shouted. "She's dead, Violet." Her voice cracked. "No one survives these things. Do you know how cold the ocean is? If the plane crashed over water, they'd have an hour, tops, to find warmth or shelter. And if they found shelter, or crashed on land, we would've heard about it."

"You don't know that."

"I do! It's a fact!" she said. "Our mom is gone. You are making this so much harder for me and Dad and yourself!"

My heart pounded in my rib cage. It took everything not to lunge at my sister. If she wanted to hurt me, she could've simply slapped me. It would've hurt far less.

Dad swung open the door. "Girls, what's going on here? What's the screaming about?"

A thick silence filled the room. That warm family moment I'd had earlier in the kitchen was gone, replaced with a chill in my lungs.

"Violet, honey, you're crying. Let me help." Dad plucked a tissue from the box on my shelf, but his careless hand knocked down my ceramic 1976 Enterprise model. It fell on its side with a resounding slam that warned of a crack.

"No!" I rushed to the shelf to check it out, but I was too late. There was a split right down the middle.

"I'm sorry," Dad said sincerely, handing me a tissue. He ran a shaky hand through his hair. "I'll replace it tomorrow. I promise."

I could barely nod. There was no replacement. Yeah, you could buy the model anywhere, but Mom had given that to me for my eleventh birthday, with the promise she'd take me for my first flight.

We'd gone on that flight, and I'll never forget how blue the sky had looked that day as we'd cut across it, or how she'd smelled exactly like vanilla.

My brain felt like it was on a treadmill, and my body was tight. Too tight.

Tight tight tight too tight too overwhelming too much.

"I think it's best if we all see a counselor," Dad said. "This is a lot to handle. I'll make some appointments for tomorrow or as soon as possible."

No. Oh hell no.

I couldn't handle this. Any of this.

I looked to the clock on my desk. It was past three p.m. now. This was even worse. Officially, it had been over twenty-four hours since Mom had disappeared.

"Excuse me." I stood up and headed to the bathroom. I was useless against my old habit. I knew it was bad, but it was the only way I could get my head clear again.

I locked the door, then fished out a safety pin from the sewing kit under the sink.

Something stopped me. I didn't want to do this. Not really.

I didn't open it.

I was frustrated, so damn scared. There was one thing I had control over, and it was scratching the tip of that sharp pin against my lower arm until bright red blood seeped out. Every time I cut, the burning pain felt like a deserved punishment for feelings that were too big for my body.

A small voice in my head screamed, *Hey! Don't do this!*

The voice sounded a lot like Mom. Maybe because in the past, it had been her.

It had been forty-three days since I'd last cut. Mom knew. She'd pulled me aside and told me how she used to harm herself when she couldn't handle the emotional pain. Physical pain was fixed easily; emotional pain, not so much.

"I used to do this too," she'd said. *"It's not the way to fix things. Trust me."*

"I don't know what you're talking about," I'd said.

Mom had taken my wrists gently in her hands. "You can hide it from everyone else, but not me. I know you."

But if she was gone now, who would understand? If I told someone else, who would see me for what I was instead of just something broken that needed to be fixed?

She's not gone. She isn't.

I snapped my hair tie against my wrist. Hard. It stung.

Not like a cut, but enough to dull the thoughts, if only for a few seconds.

It snapped me back into reality.

I still hadn't cut. I could keep my forty-three-day streak for now.

Fifty days, Mom had said. *It'll be a milestone. That way, you'll know you can beat this.*

I could make it to that fifty-day mark. I had to.

CHAPTER FIVE

DAY TWO – MORNING / AFTERNOON

The next day, Savannah went back to school.
Dad said I didn't have to, so I opted to sleep in. A few days missing out of my junior year wouldn't kill me. Unlike my sister, I wouldn't combust if my GPA wasn't perfect. I liked school, I liked learning, but I wasn't going to pretend I was some Ivy League prodigy like Savannah. Besides, I couldn't stop thinking about last night. I was dying to hit my fifty-day streak. The sting of a rubber band was the closest I'd come, and even that was too close to cutting. When Mom got home, maybe she'd have some advice.

I also needed time for my plan. Savannah was busy with Astronomy Club until at least four p.m., and Dad said he would be at the police station and meeting with other government officials and airline officials today. He felt horrible about not being home with me, but it worked. That way, I had at least a couple hours to take the train into the city and find Dr. Madison, my mom's therapist.

Maybe she could give me new information.

Getting past the reporters wasn't easy.

There were four vans parked outside and a complete mob of people. It had taken me this long to realize that the big news channels, the real news, were busy getting actual information and not stalking my house. It was only the tabloids who thought some sixteen-year-old kid crying would be a good headline.

I held my chin up, pushed my sunglasses on, and channeled my best Audrey Hepburn.

"Violet, did your mother tell you what she was going to do?"

"What did her last text mean to you, Violet?"

"Was your mother the type to do this?"

I cleared my throat and pushed past them, not looking at a single one. I didn't need their questions, even though I wanted the same answers they did.

I walked off toward the train and, eventually, they stopped following me. *Eat that, paparazzi.*

When I got to New York City, I felt at home.

I knew it was cliché to love this big, dirty, grimy place, but seeing skyscrapers pointing toward infinity made my heart do backflips. I still wasn't sure what kind of career I wanted in the future, but I knew it would involve the city and those shining Theater District lights.

The office was easy to find.

When I got off the elevator, I walked through an airy hallway with identical brown doors until I found 5G, then halted.

I'd specifically planned to arrive at 12:50 p.m., and I made it just in time. Most therapist appointments were fifty or sixty minutes, so if I arrived at ten minutes to the hour, I figured I'd have a good chance of catching Dr.

Madison alone. The last thing I wanted to do was knock and interrupt someone's session.

"Violet? Violet Ashby?" A guy in the waiting room eyed me up and down, and it embarrassingly took me more than a second to realize it was Landon Davis, the guy from Savannah's grade who messaged me the other day. I should've known, from the Mets cap he wore. It was mostly Yankee country out here, but Landon had always been different in that way.

"Hey," I said. "What are you doing here?"

"Oh, you know, just here to collect some tips on how to adopt a kangaroo."

I blinked at him. "What?"

"Violet, I'm kidding. I'm probably here for the same reason as you."

"Oh, right." It was a therapist's office, after all. Not a lot of options.

He squinted and tilted his head, letting chestnut curls fall sideways. He wore a red flannel shirt, buttoned to the top and rolled at the sleeves. "You can sit while you wait," he said.

I tried not to stare at the knitting needles and wound-up pink yarn in his hands.

I'd never seen anyone knit before. Not in real life.

His fingers wrapped clumsily around the yarn, but the needle looped effortlessly. It was transfixing, watching his hands. Watching him.

"I don't have an appointment." Saying it out loud made me realize how bizarre I sounded. Barging into a private practice wasn't illegal, was it? Could I be arrested for this?

"I bet she could squeeze you in, with everything going on," he said.

I nodded and placed my purse down on the chair. It

felt heavy with my book and water bottle in it. "It was nice of you to send a text about my mom."

I'd always thought he was kind of cute, but we weren't even friends. Friendly, though, I guess. The type to say "hey" in the halls—but we'd never hung out together.

"Sure." He cracked his knuckles on both fists. I couldn't help but notice the sexy veins traveling up and down his smooth arms, up to the roll of his flannel. Was it rude to be attracted to someone when your mother was missing? Yes, probably.

"You knit?" I asked.

"Yeah. Try to, anyway. I'm new at it," he said.

"What are you making?"

"Hm, not sure. I was following this YouTube video to make a scarf. It's more complicated than it looks."

I smirked. "Actually, it looks incredibly complicated."

He smiled back. "Look, Dr. Madison is real nice. She'll make you feel comfortable."

"Are you next?" I asked. "I didn't mean to interrupt. I'd only need, like, ten minutes—"

"You're blushing." He laughed.

Oh God. I was one of those people who blushed if someone asked me for the time. I've literally spent hours researching how to suppress adenylyl cyclase to try and stop this awful, reddening phenomenon. Spoiler alert: you couldn't. "Shut up." I clutched my cheeks, but only imagined them getting more and more like the color of spaghetti sauce.

"Sorry, I didn't mean to embarrass you." He grinned. His two teeth next to his front ones were crooked. It was charming, in a weird way. "Anyway, I'm not next. I'm her two p.m. appointment."

"It's not even one yet."

"I...like to be early," he said. "It's a thing I have."

Now who was blushing?

"I get it," I said. "Hey, wait. Aren't you supposed to be in school?"

"Emergency appointment." His face didn't betray any embarrassment, which I thought was cool. I didn't think I'd ever have the courage to admit any of that. My scars stayed hidden.

"You all right?" I asked.

"Fine, just some anxiety issues," he said casually.

"I'm sorry." I wished I could've said something useful, like I understood, but I didn't. I'd never worried in a way that seemed like something I couldn't control.

My bouts of anger and sadness, well. I could relate on that level. But having a healthy conversation where I actually said what I was feeling? I had a better shot at marrying Betsy Wolfe.

"Does the knitting help with the anxiety?" I asked.

"I think so," he said. "It's repetitive. Makes me take a step back."

"Sure. I can see that."

Wait. Anxiety issues? I thought back to ThunderRoad68. The only other information I could find on that account had been that they were also a member of an anxiety forum.

Impulse ate at me. I had to know.

"Hey Landon, are you—"

"Auditioning for the show? Yes. Are you?" he asked.

I blinked, not expecting the change in subject. "No. I'm going to design the set."

"Oh, nice!" He grinned. Damn those adorably crooked teeth. "That doesn't mean you can't be in it, though. Lots of room for extra singing and dancing utensils."

"Um. I haven't thought about it, I guess," I lied. He didn't need to know that I'd give anything to be on stage, or that before Mom had disappeared, I'd promised her that one day I would.

"I figured you would, since you killed it in acting class last year."

"You remember that?" I'd done a monologue at the end of the course from a not-too-well-known comedy. I hit each joke, and still got high off how hard everyone had laughed. But a class was one thing. There hadn't been any singing in Acting 101. Auditioning meant owning I wanted to come out from behind the lights. It meant admitting what I'd only shared with Mom.

"Yeah," he said. "Shame. You should be on stage." His hands glided back and forth as he created more stitches in the scarf. Up close, I realized how beautiful the peony color was. There was something sexy about a boy who wasn't afraid of pink.

"Where do you buy the yarn?" I asked.

"Sometimes I buy from the craft store in town, but I borrowed this one from my mom."

He quickly picked up his head and looked to me. That word. It felt like a rock on my chest. "I'm sorry," he said quickly.

"It's okay. I can talk about other people's moms," I said. Could I? Actually, it seemed extremely unfair that other people could talk about their mothers without everyone turning to stare at them. Or worse, that they knew their mothers would be waiting for them at home after school.

He took a deep breath and nodded. "I'm bad at knitting, but I'm way, way worse at talking."

"I like talking to you."

"I like talking to you too," he said quietly. "A lot."

Dr. Madison swung the door open and took in Landon, then me. "Can I help you?"

As far as therapists went, she wasn't what I'd had in mind. With a full hourglass shape, blond hair piled on top of her head, and cute ballerina flats, she reminded me of Tinker Bell. Only with glasses and no pixie dust.

"I… Uh…" *Words, words, words.* "Hi. I was wondering if you could help me. I think you know my mother, Jennifer Ashby?"

Dr. Madison pressed her lips together and stared me down.

The seconds between that and her words felt like years. If she kicked me out, I'd never know what Mom was really thinking.

"Come in." She tossed a glance to Landon. "See you at two."

"Yes, ma'am," he said.

She welcomed me inside and shut the door behind us. Her office was tiny. I tried to picture my mom sitting on the brown leather couch, among a wall of mirrors and plants that stretched toward the ceiling. The picture didn't fit.

Dr. Madison curled into an armchair across from me. "Are you Savannah or Violet?"

So Mom had talked about me. Was that a good thing? I figured most people saw therapists to discuss things that were, uh, not the best.

"I'm Violet. The younger one." I refused to sit, and instead I hovered by the window.

The office looked onto the busy, bustling street of Vanderbilt Avenue. Mom had always loved the city like I did, and hinted not so subtly that we would've grown up here if Dad had agreed to it or if we could have afforded it.

I wondered if looking out onto the lively city streets, full of people and hot dog carts and taxis, made her feel calmer. Or if it only made her more resentful of Dad.

"I'm sorry to hear about your mother," Dr. Madison said. "How can I help you today?"

I nodded. If I had a dollar for every time someone said that to me, I could fund the search myself. I explained how I'd found the card, and how it had led me here. "I know my mom didn't kill herself, and I know she would never hurt anyone else. I was wondering if…" I swallowed. "I was hoping you would help me tell everyone what they're saying isn't true."

Dr. Madison frowned. "I'm sorry. I do wish I could help you, sweetie, but that would be a HIPAA violation. I'm not allowed to discuss what patients talk about with me."

I'd expected she'd say something like that, but it still made me clench my fists. "Even if they're…" *Missing? Rumored to be dead or a suicide pilot?* "Even under these circumstances?"

"Not at all."

"There's no situation in this world where you can give me any info on my mom?"

"I can't unless I'm summoned by law somehow," she said gently. "Like a subpoena."

I wrote a note in my phone: how to subpoena someone.

When I glanced up, I caught her gaze lingering on my arm. Quickly, I tugged my sleeve down past last night's near-trauma. "Okay, well." I huffed, but I let it go. "Thanks. I guess."

"I'm terribly sorry, Violet. Wish I could do more," she said. "I always enjoyed speaking to your mother."

I'd wasted three hours of my day for this? I could've

been researching mechanical failures or remote islands off South America. A waste of my time meant less time I could dedicate toward finding Mom.

"You seriously can't tell me anything? I'm her daughter. You know that already. You know how close we are."

She said nothing. Frustration pounded in my ears.

I had to hit her where it hurt. I felt mean, but I needed info. "You must know how trauma like this messes with a person. That's your job." I didn't want to cry, not here and not now. I blinked back hot tears. I'd come all this way for nothing. I thought about telling her what the note said, but it wasn't like she had promised me any confidentiality. I wasn't her client.

"I'm sorry," she said again. I believed her, but that wasn't going to change things.

"Nothing?" I didn't know why I bothered asking again. "You can't give a scared kid any assurance that her missing mother may or may not have wanted to hurt herself?"

She blinked those cool, collected blue eyes without saying anything.

Anger pulsed through me. My wrist itched, beckoning to me for relief.

Not here, not now. Fifty-day streak is so close.

I had to hold it together, if for no other reason than to celebrate with Mom. To give her something to celebrate when she got back.

I looked to the clock on the desk. I couldn't believe it would almost be two complete sunrises and two complete sunsets without Mom. It didn't seem possible that the world could still spin, let alone spin faster toward the forty-eight-hour mark when anyone who'd survived a potential plane crash would need water.

"Forget it." I headed for the door with fury in my veins.

What good was a therapist if I was on the verge of cutting myself from anger and she sat there doing nothing?

"Wait." Dr. Madison stood. Bracelets clinked and dangled down her arms. "I can legally only report a client's information if I think they might hurt themselves or someone else."

"Okay? And you're no help to me because—" I stopped with my hand on the gold knob. "And you didn't tell anyone because you didn't think she would."

"One could infer that."

My hand slipped from the knob.

This… This changed things.

"Oh," I managed.

A lack of information was almost as good as information itself. Negative space forming a shape.

"I've been watching the news too." She sat down again, legs crossed. "It's been hard. Such little information. I can't imagine how difficult this must be for you."

"It's not exactly a fun time."

"Understandable."

Again, I tried to picture Mom here. There was a crease in the patient's couch. Could that be where she usually sat, or would she lean more toward the window? This feeling of being a stranger in someone's life I thought I knew was like reading your favorite childhood book again, only to find it had lost the luster. None of this made sense.

"Have you considered talking to anyone about this? Do you have a good support system of family or friends?" Dr. Madison's voice was silky soft. I could see why Mom had decided to see her.

But that didn't mean *I* was going to. I saw right through her "I'm here for you" nonsense. I needed help finding Mom. I didn't have time to unleash the beast of my mental health. It would be like BB-8 taking on Darth Vader alone.

"I can be a resource, if you need," she said. "Sometimes when life gets tough, it's more than okay to ask for help. I'm happy to recommend other therapists. Talking to someone could make a big difference."

"I'm all right." My brain was a big, scary place. It was best if we kept the lid on that jar.

"Are you safe, Violet?" she asked.

"What do you mean?"

"This is an extremely difficult situation. Sometimes that's hard to handle. People might want to hurt themselves, or others."

I squinted. Did she know? No. Mom came here to talk about herself, not me.

"I'm fine." I looked into the mirror behind Dr. Madison and stared at my reflection. I thought if I squinted, I could picture Mom on the couch next to me. Or instead of me.

Nothing.

"But thank you," I said. "Please let me know if you can share any information."

Dr. Madison stood. "I will. I'll keep an eye out for that subpoena, and I really do mean it. I'm happy to help."

There was a slight, heavy moment where I considered telling her everything.

How last night, I'd almost ruined my streak. How sometimes I felt like I was in a crowded room, screaming, and no one looked up.

But the moment passed and I turned the knob, closing the door quietly behind me.

CHAPTER SIX

Day Two – Afternoon / Night

As I arrived home, I was bursting to tell someone about Dr. Madison.

There was a whole new part of Mom I'd discovered. How long had she been seeing a therapist? A few weeks, or a few months? Longer?

I reached for my keys in my purse, then had that awful, sinking feeling, like when I'd whipped some eggs for cake batter, then realized they'd been expired for a week.

I couldn't find my keys in my purse because I did not. Have. My purse.

Shitgoddammitdamnshit!

I banged on the door, hoping the pounding would drum away the agony of knowing I'd lost my wallet with my debit card and all my gift cards. Even worse, my paperback copy of Malala Yousafzai's autobiography. She was such a brave person, and I was hoping to absorb some of that courage by re-reading her book. My fingernails scratched across my forearm, angry with myself for being so forgetful.

Savannah opened the door before my nails could break skin. "Hey. What's wrong?" she asked.

"I lost my bag." The only things I had on me were my train pass and a few bucks. I stomped inside the house and tried to take deep breaths. At least I had my phone, but every time I forgot something, it felt like a personal failure.

"Oh, that sucks. Do you need cash?"

"I have some, but thanks." I appreciated the thought, but she didn't get to win me back so easily. Last night had ripped a page from hell, and I had the memory of a bitter elephant. I'd never forgive her for insisting so cruelly that Mom was dead without giving her the benefit of the doubt.

Then I noticed that Savannah was wearing boy shorts and a tank top, not her usual J.Crew attire, and the circles under her eyes were more pronounced than the Ash in Ashby.

"Did you go to school today? Or did you skip Astronomy Club?" I asked.

"I went, but I…" She looked to the floor. "I threw up in third period, and Ms. Chapman sent me home."

"You okay?" I raised my eyebrows. Even Onion, lying at the top of the stairs, eyed her incredulously.

"Yeah. Fine. I ate a few of those burnt brownies last night. I think my stomach took its revenge." She cracked a real, actual smile, and for a second, I was reminded of me. We might not look anything alike, with Savannah being blonde and blue-eyed with a sharp nose, and me with my short dark hair and matching eyes, but we did share DNA. And history.

"How did the club continue on without their fearless

president?" I asked.

"I Zoomed in."

Of course. "Wait, Sav, do you have Landon Davis's phone number?"

"Uh… Maybe." Savannah picked her phone up off the coffee table and scrolled. "Why?"

I couldn't tell her about Dr. Madison. It wouldn't be fair to Landon, but also, she'd get upset if she knew I was investigating Mom on my own.

"I have his Instagram, but I don't know if he looks at that all the time," I said. "I ran into him outside and we talked a little. Maybe he remembers if I had my bag or not."

"Oh. Where'd you go?"

"Nowhere, really…outside."

"That's specific." Savannah texted me his number and threw herself on the couch. She clutched her lower side and groaned.

"You all right?" I asked. "Want me to get a heating pad? Ice pack?"

"Nah, I'm fine," she said. "Thanks."

I texted Landon, asking if my purse was at the therapist's office.

I had to admit, I grinned as I saved his name in my Contacts. Must've been those damn rolled-up sleeves. Or the way his hands moved so gracefully when he knitted. I pictured his hands again, moving so fast. On me. On my—

Ping!

Woof. Got a little carried away there.

LANDON: Sorry. I left already, I didn't see it there

Fuuuuuuuuuck.

I tugged on the ends of my hair. Why did this type of thing always have to happen at the worst of times? As if I wasn't feeling horrible enough already.

Savannah tucked hair behind her ear. "Listen, I'm sorry about—"

The front door unlocked.

Dad placed his messenger bag by the door as if it were a pair of shoes, then kicked his loafers off. It was only five. Most days, before all this, Dad would stay and write in the library or the local coffee shop until 8. But that had been Before, and now there was only After. I wasn't sure I'd ever get used to After.

"Hi, my favorite girls." He smiled too widely. Something was up.

"How did it go today?" I asked. "Did the police say anything?"

"Why don't you girls sit?" Dad gestured to the couch.

Neither of us sat. I was way too wired, and besides, I knew what that meant now. It meant bad news was coming at me like a fast-pitched baseball.

"I met with a lot of people—*a lot*—but, unfortunately, no news, really. Or at least, not much they could tell me. A lot of it is confidential," he said.

It was so unfair that we had to tell the FBI everything. They even had taken Mom's stuff, but in return, they couldn't tell us anything. Infuriating.

"They did say, though…" Dad scratched the back of his head. "The storm by Puerto Rico has gotten stronger. Agent Rosenfield told me she thinks it's going to seriously impede the search if it gets worse—and unfortunately, it's gaining strength. It might become an actual hurricane. It's going to be really dangerous for the people living there."

I clenched my fists. How awful for local residents. "So… What does that mean for the search? They'll call it off?"

My heart pounded against my chest in fury. How

could they do something like that? It was my mom out there. And 155 other people, all of whom had families and friends and pets at home, waiting on tiptoes for their arrival just like I was.

"She didn't say they'd stop searching," Dad said. "She told me they would monitor the situation and, if it gets worse, continue to search in a way that is safe for the rescue crew. They can't risk the crew's lives like that."

I didn't like the sound of that. It sounded like they'd give up.

In that moment, I wished nothing more than that I knew how to fly. That I could get on a plane myself and search the Atlantic, back and forth until I found the passengers. Every single one.

"How are you feeling, Savannah?" Dad asked. "Can I make you soup or something?"

"I'm feeling better." She flashed a smile that was as real as Kim Kardashian's butt. "Violet lost her purse, though."

"Oh no! You need money?" Dad went into his wallet.

"I don't need money, I just want my purse." I sighed.

"It's perfectly normal to be more forgetful in stressful situations," Dad said. "Plenty of studies show—"

"Huh?" Savannah lifted an eyebrow.

"I've been reading." Dad gestured to the coffee table. On it was a red hardcover, *The Parent's Guide to Grief.*

Normally, I would've told my dad to stop watching Dr. Phil, but I was actually touched. Dad usually read other crime novels to keep up with his "competition", not nonfiction.

"Thanks, Dad," I said gently.

"Why don't you paint a little," he said. "That always makes you feel better."

I hadn't thought about painting in two days, but I could

try. Maybe. It felt like a waste of time, though. "Sure."

"You can work on designs for the show!" Savannah said.

"What show?" Dad asked.

I couldn't believe I'd forgotten to tell Dad in all this chaos. Though, of course I hadn't really forgotten—it just wasn't important anymore.

"Violet didn't tell you?" she asked. "She got asked by the director to help make the set for *Beauty and the Beast,* the spring musical. Literally the only student ever in WHS history to be asked to do so."

"How do you know that?" I asked.

"Alex told me."

I narrowed my eyes. "When did you talk to Alex?"

"Vi, that's incredible!" Dad threw his arms around me. "You have any ideas yet? I bet you do. Let me guess. Are you going to have Belle fly in on the magic carpet?"

"That's *Aladdin*." Savannah rolled her eyes.

"I'm pretty sure there was a magic rug or something in *Beauty and the Beast*, too. I had to sit through it millions of times with you two," Dad said. "So, magic carpet?"

"I don't know if I'm going to do it anymore," I mumbled.

Dead silence. Savannah and Dad looked at each other, then at me. They always freaking did that. Those two didn't need words to communicate. They understood each other at the molecular level.

Maybe I wouldn't have been so jealous if I hadn't been that way with Mom.

"You have to do it," Savannah said. "You're so talented. Mr. Tariq wouldn't have asked you if he didn't think so too."

"It'll be a good distraction," Dad said. "The book says distraction is key."

"I know, I just… It doesn't feel right."

He placed his hand on my shoulder. "Mom would want you to do it. She'd be bouncing off the walls."

I wiggled away. I didn't want to think about what Mom *would* want.

My lower arm itched for me to dig my nails into it. To slice it.

Instead, I took a deep breath.

"I'm going to my room." I turned toward the stairs. "Maybe I'll paint."

"Great! Yeah, paint!" Dad said. "And if you happen to paint Belle on a magic carpet, so be it."

Their voices drifted away as I walked upstairs.

"I think you're picturing the wardrobe character," Savannah said.

"I'm telling you, child, there is a magic dancing rug in that movie."

I shut the door to my bedroom.

Painting used to be my safe space.

I could mix colors and make mistakes and it would all turn out okay. Sometimes, I could channel the frustration of wanting to cut by painting a furiously red cardinal or violently yellow daisies. It didn't always work, but sometimes, it was just the right amount of beautiful catharsis.

But when I took the brush in my hand now, the canvas stayed empty.

I sketched an outline of the stage but couldn't bring myself to fill it in. It glared at me, unfilled. Before I realized it, I'd sketched a Boeing 747, with its wings extended.

Soaring downward.

All I could think about was Mom. And storms revving up.

And planes falling from the sky.

And subpoenas.

There was only one person I could talk to about this.

I texted Alex: So, an FBI agent came to my house the other day.

ALEX: ????????

ME: It was about Mom. She wanted to know if I had info on her

ALEX: Oh! What did you say

ME: I said I had nothing. But now I think I have something… The FBI can get a subpoena, right?

ALEX: they can probably get anything they want. What info did you get?

ME: I'll tell you in person. I think I might go to the FBI office and talk to her. Can you come with me?

ALEX: Of course! Whatever you need.

ALEX: You doing okay? With everything?

ME: Trying.

We had, perhaps, the most depressing family dinner ever on record.

Dad heated up one of the casseroles someone gave us, and we all ate it in complete silence. The entire time, I stared at Mom's chair, as if somehow I could will her to come back to me.

I drew for the rest of the night until it got dark. I turned the lamp off, and my room became pitch black. My curtains were closed, because I didn't trust any reporters not to look into my bedroom if I left them open. The last thing the world needed was *Missing pilot's daughter shows tits to the world! They are small, but ok overall!*

A text lit up my phone.

LANDON: Hey. I'm outside your house. Come out

I tilted my head in surprise. I thought the text would

be from Alex.

A second text from him: Wait. That sounds creepy. I'm sorry. But I have your purse.

Third text: That didn't sound right either.

"Daughters!" Dad shouted from downstairs. "There's a boy outside. Why is there a boy outside? And is that a Mets hat on his head? He's wearing those hideous clashing colors on purpose?"

Dad was originally from San Francisco, so he was a Giants fan. He tolerated the Yankees, but something about the orange and blue Mets colors ticked him off.

I hopped downstairs. It had gotten dark outside, and it made me feel like I was sneaking out, even though I was only going to my front door.

"Can you tell your suitors to come by during the daylight?" Dad said. "I was going to lock myself in my bedroom and write, but I can't do that if random young men stop by my house."

"He's not random, it's Landon Davis from school. He found my purse."

"Oh. Fine. He can come in, then." Dad waved his hand and continued his ascent to the master bedroom. "If he stole anything out of your bag, let me know. Make sure he didn't take any tampons or anything."

"Why would he do that?"

"I'm doing a lot of research for my book, and I saw a ClickTok—"

"A what?"

"A ClickClock? TikTok? Anyway, some video where teen boys are sticking tampons up their—"

"That's fine, I don't need to know."

LANDON: There's a lot of cameras outside. Can I meet you somewhere else? I'm by your neighbor's very interesting flamingo statue.

ME: Go past the flamingo, into their yard. I'll meet you around the back.

Never thought I'd be looking forward to seeing that tacky lawn ornament.

I went through my living room and into the kitchen, then opened the door to the backyard. I caught a glimpse of Landon jogging through my neighbor's grass. He wore basketball shorts and a white T-shirt. His hair was still tucked under his Mets hat. It must've rained at some point, evidenced by the mist around him, and the dewy grass. The clouds looked like they were threatening a repeat performance.

He had my brown purse around his shoulder, and it made him look like one of those big guys who walk their girlfriend's tiny Chihuahua.

I waved to him, and he waved back as he ran to me. Sneaking by the paparazzi was a mini victory, and it made the moment more special. It belonged to only the two of us.

"Malala Yousafzai, huh?" He handed me my bag back. "Not that I was snooping, but you know. I see a book and I have to check."

"She's incredible. You should read her book if you haven't already." I took the purse back. "Thank you for this. You have no idea how much I was panicking. I thought you said you had left already?"

"I did, but I went back." Landon slipped his hands into his pocket. "I've lost my wallet before. It sucks. I would've gotten here sooner, but I put my little brother to bed."

"I'm grateful that you brought it back to me at all. Seriously."

"No worries," he said. "This might be weird, but you want to go for a walk?"

I blinked. "Is that like, a thing?"

He gave a shy laugh. I always thought shy people were more likely to be trusted. Something about the way he grinned and looked to the floor made me want to be close to him. "If you can't, it's alright. I was going to walk to the twenty-four-hour store and get some seltzer. It helps me sleep."

"Do you have trouble sleeping a lot?"

"Um… Sometimes. When the anxiety is bad, you know? Then I'm awake all the time."

Truly, I didn't know what that felt like. To be up all night, his heart probably pounding against his chest, worried about something out of his control.

But I did know what it was like to feel so sad that your chest threatened to rip open like a cave, sometimes for no real reason at all. It was hard to explain, and that was why I'd never bothered trying, but maybe… Maybe he'd get it. Especially now. Until Mom was back home, I knew I'd be staring up at the ceiling all night.

"So…walk with me?" he asked.

I glanced up toward the clouds, then quickly away. I couldn't stare into the stars, not yet. "Isn't it going to rain?"

"Maybe. That's the fun of it."

Why not?

If life had taught me anything the past few days, it was that it was short. We walked quickly through two of my neighbors' yards on the right to avoid being seen. Their lights were already off for the night. The shadows fell heavily on us, and I was thankful for the lack of fences around us.

We cut to the end of the block, then took a turn toward the main road. I kept checking over my shoulder for camera crew, but we were in the clear.

For mid-September, it was unseasonably warm, without even the slightest bit of wind. Still, the electricity in the air from the recent rain whispered that a storm was brewing.

"Check out the stars," he said. "It's kinda cloudy, but you can see a few."

I didn't look up. I hadn't been on the roof since Mom had disappeared. It used to be the habit that had calmed me before bed. The only thing that would quiet me if I wanted to cut. But I was afraid that if I looked up, I'd never want to look down again. That I'd keep searching.

Or maybe I was afraid of what I'd find. Or of the lack thereof.

"Beautiful." They were, I bet.

"So. What did you think of Dr. Madison?" he asked.

"She's cool," I said. "But I'm not the one seeing her."

"Oh? You have a twin? With the same purse?" He smirked.

"She's my mom's therapist. I was just trying to get information."

"To help?"

"Yeah. To help." I hoped that, in those three words, Landon had heard my heart. What I'd meant was, *thank you for not judging me. Thank you for not thinking I'm naive for having hope. Thank you for believing.*

He moved his hands into his pockets, and his pinky brushed my wrist.

I guessed I found pinkies kind of hot now, because it made the hairs on my wrist stand up.

By the end of the main road, each home was unlit, though some porch lights flickered on as we passed. Stepping in tandem, one by one.

"How's Savannah doing with it all?" he asked.

Every boy I'd ever talked to had asked about Savannah. Well, okay. Not every single guy, but still. It helped that I was attracted to all genders, leaving a pool of potential wide open for me and me only, not for my straight sister.

"She's handling it better than me, I think," I confessed, surprised by how easily I admitted to it. There was something about the dark that made people honest. Like our secrets could remain in the veil. "She's been quiet, kind of doing her own thing."

"Gotcha," he said.

As we curved toward the main boulevard in town, where dim store lights twinkled from signs left on, we made a right and walked into the store.

Landon picked out a seltzer and asked me if I wanted anything. I said no, even though I was eyeing the Reese's Pieces. Peanut butter inside that crunchy outer shell was my weakness.

On the way out, I looked up at him. "Be honest. Did you like Savannah when we were younger?"

Landon did that embarrassed, too-genuine-too-cute laugh again. It started in his chest and bubbled to his soft pink lips. "Not *liked* liked. But liked."

"Ah. I see."

"Brunettes are more my thing."

I'M A BRUNETTE, I wanted to yell, but it appeared his eyes were functioning.

I wasn't sure if his honesty smothered me or ignited me.

The air outside felt even warmer than it did before. We walked side by side, arms brushing here and there.

"But crushes don't mean anything at that age," he said. "I probably had a crush on every girl in our class."

"Same. Perks of being bisexual."

He side-eyed me, the same way everyone did when I mentioned that. I was proud of the way I was, but sometimes being bisexual was like running a race with your ankles tied together. If you dated a guy, people said you were really straight. If you were with a girl, you were actually gay. There was no winning. It only made telling people harder.

"You knew that, right?" I asked. "I dated Lauren Meadows last year? Very non-dramatic breakup, but everyone seemed to care anyway? And then, earlier this year, I sort of dated a guy from another school, but it was only a fling, really."

"Actually, I didn't know you were bi. I thought you were a lesbian. So, thank you for that brief but educational dating history. I'll take better notes next time."

"Are you going to share your brief but educational dating history?" I quirked an eyebrow.

"Sure. Close your eyes."

I did. The split second of not knowing was thrilling. Was he going to show me a graph of his dates, show me a photo of his girlfriend? Maybe even lean forward and—

No. That'd be strange. I didn't even have time for that now.

Instead, he put his warm, soft hands over my eyes. "What do you see? That's been my love life."

"I doubt that." I laughed as he removed his hands.

He turned pink, and then I followed suit. Goddamn adenylyl cyclase.

We walked in silence for another few minutes. Comfortable silence, though, like my favorite cardigan.

"Hey," I said. In the cover of the dark, I felt comfortable asking him. If he didn't give me the answer I was looking for, I was safe under the dim street lights. "I meant to ask you earlier. Are you ThunderRoad68?"

"Am I what? You mean like, the Springsteen song?"

"That's a song?"

Landon laughed lightly. "You know, Bruce Springsteen? "Thunder Road" is one of his best songs."

"Oh," I said. "I saw that screen name post stuff defending my mom, and I was wondering if it was you?"

Landon stopped and looked at me, confusion written on his handsome face.

I had my answer.

"Never mind," I said.

With the post in the anxiety forum and the post in the community group, it made sense. But I guessed that fit a lot more people than I'd thought.

"Sorry. I don't know what you mean." He wrung his hands in front of him, as if he were trying to knit with nothing there. "If it helps any, I don't think your mom should be blamed."

"So, what do you think happened?"

Landon scratched the side of his head. "I have no idea. I've seen the news report on it, but I don't understand a lot of it. People on the news keep talking about cyberhijacking, like a hacker taking control of the plane from the ground or somewhere remote. I mean... I guess it's possible, because I don't see any scenario where your mom did this on purpose."

"Right. And cyberhijacking itself is new. There's no precedent for this sort of thing. I saw online that people were saying the government could be concealing negotiations with terrorists or cyberhijackers because they don't want to tell everyone." I tried to control my tongue. I didn't want to sound like one of those people who believed there had been no passengers on the 9/11 flights or that the earth was flat.

But this was my life. My mother. His belief that she might not have crashed on purpose made my heart grow three sizes.

"I don't really have a good guess as to what happened either. But I know she didn't do this on purpose, and I know it sounds impossible, but I think she's okay," I said.

She had to be.

"Your mom was always so nice," he said. "I remember a birthday party for Savannah at your house, way back when. We painted our own masks, but mine came out kinda odd-looking. I'm not good at art like you. So she helped me make a new one."

I couldn't help but smile. I didn't know that story. I didn't even remember that party. But I was happy Landon did, even if he'd said Mom "was" and not "is" nice.

We ended up back at my house.

The camera crews had left for the night—perhaps they'd figured we'd gone to sleep. It left a peaceful quiet around my house, one I hadn't felt in days.

Onion's tiny face appeared in the window, beckoning me inside.

"Thanks for the purse," I said to Landon.

"I scored these too." He extended his hand and slipped me a package of Reese's Pieces.

"How did you do that?!"

"You looked away for a second. I saw you staring at them." He smiled.

Oh my GOD. I am dead. "That was so sweet," I said a bit quieter than I would've liked.

Landon nodded. "You can make it up to me by lending me the book when you're done. And if you get an appointment with Dr. Madison, let me know. We can be waiting-room buddies."

"Sure." Nope, no intention. "Get home safe."

Hc took two steps forward, then stopped. Crickets chirped in the oak in front of my lawn.

"Hey," he said. "Not to sound weird, but I still think you should audition for the show."

I shook my head. "I can't. I'm still figuring out everything with my mom."

"I know. That's why it makes more sense to do it," he said. "I'm scared too. I can't sing, but I want to. It wouldn't be true to myself to pretend I don't."

"I'm not scared," I lied.

"Oh, okay." He smirked. "Sure." How could this boy make me feel warm without even touching me?

"Night, Violet," he said, and headed back home.

I walked into the house carefully, placing one foot gently in front of thc other. I'd only gone around the block, but Dad would've asked way too many questions if hc saw me coming back with a boy. I didn't want to makc it "a thing."

The first stair didn't creak. Two steps, no creak. As I reached the third—

"What are you doing?"

I clapped my hand over my mouth so I didn't scream. Freaking Savannah, hovering outside the bathroom door like the Babadook. "Nothing," I said.

A roll of thunder roared behind us. I guessed the sky had decided to rain after all.

"Where did you go? Was that Landon Davis?" she asked.

"He found my purse. I left it at the library." The lie rolled off my tongue far too easily.

"Oh. That's good." Savannah rubbed her eyes. "Hey,

Dad wanted me to ask you. Do you like roses or a mixture of flowers better?"

"For what?"

She clenched her jaw.

Oh. *Oh.*

I wasn't interested in any memorial. Nothing of the sort. It hadn't even been two full days yet.

"Whatever," I mumbled.

"Okay." Savannah tucked hair behind her ear. "You know what it reminded me of, though? Remember the time when Mom showed us how to make origami flowers? I was awful at it, but yours looked like an actual flower! That was so fun."

A flash of Mom: her hands smoothing my hair into a braid, watching my fingers fold a pink piece of paper into the petals of a rose. I sat in her lap, Savannah to my left. Mom hung my origami flower on the fridge for weeks. The world had been quiet then.

I clutched my bedroom doorknob so tightly my knuckles went white. I wasn't sure if I'd ever know that feeling again.

And how *dare* Savannah talk about Mom like that when she'd given up on her so easily? How dare she?

"Pick whatever flowers you want." I shut the door behind me, the coveted last word.

In my room, I researched the case some more.

Dad and Savannah were ready to give up on finding Mom, but I wasn't. Their denial drove me harder and harder. I trusted Mom to come back home; why couldn't they? I hit enter in the search bar a bit too hard.

Tomorrow was day three. People couldn't live without water for three days, and with the storm off in the distance... It didn't feel like people were racing against the clock like

I was. It was as if no one else realized we were coming up to a tight deadline.

Maybe they had landed somewhere safely and couldn't communicate...

I had to tell myself that. I needed something.

Something tangible.

I crept toward my parents' bedroom. Dad was asleep, so I took each step slowly and carefully. I gently opened the door to my parents' walk-in closet. Dad's stuff had mostly been moved out, so it was all Mom's. One side of the closet was starkly empty.

I spotted my mom's favorite tan cardigan and smoothed my fingers across the sleeve. She'd worn it the day I'd gotten my learner's permit. I remembered hugging her so tightly after I'd passed the exam, and how she'd taken me for chocolate ice cream next door.

"Just because you have your permit doesn't mean you can take the car whenever," she had said.

"I know. I'll ask first," I'd responded.

"I'm going to miss driving you around," she'd sighed.

I took the sweater off the rack and tossed it on. It was the closest thing I had to a hug from Mom right now. When I slipped my hands in the pockets, something sharp poked my cuticle.

A pair of small flight wings, a badge. I was struck by the brilliance of the gold and the structure of the model. I wasn't positive, but I thought I recognized it from her uniform. Maybe her old one. In the other pocket, there was a crumpled photo and a necklace in the shape of an M.

I held it up. It was silver, with rhinestones on it. She didn't wear jewelry much, but I'd never seen her wear this one at all. M? It must've stood for Mark, Dad's first name. Or Modern Airline, the airline she flew for? No, that would be weird. Companies didn't do that.

In the photo, Mom looked way young. Her hair was shoulder-length, even though all my life, she'd had a pixie cut. She was hugging a man I didn't recognize, standing in front of a military jet. He was tall, decently handsome, and definitely not my father. On the back, Mom had written "June 1991."

Not very informative, Mother.

"Hey." Footsteps creaked into the bedroom. Dad. "You okay in here?"

I quickly slipped the wings and photo back in my pocket. "Yeah. Hey, can I wear this?" I held the necklace up.

"Uh." Dad blinked his sleepy eyes as he walked into the closet. "Sure? Why not?"

"When did you give this to Mom?"

Dad came forward and took the necklace in his hand. "I didn't."

CHAPTER SEVEN

DAY THREE – MORNING

For perhaps the first time in my life, Dad had made a full breakfast for Savannah and me.

Eggs with cheese, sliced bananas, the whole thing. He even had bacon going, which had been half the reason I'd gotten out of bed. I scooped a bunch of it onto my plate.

"What's the occasion?" I asked.

"Can't a dad make breakfast for his daughters when they're going through a hard time?" he asked.

Savannah sipped on green tea in a black thermos. "And? You're up to something."

"*And* I wanted your opinions on something, because I have to make some calls today," Dad said. "Would you prefer your therapist to be a certain gender?"

I put my fork down. "It's way too early to have this conversation."

"I know, I know," he said. "But I'm making an appointment today, so you might as well tell me."

"I'm open to any gender," Savannah said.

I narrowed my eyes at her. How was everything so freaking easy for my sister? Memorial flowers—roses! Airing out all my issues—no problem!

It wasn't even like I'd be able to see Dr. Madison. If I was going to see a therapist, I might as well see one I could get more information from. But she'd made it clear she wasn't going to break ethical rules.

"I'm not going," I said.

"You are." Dad shut off the oven and turned to face me. "I know you're not happy about it, and I get it. If you want to continue this conversation another time, fine. But I am making an appointment and your butt will be in that seat." He then looked to Savannah. "Butts. Plural."

"This is such crap." I dug my nails into my arm underneath the table. I went deeper and deeper until the white, sharp edges threatened to break skin.

Fifty days, Violet. Almost there.

If I could hang on to a streak that long, maybe I could hit seventy-five. Then one hundred. Then maybe forever.

I dropped my hands back onto the table and shoveled a huge bite of eggs and bacon into my mouth to distract me.

All of this was so unfair.

I stared at the empty seat at the breakfast table, wondering why the hell Mom was taking so long to show up. By three p.m. today, we were going to hit the dreaded seventy-two-hour mark. My insides were practically crawling out of my skin with anticipation.

"We can talk more in the car, okay? But we gotta go. I'm not being late." Savannah sipped the last of her tea and pushed her half-eaten plate forward.

"You're not going to finish?" Dad asked.

"I don't feel great," she mumbled.

"I'll eat your bacon, then." I reached across to her plate.

"Stomach bothering you again?" he asked.

"Just my period, probably," Savannah said.

"Oh, all right. I did a run to CVS yesterday and picked up some tampons because I saw we were running low. Hope I got the right ones. That TikTok video really freaked me out. I don't understand why boys are sticking them up their—"

Savannah coughed and took a gulp of tea.

I sighed and tried to pretend I didn't find it sweet that he'd run an errand for us as I ate what was left on my plate. "This therapy discussion isn't over." I pointed my fork at Dad.

He took it and chucked it into the dishwasher. "I accept that challenge."

I followed Savannah to the car and slipped into the front. "He really had to throw that on us before our first day of school?"

"Your first day of school. I've been back since," she said.

"You threw up and got sent home. Doesn't count."

Savannah side-eyed me. "You're snippy this morning."

"Maybe getting ambushed about roses or whatever last night didn't help." I crossed my arms and looked out the window. The idea of talking was exhausting. No words would ever be able to tell my sister how I felt. We communicated in two separate languages. I was tired of wishing I could have one of those sibling relationships where we had tons of inside jokes and memories together. It was never going to happen.

"Hey, listen…" Savannah stopped at a red light. She placed her hand on my shoulder, which I couldn't remember her ever doing before. Her hand was warmer than expected. "I-I'm…"

Incapable of saying sorry? I wanted to blurt. *Much like a young Maleficent?*

"Everything is going to be okay today," she said. "And if you need me, find me."

I nodded. "Yeah."

The one person I wanted to find, I couldn't. No one could.

"Look, you want to make it up to me? Then I need a favor," I said.

Savannah side-eyed me again. "I'm afraid to ask."

"Drop me off at the jewelry store. The one in town, with the lady with the frizzy blonde hair," I said.

"What?" Savannah raised an eyebrow. "Why? What are you buying jewelry for?"

I held out the necklace and photo, secure in my pocket. "Have you seen Mom wear this before? Is it definitely hers? And do you know who this guy is?"

Savannah glanced at both items, then to the road. "I have no idea."

"Okay. Drop me off, then."

"It's not even eight a.m. yet. She probably doesn't open until nine or ten. What are you going to do, sit around for a few hours?"

"If that's what it takes."

For once, Savannah did what I asked. I guessed guilt about being a literal demon to me the past few days was welling up inside her.

I only had to wait a little over an hour, and I got some tea at the café next door.

While I was there, I browsed Mom's friends on Facebook, but didn't see any that matched the man in the photo. Based on the fact that I'd found the necklace with the photo, I assumed one had to do with the other. I could be wrong, but I had to follow any lead. Anything at all.

When she arrived, the jeweler, Ms. Elmwood, seemed surprised to see me so early. She had barely gotten behind the counter before I'd opened the shop door.

The jewelry store was small, with high ceilings and green-painted walls. The displays were clear and shiny, and the entire store smelled like an old book. A dozen clocks lined up on the wall reminded me of how quickly time was getting away from me.

"Good morning. You're one of the Ashby girls, aren't you?" she asked.

"Yes," I said quickly. "And I'm sorry to ambush you so early, but I need your help."

"I'm so sorry to hear about your mother. She was just in here the other day. I can't believe she's gone so suddenly," Ms. Elmwood said.

"She was?" I raised my eyebrows.

"Yes. Two days before the crash, I believe."

I tried not to wince. There had been no *crash*. No debris, nothing. The worst thing about all of this was Mom being gone. The second worst was the assumptions.

"What was she doing here? What did she need jewelry for?" I asked.

"She wasn't buying," Ms. Elmwood said. "She was selling. Quite a bit."

Selling? I hadn't gone through my mom's necklaces and things. I didn't know if anything valuable was missing. Why would she get rid of things?

"A lot of people come in here to sell before they…" Ms. Elmwood tilted her head. "You know. It's common. Makes things easier on the family."

I clenched my jaw. Nothing was easy for my family, and

I did not appreciate her insinuation.

"I did phone the police when I heard," she said. "They said on the news they were open to any tips. Just so you know."

Great. I fought the urge to smack her across the counter. *Give them all the more reason to think this was on purpose!*

"Whatever. I came in here because I wanted to know if she purchased this here, or when she did." I placed the necklace on the countertop. It made a small *click* against the cool glass.

Ms. Elmwood held it up under the light. "She had this with her the other day."

My heart pounded against my rib cage. "Really? She bought it here?"

"No, she had it with her. It was tangled up in the other jewelry she was selling. She took it out and said she didn't want to give it up, that she'd gotten it from a school boyfriend."

School boyfriend? Mom had only had one serious boyfriend in high school, and one in college. Neither of their names started with *M*. But hey, it was something. Maybe there was a nickname, or someone less serious.

She held it to the light again. "This is an older piece. Not really in style anymore. I haven't sold this style since the early 2000s, maybe."

So, before I was born.

I grabbed the necklace back. No way I was going to school now. I had yearbooks to sift through.

"Thank you!" I chirped, and then I was out the door.

I took a rideshare back home. The twenty-five dollars was worth it. I didn't want Savannah or anyone else to know what I was doing. School could wait. For the first time, I actually felt like I was making headway.

And besides, Mom had said to keep this between us.

As soon as I got home, I scoured Mom's high school yearbook. I sat on the gray carpeted floor of her bedroom and scanned the names of everyone who'd written a message on the back.

Have a great summer!

Math class was bogus but you made it fun

You're rad, Jenn!!

All these notes made me smile, and I wondered how these people felt about seeing Mom's name on their TV. That said, none of them were any guys whose names started with *M*. I looked through every photo, but I didn't see anyone who could be a younger version of the man in the army photograph that I found.

Her college yearbook was next. I didn't even know colleges had yearbooks. It was much smaller and barebones than her high school one. Again, no messages from anyone beginning with *M,* and none of the photographs resembled Mysterious Army Guy.

My last hope was Facebook. I detested that old-people website, but Mom did check it occasionally. It was the only social media she had.

I started toward Mom's laptop but stopped short. Agent Rosenfield's evidence team had taken it the other day. I didn't know her passwords, but I could guess based on old ones I'd set up for her using my own phone.

SavannahViolet0406

OnionDog255

CherryBlossoms0406

Finally. It was *SavannahViolet255.* Thank goodness my parents were technologically inept.

Hi, Jenn! Facebook welcomed me. *What's on your mind?*

If only I knew.

I didn't let myself look at the photos. I wasn't ready for that. My heart already ached for her, and I didn't want to make it worse. The time between people being able to survive without water and dying was closing in far too quickly.

First, I went through her small friends list. There were a few guys with last or first names starting with *M* that I wrote down. One struck me — Miles Miller.

I put my pen down. Why did that sound familiar?

I clicked on his profile. He wasn't Mysterious Army Guy, but I instantly remembered why I knew his name when I saw his face.

Coiffed blond hair, thick dark glasses. He'd been on the news the other day, the first day after it had happened. He was the founder of a cybersecurity tech company.

"*Cyberhijacking is extremely possible,*" he had said. "*My team has done it.*"

Could he have been part of the plan?

I had to find Miles Miller.

CHAPTER EIGHT

DAY THREE – AFTERNOON

I sent Miles a message. This was the mysterious boyfriend? He was the polar opposite of Dad. Miles looked uptight, and on the news he seemed to be a know-it-all, like a wannabe Elon Musk. Dad was more of a hippie, artsy type.

While I waited for his response, I did more research on him and his company. He had been in the military, too—in the nineties, like Mom had.

Quickly, I ran back downstairs, where the photo albums were. Mom didn't keep too many photos from her time in the army. She didn't like to talk about it, so we didn't ask.

But I found Miles. He was in one photo with the whole unit and another with Mom and a few other people. I searched the album twice over for the Mysterious Army Guy, but nothing.

Finally, I got an answer. He responded that it had freaked him out to receive a message "from Jenn", but he would be happy to chat with me today.

But this should be an in-person conversation, he said. *They track everything I say online or on my phone.*

They?

I wasn't naive. Even if this guy was my mom's friend, and he wanted to meet in a public place, it did feel unsafe. I'd never do this normally, but time was against me.

In a few hours, we would be at the three-day mark. The dark zone, where my thoughts were too afraid to go.

I was running out of time.

If he knew anything, anything at all, it would be worth finding out. Especially if he knew Mom well and could help clear her name.

Part of me wanted to ask Dad to come with me or if he knew who Miles was, but he'd never understand. Neither would Savannah. It wasn't like she'd ever come with me anyway. There was Alex, but I knew auditions for the musical were coming up and she'd be busy. Besides, I was already making her come to the FBI office with me.

There was one other person who might be willing to help.

ME: Soooo say hypothetically, I needed to ask you a favor, would you be interested?

LANDON: If you hypothetically needed a favor, I would hypothetically be happy to help. What is it?

I explained to Landon briefly what was going on, and asked him to meet Miles with me in the local park today after school.

LANDON: Sooo let me get this straight. You want me to come with you to meet an old guy you don't know that you met online?

ME: … kind of yeah!

LANDON: lol ok. I don't want you going alone. So

sure. I have a free period last period, so I can meet you at the park at two p.m.?

ME: You are perfect

My face flushed. Did I really just type that?

But ugh. It was kind of true. Nice, cute, knits, willing to meet a rando in the park with me.

Landon must be a secret serial killer or something. No one had it that put together.

ME: I meant like, perfect! Like, that sounds good!

He didn't reply. I tried not to kick myself about it, considering he was probably in class.

Still.

I was such a clown.

I walked to the park a few minutes before two p.m. I had the necklace and photograph securely in my jeans pocket. Miles was already there, sitting on a bench under an oak tree. He was too busy looking at his phone to notice me. His too-large glasses hung on the edge of his pointed nose.

"Hi!" Landon jogged up behind me. His cheeks were lightly flushed with pink. "Sorry I'm a little late, Mr. Tariq wanted to talk about auditions."

"Oh yeah?" I grinned. "Are you going to try out?"

"Hmm, maybe. I'm not that good of a singer, but I've always wanted to try," he said quietly. "Anyway! How are you doing with everything? You okay?"

"I'm fine," I lied. I was anything but fine. It was like every molecule in me was crackling with electricity, knowing we were getting too close to the seventy-two-hour mark. "But thanks for coming with me. The guy is right over there."

Landon glanced at Miles, then back to me. "Okay, I'm ready," he said, as if he were going into combat. He stood straighter and clenched his fists.

"Miles?" I asked as I approached. "Hi. I'm Violet."

"Violet!" Miles stood up and reached over to shake my hand. "Wow. You look just like your mother. Only with darker hair, I suppose. But just as lovely."

"Thanks," I said.

When I was younger, people said I looked like my mom all the time. Now, they didn't say it as much. I hoped that didn't mean I didn't resemble her anymore.

"I was wondering if you could help me with a few things," I said.

"Ah," he said. "You know about the cyberhijacking, then?"

Landon and I looked to each other, then back to Miles.

"What do you mean?" I asked breathlessly.

"Sit." He moved aside on the wooden bench.

My legs practically gave out as I sat next to him. Landon didn't sit. He stood, arms crossed, as if he were my bodyguard. My pink-scarf-knitting, anxiety-having bodyguard.

"I saw you on the news, talking about it," I said. "Is that what you're referring to?"

"Yes. You're familiar with my company, right? Ajax Systems? I'm one of the nation's leading cybersecurity experts, and my company is internationally recognized," he said.

I didn't really know what it meant to be an internationally recognized cybersecurity start-up, but it sounded good. Like Miles knew what he was talking about.

"I believe US133 has been cyberhijacked by a remote foreign body," he said. "Or perhaps a domestic threat. The evidence is clear. It's been done before."

"Sorry to ask, but what are you talking about?" Landon asked. "I've never heard of cyberhijacking until the other day."

"In 2016, the Department of Homeland Security hacked into a Boeing 757 that was parked on a runway in New Jersey. They pulled it off using the radio frequency communications." Miles's voice was quick and staccato, as if he had more to say than his breath could handle. "The public only heard about this hacking a few years later, in 2018, because the government knew there would be panic and wanted to fix the glitches before they released this information. But, of course, my team knew of this long before then. Someone could even use the wifi on board as a potential hack, if they knew how. So we're looking at remote threats on the ground, and threats within the plane itself. This major threat has been sitting under the public's nose."

Landon quickly typed something into his phone. "He's right, that did happen," he whispered.

I hadn't heard of this hack, and Mom had never mentioned it. My breath quickened. So it was true? Someone could have potentially hacked into the plane's computer from the ground? I thought of all the implications that could've had. For Mom, for her passengers... I didn't understand why someone would do something so terrible.

"So, you think that's what happened here? Why would they do that?" I asked.

"Well, I can't answer to the motives of a malicious person, but I can say that in this day and age, to not find a United States commercial airliner within a few days is... unusual," he said.

I thought back to other planes I'd heard about. MH370 was still missing, many years later. Air France 447 had been found, but it had taken about five days. Neither of those had exactly had the ending I was hoping for, but they still pointed to the fact that searching could take longer than a few days.

We were only on day three, but even that felt too long. It was as if my brain had been replaced by a clock. I could barely function, only count the minutes as they sped away from me.

"Think about it," Miles said. "My suggestion is that the government absolutely knows where the plane is. I don't mean to scare you, but I believe someone remotely landed the plane—safely—and is demanding a large ransom from the government. They're hiding it, of course, so as not to instill panic. Remember the early weeks of the coronavirus pandemic? Mayhem. Empty grocery store shelves. The economy took a nosedive. 9/11? Ah, wait, you weren't born then, were you? Well, case in point, there was panic, and the government learned their lesson. Think of all the canceled flights and how much money they'd lose if they announced they'd let a huge security threat like this happen again."

My head felt like it was being crammed with way too much information. It made sense to me, I guessed. But would it really be possible to hide something like that from the public? Such a big safety threat?

"What about all the people on the plane?" Landon asked. "They have their cell phones, couldn't they call for help?"

"It might surprise you, Gen Z child, but not everywhere in the world has cell service. The ocean is quite vast," Miles said. "And not if they were taken hostage."

"So… You think my mom is being held hostage?" I said slowly. I hated the idea of her being scared, but that would mean she was alive. Not crashed, not in the middle of the frigid Atlantic.

"That is my assessment, yes," Miles said. "I imagine this cyberhijacker would keep everyone on the plane and hold the plane itself as ransom until they got what they wanted. Perhaps they were already on a remote island in the middle of the ocean, for example, and had the plane land there. Then these hijackers took physical control."

I pictured my mother and 155 other people, sitting on a remote island somewhere. Was there food, water? The hijackers would want to keep them all alive, I assumed. I hoped.

"I know your mother. We don't communicate regularly, but I know the type of person she is," Miles said. "She would never do this on purpose."

"Yes! Right," I said quickly.

"It's infuriating that the media has been saying so," he said. "It's a waste of resources."

Finally.

Finally someone else who agreed with me that things might be okay. It was like the sun peeking out after a storm. I fought the urge to hug Miles, this odd stranger. All I wanted was someone as certain as me that she wouldn't do this on purpose, and that she might be okay. Even if the details were fuzzy. Even if it didn't make perfect sense.

"And I was in the army with her, as you know. She's a talented pilot. Accidents happen, sure, but she is skilled and fierce as any," Miles said.

"I'm sorry, I just find all this a little hard to believe," Landon said. "This kind of stuff seems…like a movie or something. Like it can't really happen."

"It's already happening," Miles said. "My entire company is dedicated to stopping hackers like these and learning more about these groups. In 2017, Russia cyberhijacked our electricity grid. You hear almost daily about meat-packing plants being hacked, hospitals. The gaps in our systems are dangerous. This has happened before, I believe it is happening in this case, and if the government doesn't address the system flaws, it will absolutely happen again."

Landon pulled out his phone again and stared at it with knit brows. I assumed he was verifying everything Miles had mentioned.

"We got lucky with the grid hijack," Miles said. "Imagine no lights, no power? It could affect us for months on end. People would die, the economy would tank. It would set us back years. That's why you don't hear about these things. Fear."

I could barely focus on what he was saying. I was still picturing Mom on a remote island, kidnapped by some awful hacker people. The idea of her being scared, hungry, missing us… It made goose bumps poke at my skin. I was the last person she talked to before she disappeared. That made me feel even more like this fell on my shoulders.

"I wouldn't be shocked if your mom knew about these gaps. Jenn is a smart person," Miles said. "And we'd talked about this in the past. A few years ago, maybe."

My mom wasn't the most tech-forward person, but she was probably more savvy than most people her age. Is that what she'd meant, though, in the letter?

None of this was supposed to happen this way. I am just asking you to trust me. This wasn't my original plan, but I do have a plan.

Had she known this would happen somehow? It didn't make sense. If she'd known about it, why put herself at risk? None of this made sense to me, but she was asking me to trust her. That I could do.

"Are you working with the government on this?" I asked.

"They've contacted me and we've spoken extensively. That is all I can say."

I tried to ignore the hope welling in my heart. It sounded like Miles could be right. That Mom could be okay, and that there was a lot of information not being shared with my family or the public to keep everything under control.

But what if he wasn't right?

I tried not to think about it.

"I came here to ask you something." I took the necklace from my pocket and showed it to him. "Does this look familiar? Did you give this to my mom?"

Miles barely looked at it. "No, not me. Why?"

I explained how Ms. Elmwood, the jeweler, had said it had been from a school boyfriend, but I hadn't found any names starting with *M*.

Miles gave a small chuckle. "If I had to guess, the man you're looking for is Matthew Bryant."

Matthew Bryant. The name didn't ring any bells. None at all.

"Is it this guy?" I took the photo out and showed it to Miles.

"That's the one," he said.

CHAPTER NINE

DAY THREE – AFTERNOON

In the end, I hugged Miles. I had to.

He said he didn't keep in touch with Matthew Bryant or too many people from his army days, so he didn't have contact information or know much about him. All he knew was that there were rumors that Matthew Bryant and Mom were a couple, and he saw them flirting a lot (ew). Miles wished me luck, and Landon and I went on our way. He offered to give me a ride to the train station so I could meet Alex.

I was invigorated to go meet Agent Rosenfield. I now had two things to ask her about – Matthew Bryant and the subpoena for Dr. Madison.

"Are you sure you're okay?" Landon buckled his seatbelt, then watched to make sure I did the same as I climbed into the front seat. His car was shockingly clean and tidy for a teenage boy's. Not a fast-food wrapper in sight. Only notebooks and papers in the back seat.

And a worn-looking beige teddy bear.

"That's my brother's," he said quickly. "I swear."

"Sure." I laughed. "How old is your brother?"

"Nine," he said.

"Big age gap."

"Yeah. I take care of him a lot. Pick him up from school and stuff to give my parents a break. They work pretty wild hours," he said. "But really, I want to make sure you're okay before I drop you off. That must've been a lot for you."

"I'm fine, I guess? I believe Miles. Since day one, I've believed she was okay. It's so nice to hear someone else agree."

Landon paused. "I get it… I just… Everything he said felt strange. Like it can't be real. I don't want him to give you all this false hope for nothing."

I looked toward the trees rushing past us as Landon drove. Blurs of green and brown.

"It does seem far-fetched," I said. "But this entire situation is far-fetched. So, honestly, I believe it. My mom would never do something like this on purpose."

He nodded. I could tell he didn't believe Miles's theory. And that was fine.

He didn't read Mom's letter. He didn't know what I knew.

No one did.

"Thank you for coming with me," I said. "I really do appreciate it. I'm glad he wasn't a creep, but it made me feel so much safer with you there." I wasn't ready to admit it yet, but Landon did make me feel that way. Like he was a warm fire on a frigid day. Hell, he even *drove* responsibly. Two hands on the wheel in the nine and three positions.

"Happy to help!" Landon pulled up to the train station parking lot.

Alex was already there, up on the platform. Her beautiful curls blew in the wind.

Landon looked to me with those deep brown eyes. "Let me know if you need anything else, okay? I've never driven in the city before, and… I'd probably puke just trying, but if you need me, I'll come pick you and Alex up."

A boy who was willing to face New York City traffic for me was a guy I wanted to keep. "Thank you."

There was a quick buzz of an impulse for me to lean over and kiss his cheek. I fought it — I'd already made him think I was super bizarre with all this cyberhijacking stuff.

Instead, I awkwardly patted his shoulder. Two long pats. Like a grandmother.

I was destined to be single for life.

After I left the car and headed for the platform, Landon waited until I reached Alex before driving away.

"Hi!" she grinned. "I love that cardigan. Can I borrow it tomorrow? It'll fit perfectly for me trying to look like Belle but not obviously. You know?"

I glanced to my light-blue cardigan. "Sure. I'll probably come in and sit in on auditions. Mr. Tariq asked me about it a while ago."

Audition day for the school musicals was like the Oscars for Alex — once a year, and she stressed about it until everything was over. I knew she'd get a good part in *Beauty and the Beast*, but Alex was bound to have a mental breakdown or two.

Actors.

I was a little jealous, though. It was probably fun to imagine yourself in a part and memorize all the lines just in case. Not that I ever did that. So not me. I did not

ot k

sing through the entire soundtrack to *Rent*, all parts, just in case someone ever needed me to fill in for Maureen or Roger.

"You'll kill it," I said.

"I better, but I can't talk about it until then, because it's bad luck." Alex had a lot of theater beliefs surrounding luck, like not saying a certain Shakespeare title in a theater, or doing a certain vocal warm up before every show. I didn't dare question them.

"So," Alex said gently. "What is it that you're going to tell this FBI chick? Did you learn anything new?"

I couldn't believe how much had happened since I'd filled Alex in. I told her about Dr. Madison, the photo, the necklace, everything. It wasn't that I expected to get ahead of the FBI with this info, but they were simply going to tell me Mom was dead and I wasn't ready to hear that.

I *needed* to make Agent Rosenfield order that subpoena, even if I had to hack into her computer to do it myself. It was the only thing keeping me going right now. I knew it was ridiculous to keep up hope, but I couldn't bring myself to give up on the one person who'd never given up on me.

I wanted to look up, to see how cloudless the sky truly was, but I couldn't. Not yet.

The train pulled into the station with a thunderous roar. We took seats across from each other so we could both have a window.

"I've gotta google this Matthew Bryant guy. You start on page five, I'll start on page one," I said.

Ever since I'd heard the name a half hour ago, I was desperate to lunge into the search. So far, though, Google wasn't very helpful. Apparently, Matthew Bryant was a common name. When I typed in "Matthew Bryant age 50", it still wasn't useful. I tried our town name and county instead—nothing. There were at least ten different Matthew Bryants in the area: engineers, doctors, plumbers.

When I typed in his name with "army", some LinkedIn profiles came up. I showed them to Alex.

"None of these look like the guy in that photo," Alex said.

"I mean, that photo was taken, like, thirty years ago. You think he might look different now?"

"I guess," she said. "This whole thing is so confusing."

"Tell me about it," I said. "But I don't know, talking to Miles earlier confirmed what I already felt. I really think it's a cyberhijacking, and that Mom is okay. I can't prove it, but I know deep down that she's not…that it wasn't an accident, and that it definitely wasn't on purpose."

"That would be the best-case scenario, I guess." Alex sighed and leaned back in her seat. "So, if it wasn't Landon posting in the forums, who do you think it was?"

"No idea. I'll have to do more research on the account name," I said.

It could've been a stranger, lying about knowing her personally.

But something about the posts seemed genuine.

I wondered if Dad missed Mom as much as I did. It was weird to think that. Yeah, I'd known her my whole life, but Dad had been with Mom even longer than that. And these new strangers I'd learned about, Miles Miller and Matthew Bryant, had known her even longer.

Did that mean they all knew her better than I did? "I hope I didn't make Landon think I was weird by asking," I said.

"Why do you care?" Alex smirked. "You're afraid he won't talk to you anymore?"

"Shut up." I rolled my eyes.

"It's really sweet that he came with you to talk to that cybernerd guy," she said.

"It is," I said. "He's so nice. I can't believe we've gone to the same school this whole time and barely talked until now."

"I think I follow him on Insta." She leaned forward so I could see her phone. She clicked on Landon's profile. It showed mostly photos of him playing the guitar by himself or with friends. I guess I followed so many people, I hardly noticed his photos before.

A text notification popped up at the top of her screen.

HOT GF: Come over later?

I blinked. I'd been pretty shocked over the past few days, but I hadn't expected to see that. "Who's HOT GF?" I managed. "You're seeing someone?"

"It's...Well... Kind of." She squirmed away from me.

"You are? How serious?"

"Um... Somewhat. Decently serious, I guess," she said. "I really like her, and I'm, like, 98.5% sure it's mutual."

"You have a girlfriend?" I squeaked. "Why didn't I know about this?"

Alex in love was a new phenomenon. Last year, she'd fallen hard for a girl at another school who was particularly pretty but not particularly interested in Alex.

I wanted to see my girl happy, but the idea of her broken-hearted didn't sit well with me. She was the type who was still holding on for her perfect first kiss— fireworks, the romantic sort of rain following a picnic— and would settle for nothing less.

Pretty badass, if you asked me.

"It felt so vapid with everything going on with you," she said quietly. "It's insignificant."

I reached for her hand. "Al. It's not. Tell me about this girl."

"Going from cyberhijacking and plane stuff to discussing girls still feels weird." She gave a small laugh.

"Come on. What is she like?"

"She's super smart," she said. "She's beautiful. Blonde. Incredible legs."

I smirked. "You love legs."

"I do. I really do."

Two peas in a queer pod. "So when can I meet her?" I asked.

"Uh…" Alex picked at the fabric lining of the train seats. "I want to wait until things are official between us."

I raised my eyebrows. "But it's just me."

With all of Alex's former crushes, she'd introduce me early on so I could charm them. The idea was befriend them, talk up Alex, get them to date. It would be a flawless plan if Alex didn't continually fall for girls who didn't know of her existence. Or straight girls.

"I know, I know. But I don't want to scare her," she said. "You understand, don't you?"

"Of course." I did understand. But I also couldn't help wondering if Alex didn't want to introduce her to the girl whose mom had allegedly killed 155 people. If Alex wanted a shot at normal, I didn't blame her. I would've given anything for "normal."

"It's not that," she said quickly. "It's really not."

"Okay."

"No, Vi. You need to believe me. It's not that." The sincerity in her voice was genuine enough for me to believe her.

Still, it stung.

"Okay," I said.

"It's just… This is different." She shook her head. "I don't want to talk about it. Tell me about Landon, please."

"No thanks."

"Come on! Hey! Wait, let me do your tarot."

"What? No! We're on the train," I said. "Besides, what if it says something bad?" I couldn't handle any more bad news.

"It won't."

"You don't know that."

"Violet, play along for once." She reached into her bag to retrieve her collection of tarot cards. She spread them out on her legs, along with a quartz crystal. "Besides, we're not asking about bad stuff." A mischievous grin spread across her face. "I want to see if it says you're in love."

"Oh please." Like I could even handle a relationship right now. I could barely handle getting dressed in the morning.

"Choose one," she said. "We'll keep it simple."

I did. For the record: I did not believe in this stuff. But maybe there was a Priestess of Lost Planes card or something.

"Ah. The Tower." Alex nodded. "I figured that would be it."

The card showed a medieval-looking tower under siege. Fire and flames, generally nothing that said *Mom will be home soon*.

"This means something disrupted your usual harmony," she said. "The lightning represents that change. But it also represents an awakening. Truth. Basically, honey, follow your intuition."

"Okay." I tried not to roll my eyes. No shit something had disrupted my usual harmony. Anyone watching CNN the past few days could've told me that.

"It can also mean you're looking to buy a house. Are you looking to buy a house?"

"I get paid seven-fifty an hour selling pickles. So, no, I'm not looking to buy a house."

"Mhm," she said. "Then yeah. From destruction comes creation. Be the tower, Violet."

"I'll try my best."

We pulled into Grand Central.

I stood, but the train lurched forward and I lost my balance. I didn't feel much like a tower.

The FBI office was a seventies-style, nondescript glass building in the financial district.

As Alex and I took the elevator up and then sat in a lavish waiting room with faux waterfalls and leather seats, I wondered how all these businesspeople passing by were going on with their lives. A plane with 155 people had gone missing, but corporations still functioned and the receptionist took our names down. I didn't get it, and in a way, I was jealous.

Even of Alex, who sat beside me doing math homework. "Savannah isn't coming, is she?" she asked, without looking up from a quadratic equation.

Is the Pope Jewish? Are the ice caps fine and dandy? "No. I'm not sure if she knows I'm here, so don't say anything to her."

"Ah." Alex rolled her eyes. "Have you two ever considered actually communicating?"

"No, that would be outrageous."

"Right."

Agent Rosenfield appeared from a hallway behind the receptionist. Black suit, black tie, intense gaze. Intimidating as hell. "Hello, Violet. Violet's friend," she said.

"Alex." She extended her hand, and nobody could miss the legs-to-neck-checkout she gave Agent Rosenfield. *Ugh*.

"Wonderful." As Agent Rosenfield led us down the hall, she glanced over her shoulder, as if searching for something. "Is your father on his way?"

"Yeah, but he'll be late. He's working." I was becoming a fantastic liar. I only felt the slightest bit of shame creep up my neck. "But he did give me this." I slipped her a forged contract.

When I'd texted her that I wanted to visit her with information, she'd sent me an email with a parent permission slip. It *did* cross my mind that I was lying to probably the smartest people in the world, but hey, no way was I telling Dad I had possible dirt on Mom. He'd been through enough.

"Great." She barely looked at it, thankfully.

We passed through the open offices, and a burst of energy hit me in the chest.

This room was a living, breathing thing. People's excited voices buzzed in the air as tons of screens flashed with stories and razor-sharp images. So many wires traveled up and down. I was desperate to follow each one into its plug.

I could picture exactly how I'd draw this as a theater set. A movie set, even.

"Cool," I whispered.

"It is cool." Agent Rosenfield grinned; the first real smile I'd seen from her.

Her office was the opposite of the open space—quiet, neat, and tiny.

I peeked at the picture frames on her desk. No wedding photos, no children. Only Agent Rosenfield shaking hands with a former president and the New York governor, then a picture of her and a woman in a hijab posing by a lake.

Alex and I sat across from her. I refused her offer of tea or coffee, but Alex took a hot chocolate.

Agent Rosenfield sat and clasped her hands. "So, what is it you wanted to tell me?"

"Remember, everything you say is confidential," Alex said.

"No," Agent Rosenfield said bluntly. "It's not. Not at all."

I assumed it wasn't, but I appreciated Alex for asking. "So... If I tell you something you don't already know, you can use it against Mom?"

"If I had to, yes," Agent Rosenfield said.

I bit my lip. I figured that would be the case. But all of this was too important to stop now. "That's fine. Before I tell you, I want you to tell me something," I said.

"Try me."

"Tell me everything you know about this case."

"I can't do that," she said.

"Can you tell me if you're leaning toward it being a cyberhijacking? I know you talked to Miles Miller. I know he's involved somehow."

"Look, I'm running this investigation. To keep it running properly, I can't tell you the details. This is an incredibly confidential investigation," she said.

"But I'm family. This is my mother we're talking about! We're running out of time!" I tried not to yell in the FBI office. I wasn't trying to get arrested. But damn, they were dragging their feet on this as if every second didn't count. "It could easily be cyberhijacking. In that case, can't you trace some IP address? Just freaking... I don't know, find her?"

Don't cry, don't cry, don't cry. I blinked back tears.

"I know it's your family on the line, and I know you are desperate for information," Agent Rosenfield said gently. "I get it, but you have to understand we keep this confidential for a reason. It's to make the investigation more efficient. I can go over logistics with you, if you'd like."

"Fine," I huffed. "Give me the logistics."

Missing in the Atlantic by South America, fair weather but a storm forming in the distance, no distress signal, and the glitchy way the transponder had turned on and off twice within fifteen minutes. Five continents had sent out fleets and planes to search, but so far, nothing.

Because of the way the transponder had turned on and off, it had interfered with the way the radar could tell where the plane was, so the size of the search area was way larger than it should've been. A plane at full speed could go at least 150 miles in only fifteen minutes.

"And this storm coming, Violet," Agent Rosenfield said gently. "If weather predictions are correct, then it is going to directly interfere with the search. It already has, since there is an area the crews haven't been able to safely search today. In the next few days, it will likely be declared a hurricane."

"Does that mean they'll stop searching?" The fear made my voice waver.

"Not necessarily, but I have to be honest and say it will certainly impede things in a major way."

I looked to my hands and tried to blink back tears. I hadn't heard a single piece of good news since any of this started.

"Additionally," she said, "Homeland Security is working to clear all the passengers on the plane. That means they are doing a proper investigation to be sure those passengers aren't responsible for the plane's disappearance. As of this morning, they've cleared twenty."

"Twenty?" That was nothing. There were over a hundred people left. With that tortoise speed, it would a month to clear all 155 passengers.

I didn't have that kind of time.

Mom didn't have that kind of time.

I thought of all those people. All their families, all their friends. It was unimaginable. The idea that my family wasn't alone somehow made it worse. This type of suffering shouldn't be shared.

"That's way too slow," I said.

My nails found their way to my wrists. My self-harm often happened on auto-pilot. The pain of digging into my soft skin made me realize what I was doing, and I dropped my hands to my sides.

"I know it's frustrating," Agent Rosenfield said gently. "I feel where you're coming from."

"Do you?" Alex's face was blank, but her words strong. "Violet has been through hell. Her mom is gone, and she doesn't know why or how. You didn't know Mrs. Ashby, but I did. I do." Alex took a gulp of hot chocolate. "When I was nine, I was in a car accident and lost my left eye. Everybody freaked the hell out, even my parents, and treated me like I was different. Like I was this fragile thing who was suddenly less capable. But not Mrs. Ashby.

"She changed my bandages after the surgery and treated me the same as she had before. She told me that I can do it, and put the video game controller back in my hand. Without her, I might've never played video games again and realized I want to design them. And, honestly, I probably would've just given up on everything."

My fingers tapped against my wrist, begging to dig again.

Alex tucked hair behind her ear. "That is not a woman who kills 155 people. So imagine if that person was out of your life, and suddenly being pointed at as a criminal? That's what Violet is going through."

Wow. For once, me and my big mouth were left speech-less.

It had been six years since that accident, and Alex had never told me any of that. I imagined Mom's gentle hands smoothing the bandage onto Alex's face, calming all her fears. The same thing she used to do for me when I was afraid.

I reached under the table to squeeze Alex's hand.

She squeezed back.

I knew Alex always had my back, but it made me feel stronger to see it in action. Lately, I'd felt alone, but this was a reminder that I wasn't.

"I admire that, Alex, and I admire your bravery, Violet. I'm so sorry all of this is happening to you," Agent Rosenfield said. "So let me also divulge something personal to you. I do know how you feel." She tapped her expensive-looking pen against the wooden desk. "I wasn't assigned to this investigation. I asked for it. My friend, my very, very good friend, was a passenger on that flight. She was flying home from doing medical work in Brazil.

"This is someone I grew up with, that person I looked to every time the teacher said to find a partner. We stayed like that, even as adults. I've barely slept since I heard the news. And having to deal with my colleagues suspecting her of terrorism? I'm torn between wanting to take a leave of absence and defending her because I know no one else will. Getting out of bed every morning is…difficult. To say the least." Her face was hard, unmoving. "I need to know what happened to her. That is why I do what I do. The truth isn't always going to be handed to you. Sometimes, you have to fight for it."

The beat of my own heart echoed in my ears. I hadn't expected that. Not at all. Her bravery, words so honest that they chilled to the bone. I wanted to feel that way about myself. I wanted to be so sure I could solve this mystery.

She tilted the photo on her desk toward us, the one of her and the woman in the hijab.

"You may have heard of her. Ayesha Ahmad," she said.

I had. I certainly had. The news had been as awful on her. When commenters discussed passengers possibly hijacking the plane, her name was always the first to be brought up. "Oh. I-I'm sorry."

She nodded. "I didn't even know she was on the flight until her husband called me to tell me and asked if I could help. She's an incredible doctor. Incredible person. For a few years, she thought she wanted to be a vet, but she couldn't take seeing animals hurt, dying. So she decided to help people instead. That's what she always said—she wanted to be a helper. Maybe that's why we bonded so quickly. I don't know. She's so much better at it than me."

She tilted the photo back toward her and took a moment with it.

"So, I know part of what you're going through. I can't imagine all of it, of course. Losing your mother." She looked to me. "I don't pretend to understand that. But I'm coming from a genuine place, and I think we can aid each other."

No wonder this woman worked for the FBI. I suddenly

realized how false confessions happened. I *wanted* to look into her deep green eyes and tell her my entire story.

"I think so too." I swallowed. "Who's Matthew Bryant?"

She blinked. "How do you know about him? Did your mother say something to you?"

"No. I found a photo of him and my mom, and I did some digging."

"He is an important part of my investigation," she said. "Before takeoff, your mom had a three-minute cell phone conversation with a number linked to a man named Matthew Bryant. They had many phone calls leading up to the flight."

My hands were shaking so hard that I could barely grasp the photo in my pocket. "This guy?"

Agent Rosenfield peered at it. "Yes, that's him. This must be an old photo."

"1991, it says on the back," I said.

"Hm. May I keep this?"

"Uh... No?"

"I'm sorry. My asking was a formality. This is evidence now." She reached for the photo.

"Wait!"

Quickly, I took a photo of the original with my phone. They couldn't take that from me. "That's okay, right?"

"Yes." She took the photo from me and placed it into a sealed bag. "I'm sorry. I hate to do that."

"Whatever," I mumbled. I had better photos of Mom, but it stung to see the FBI take yet another piece of her away from me. We were officially over the seventy-two-hour mark now. Every minute that passed took her further away from me.

"But who is this guy? Why was she talking to him right before takeoff?" I asked.

"That is confidential as well," she said softly.

Did this mean Mom was complicit in something?

No, no. It had probably been a simple conversation. I bet Mom met plenty of people. She wouldn't be able to name all of my friends, so why should I be able to name hers? No, it didn't make her guilty of anything.

But it did make a flame of anger lick me. I hadn't been the last person she'd talked to before…before it happened. Because of the text, I'd thought it had been me.

Silly, but it had made me feel important. Connected to her. Like being the last person to talk to her made me the only person who could save her.

I guessed I'd been wrong. "I see," I mumbled.

"So, is that what you came here to ask me?" she asked.

"Yeah. But one more thing."

I looked to my shoes and debated if I should tell her about my idea to subpoena Dr. Madison. They'd already investigated Mom. They probably already knew everything. I felt useless to even suggest it—what if they used the stigma of mental health against her? Oh, she was crazy, therefore she killed 155 people. Or worse, there could've been something that I didn't know. Something that made Mom seem guilty.

But if I didn't mention it, I might lose out on the one piece of truth in my favor.

"Have you investigated my mom's therapist?" I asked. "If you subpoena her, Dr. Madison has to tell you what my mom said."

"Yes, we did reach out to her. Your mother has been going there over a year, according to her credit card information," Agent Rosenfield said. "The subpoenas can take a long time, and time isn't a luxury we have right now. It's a complicated process with sensitive information."

"Please," I whispered. "Dr. Madison knows my mom would never hurt anyone. Please let her tell you that. I don't care how long it takes."

"I didn't say I wouldn't do it. I just said it might not be the magic answer you want." Agent Rosenfield slid a piece of paper across the table from me. "I filed the request yesterday."

It sure sounded like magic to me.

CHAPTER TEN

DAY FOUR – AFTERNOON

The next morning, a chill swept through the September air. It was finally starting to feel like fall. Even the leaves had changed from green to Golden Delicious apple-yellow, seemingly overnight.

I decided to go to school. All my sleuthing made me exhausted down to my bones, and honestly, I was craving some type of normalcy. It was as if going about my normal routine could bring Mom back to me.

Plus, Dad said I could skip history, and Savannah offered me a ride.

"Glad to hear you're joining me today." She was dressed in jeans and a V-neck, ready to go. She even wore eyeliner, which was unusual, considering I wasn't sure she owned any. "You're actually planning on going, not making me drop you off at random stores?"

I shushed her. I didn't want Dad to hear. "Yes, I'm going."

We said goodbye to Dad, who dutifully made sure we

had our lunches and an extra granola bar, just in case. It made me feel even worse for lying about going to school yesterday.

"You sure you're up to school?" I asked Savannah as we got outside. "You looked pretty bad yesterday."

"I have a math test," she said.

The sun felt warm on my skin, and I was grateful for it. "I think they'd understand, given the circumstances." A bunch of my teachers had kindly emailed me and told me they didn't expect me to come to class until I was ready, and not to worry about assignments.

"Stanford will not understand." Savannah unlocked her silver sedan and got into the front seat. It was dented and used, but hey, it got the job done. I'd contributed many pickle store hours so we could share.

"Right. And there are no other colleges on this Earth besides Stanford, unfortunately," I said.

"That's correct."

Savannah hadn't been officially accepted yet, but we'd toured the school as a family and all fallen in love. We were under strict instructions that our fingers had to remain crossed until she got that fateful letter in the mail about her acceptance.

She turned the engine on, and then we were off.

"Wow, less cameras today," Savannah said.

Only two news trucks were outside our house this morning, a stark contrast from the buzz of the past few days.

Last night, when I'd turned on the news, the newscasters had been talking about the tropical storm by Puerto Rico. They'd hardly mentioned US133. I was thankful for the privacy, but I still wondered if a lack of public interest meant fewer answers coming my way. Again, I was envious that other people could turn the other cheek to this. That their lives could continue unscathed. An entire airliner was missing, and people were still going to work and doing dishes?

Then again, they hadn't lost anyone. They hadn't lost their mom.

"I know," I mumbled.

And what if Mom and her passengers really were okay, either on some island or held hostage by hijackers, and then this hurricane swept through? I was powerless to stop any of this. Worse, I felt alone again.

"Are you nervous at all? To go away next year?" I asked.

Savannah shrugged. "Yeah."

"Really? You seem so excited."

"I am, but I don't know anyone in California," she said. "It's so far from you and Mom and Dad."

I couldn't help but smile that she'd included Mom too. Maybe it had been a simple reflex, but whatever. "You're going to love it. You'll get all As, become, like, the youngest astronaut in history, and have all the astronaut boys wanting to be launched into space with you."

She hesitated. "Thanks for the vote of confidence."

"I don't know what I'm going to do without you," I said.

She gave a small laugh. "Are you kidding? You'll be fine. You're going to be so busy with school and theater that you won't even notice I'm gone."

I forced a small laugh too, even though I knew she was completely wrong. I already missed my sister, and she was still here.

• • •

After classes, I met Alex in the music hallway. Glass cabinets showcased trophies of theater festivals past as we walked in step.

"Okay, so yesterday was really cool," Alex said. "I felt like a spy just being in that building."

"I know, right?"

"I really hope Agent Rosenfield can help you," Alex said.

"Me too." I wanted that more than anything. With all this time passing, I felt Mom getting farther and farther away from me, like a balloon let loose into the sky. I needed to hold her close. Even if I ultimately had to let her go, I needed her with me now, until I could at least prove her innocence.

I rubbed my thumb against the wings from her uniform in my pocket.

"But, hey, this is your big day, okay?" I said. "We can talk about my mom anytime. You're going to kill your audition."

"Or I'm going to forget all the words and vomit and die."

"Or you're going to kill it." I rolled my eyes. "Do you want to go into a practice room? I'll listen again."

"Yes please."

I'd heard Alex sing "Part of Your World" from *The Little Mermaid* about a thousand times. In fact, I never needed to see that movie ever again. Alex's voice was like a cool sea breeze, and I knew she'd be a shoo-in for one of the Silly Girls. Belle was most likely going to be played by Brittany Thompson, a girl with a beautiful voice who had been the lead in everything since elementary school.

Alex still threatened to quit school forever if she didn't get Belle, though. But regardless, as a certified theater nerd, audition day was one of my favorite days of the year.

It made my cells tingle to guess who would get what role, and watching my classmates give their all was like seeing them in their rawest forms.

We walked toward one of the two practice rooms in the music wing. They were fairly soundproof, but the doors had huge glass windows that had to remain visible at all times due to some unfortunate fornication issues last year.

Before I got close enough to see through the glass, a voice singing "Bitch of Living" from *Spring Awakening* wafted through my ears. He was okay—a little weak-sounding, but he had a ton of emotion behind it. If I were the director, I'd give him a callback.

"He's good," I whispered.

"His pitch is off, and I doubt he knows that song is about masturbating." Alex scowled.

"I doubt he's in competition with you."

"Oh yeah." Her posture relaxed. "He's fine."

We took two steps closer, and the singing stopped. A boy in a green flannel shirt turned to face us. Of course, it was Landon.

He opened the door, his cheeks red.

"Landon!" I grinned and fought the urge to fling my arms around him. "I had no idea you could sing!"

He looked to the floor with that shy smile, and I swore—I *swore*—that boy's lips would be the death of me.

"Kind of, not really. I'm more of a guitar guy," he said. "But I figured I'd try out."

"Are you trying out for Beast or Gaston?" Alex always went for the jugular.

"I just want to be in it." He tugged at his sleeves. "Given any more thought to auditioning, Violet?"

"Nah. I'm good with crew." I glanced at Alex. "And moral support."

"Can you be my moral support, too? This stuff is scary." Landon reached forward and moved a piece of hair from my shoulder. I did *not* like the way his fingers on my skin made me quiver.

My body thought otherwise.

"Um, okay, I need the practice room." Alex pushed past him and dragged me along. "See you on stage, Landon."

"See ya." He waved as he walked off.

"Pull a tarot. I want to see if you're in love." Alex whipped her deck of cards out.

"What? No!"

"He looked really nervous around you."

"Well, he—" I caught myself. It wasn't my business to tell Alex that we'd met in a therapist's office, and how he'd opened up to me about his anxiety. I hadn't meant for him to be a secret, but a wall was thickening between Alex and me. "Maybe a little."

"What did he mean about auditioning?" Alex asked. "Were you thinking about it? That would be so fun!"

"He misunderstood." How could I compete with Alex's voice and charisma? I couldn't. There was no point in me standing on stage to audition and embarrassing myself. Even if I did, who would I perform for? I'd promised Mom my first performance. I couldn't let it happen until I brought her back home. "Let's go rehearse, Belle," I said.

We walked off to the auditorium together. Alex found her seat, and I found Mr. Tariq. He had a pad and paper ready to go, and wore a tie with music notes on it. That was his "good luck to the cast" tie, as he told us each audition day.

"Sit anywhere you'd like," Mr. Tariq told me. "Take some notes. Maybe someone's audition will inspire you for a design. And if it does, tell me."

"Okay." I went into the crowd and sat next to Alex.

I needed this. I needed to pretend I was a normal high school kid who had nothing better to do. Even if the world around me was somersaulting.

First up was Alex. She came to the microphone and held her hand to her throat like a dramatic opera star. "Alex Marquez, mezzo-soprano, eleventh grade, birthdate January twenty-sixth, 2006. Inspired by the legendary Idina Menzel, similar in vocal style to Lea Michele, been taking voice lessons for three years now."

"We know who you are, Alex," Mr. Tariq said. "Get on with the song."

Her voice sailed all the way to the back of the auditorium when she sang. Her eyes were closed for all the high notes, and she sounded like a Disney princess. Her stage presence was killer. I crossed my fingers for her under the table the entire time.

When she finished, she plopped down beside me. "I'll end myself if I have to be a dancing utensil."

"You'll be the best fork anyone's ever seen," I whispered.

"Fork you." Alex crossed her arms.

Landon was next.

He stepped onto the stage and slicked his curls back in a way that totally did not make the hairs on my arm stand up.

His tongue glided over his top lip as he said, "Hi. I'm singing "Waving Through A Window" from *Dear Evan Hansen*."

"Song change," Alex whispered. "I hope he didn't hear me earlier."

Not going to lie, Landon had a shower-singer type of voice. Nothing impressive, but the notes spun around my head with his confidence.

He looked into the audience the entire time, and when he belted about wanting to speak but no one hearing, his genuineness brought tears to my eyes. I knew exactly how that felt, to be immobilized by waiting, no matter how much you spoke out.

Story of my life the past four days.

I whipped out my sketchbook. Something about his words had curved like I imagined the petals on the rose in the Beast's library would. Circular, but not quite perfect. Like how he'd poured himself into those notes, that song. The same way my art was like taking a part of me and showing the world.

"What are you doing?" Alex whispered.

"Taking notes."

"Nice," she said, with a hint of pleasant surprise in her voice.

Mr. Tariq stood and clasped his hands together. "I'd like some of you to read for parts." He doled out a few sides with scenes to about ten people, including Alex and Landon.

"Landon, can you read for Lumière? And Ashley, can you read for Babette?"

Ashley was in my grade, and I tried to ignore that she was prettier than me with her long, flowing black hair as she stood up on stage with Landon.

"Babette? Which one is that, one of the Silly Girls?" Ashley thumbed through the script.

"No, she's the feather duster," Landon whispered.

"Oh." Ashley rolled her eyes.

"Seriously?" I whispered to Mr. Tariq. So what if Babette wasn't a lead? She was a speaking part, and seemed like a lot of fun to play. She was kind of a ditz, but lovable and had a ton of comedic lines. Plus, the costume would probably be sparkly and decked out in feathers.

"Everyone is entitled to a diva moment." He shrugged.

I disagreed.

"This is going to be good," Alex whispered.

"There's only, like, three lines on this page," Ashley said. "How am I supposed to show I can act with three lines?"

"Easy," I said a bit too loudly. "You read three lines with good acting."

Landon snickered, but put his script over his mouth to hide it.

"Do your best," Mr. Tariq said.

Ashley sighed and read her lines with Landon—badly, if I might say so.

"*Ah Babette!*" He read the line a bit drily—then reached for her hand but missed. On the second time, he took it and mimicked a kiss. His lips didn't touch her skin, but something like jealousy flared in my chest.

Ashley read her lines about her hands that had become feathers, but with absolutely no charisma, no uniqueness. No talent. If she were hooked up to a monitor, it would say she'd flatlined. Not that I was biased.

As they continued to read, Landon didn't even look up from the script. I couldn't help but wonder if he was too aware of everyone staring at him to unlock what was inside. There was a spark in him, I knew it. I'd seen it during his song. But he didn't seem to be able to muster it up on that stage.

When they finished and he looked to the director's table, I gave a thumbs-up.

"Try again, this time with more gusto," Mr. Tariq said. "Don't worry about the accent or the scene itself. I want to see what's in your imagination. Same for you, Landon. Think bigger."

"Then can I try a different scene?" Ashley asked.

"Maybe with Belle? Sorry, it's just this scene is really short. It's hard for me to *imagine* anything with a small character."

"Small character? What?" I couldn't help myself. Word vomit was my specialty, especially when no one had asked me. "Babette is a fantastic role."

"Violet, shut it," Alex whispered. "Let my competition ruin herself."

"I can't focus if your little assistant director doesn't stop talking," Ashley said.

I stood up. "I'm not the assistant director, I'm crew. You'd know that if you'd ever looked behind the curtain to see who was giving you some light on stage the past three years."

Actors.

Ashley read again, this time somehow worse than before. Every molecule in me was raging. I knew exactly where to fix each instance where she'd gotten it wrong. Her tone was all off—way too much attitude, not enough fun. It was messing Landon up, and I had to admit, he was... less than stellar this time.

I couldn't focus for the rest of the rehearsal. No one else read for Babette, which meant she'd probably get it, and she would do a horrible job. NOT that I cared about her acting career or the fact that she'd feel Landon's presumably to-die-for-soft lips on her hand five nights a week during rehearsal, but I didn't want it to screw him up.

Mr. Tariq stood up to dismiss everyone from rehearsal. "Thank you all again. Landon, Violet, can you two stay back?" He turned to me and passed me the script. "I want you to give it a try, to read for Babette."

"Me?"

"I need to see the scene again with someone else. A

fresh take, if you will."

"Um… Okay." I went to the stage, where Landon still stood. He flashed me a crooked smile. Up close, it was obvious how hard his hands were shaking. It was also obvious how adorable his freckles were under the warm stage lights, but I had to ignore that right now. "You got this," I whispered.

Landon nodded and began the scene. His whole posture changed as we stepped closer. He stood straighter and extended his arms with purpose this time, as if he were truly supporting heavy candles.

At his next line, Landon took my hand and actually kissed it. I tried to ignore how soft his lips felt, how I wished they had lingered just a bit longer. He then did a fake sneeze as if to react to my fake feathered hands. He did it so genuinely, I thought it was real.

"My feathers!" I put on the waterworks and took my hand back as if Landon's lips were ice-cold.

We continued with fire. For a few minutes, I was out of my body, out of me, and a stranger to my situation. I was *living.* I forgot all about US133. Everything was in the here and now. I hadn't felt that way in a few days now.

And looking into Landon's eyes when we finished, I knew he felt the same way. The world had only been ours for a little while.

A few of our classmates still lingering in the auditorium clapped.

"That was so good!" Alex called from the audience. I hadn't realized she'd waited for me.

"Excellent work, both of you," Mr. Tariq said.

As we descended the stage, Landon held my hand to help me. I climbed down a tad bit slower, only so I could bask in the warmth of his hand in mine. I refused to make eye contact, because I didn't want him to see the way my cheeks burned with red.

"So cool, dude," Alex said to me. "I didn't know you had it in you."

"Honestly, I didn't either." My heart rate spiked. I couldn't focus on anything besides what I'd done. Stepping outside of myself was powerful.

I needed a few minutes to process everything. So I picked up my pencil and sketched the roses again.

On his way out, Landon came over to me with a huge grin on his face. "Violet, thank you so much. I couldn't have done that without you."

"Of course you could have!"

"No. Seriously. I was so nervous until you got up there." He shook his head. "And you were awesome! Wow. I really hope you get the part."

Goddamn adenylyl cyclase taking over my face. "I don't think I've properly auditioned," I said. "I was just showing Mr. Tariq an alternative."

"Really?" Landon's face fell. Disappointment etched his face to replace that joy, and it felt like I'd accidentally kicked Onion. "That's…a bummer. I thought we'd have fun."

My face burned hotter. "I mean, I'll think about it," I blurted out. I couldn't let him down. He'd shone so brightly out there.

"Okay. Well, good job anyway." He gave a small smile, then headed out of the auditorium.

Alex clutched her hand against her heart. "True love does exist."

"Oh, hush," I said. "He did give me Reese's Pieces the other day, though."

"Wait, what? They're your favorite!"

"I know!"

"That's freaking adorable, oh my God," she said. "Oh, take a tarot!"

"You're so annoying." I really, really didn't want to admit that I was curious what my card would say if I did indeed pull one.

"I'm going home to lock myself away until the list is posted," Alex said. "Call my house phone if you need me."

"Yep," I responded, but I'd already been pulled back into my work on the sketch. I had to get the roses just right. They were still too circular. They needed to be more organic, like the way the edges would be frayed in nature.

"You did great, Violet," Mr. Tariq said. "Your mother would be very proud."

The interruption pulled me out of it.

Would she? I suddenly felt ridiculous thinking about the red of roses and the shine of fake stained-glass windows for a school musical when Mom was gone. It was like only searching for the back of an earring when you knew the diamond stud was gone too.

"I think the set designer would love to see that at the meeting. Create a color swatch, if you can."

"Mm. I'll try." I put the pen down and looked up to the empty stage.

"Your reading was fantastic. If you'd like to audition, you can go up and read something else."

"Oh. Um…" The decision felt too heavy to make in only a few seconds. It was easier to say no, even though I wanted to. "No, thank you."

"Everything okay?" he asked.

I don't know, I wanted to say. Everything with Mom felt so entirely wrong. But I'd forgotten about it when I'd been acting, focusing on the story and nothing else.

He placed his hand on my shoulder. "It's hard to create

when everything feels wrong, but that's the most perfect time to do it. That's when you need to do it most. But be gentle with yourself. Grief is hard."

I smiled up at him. "Thanks, Mr. Tariq."

"Sure. Call me if you ever need anything. I'll leave the auditorium unlocked for you, if you want to stay here." He headed out, and I was back by myself.

This time, though, I couldn't get the pen to move. My mind was racing far too much.

"Art feels pointless without you," I said out loud. My voice echoed in the empty room. "And I miss you."

I tapped my pencil against the sketchpad. Not like I expected anyone to answer, but still. A sign would've been nice. I'd heard of a lot of people seeing signs from a loved one when they were missing…. Why couldn't I?

Maybe it was because she wasn't gone.

My stomach suddenly roared. I guessed I hadn't eaten enough at lunch.

"Violet?" Landon's voice rang out from the back of the auditorium. "Did you just say something?"

"Oh, no. That was my stomach making sounds like a hydrogen bomb." *Super hot.* I wished I was one of those girls who always knew what to say. But no, I was the girl with the stomach begging for french fries. Which… sounded terrific right now. Since all this had happened, I hadn't been the best at eating anything that remotely resembled a vegetable.

Landon laughed lightly. "Well, you want to grab some ice cream or something? My treat. You've got to remember to eat."

I looked up toward the lights. Maybe signs came in different ways. "I'd love that."

CHAPTER ELEVEN

DAY FOUR – LATE AFTERNOON

"Dip the fries in the shake," Landon said.

"What? No way, ketchup only," I said.

A week ago, if someone had told me I'd be hanging out outside a McDonald's with Landon Davis, just the two of us for the second time, I'd have thought they were joking.

We'd never talked much before, but now we were sitting only inches apart on one of the benches outside, with our legs brushing against one another. We faced toward the McDonald's, people-watching as we ate.

"You're missing out." Landon dipped a large, salty-looking french fry into his own chocolate shake. He slowly put it to his lips. "Excellence."

"Okay, fine. Hit me."

Landon dipped one of his fries into my vanilla milkshake and held it up for me as I took a bite. I tried to ignore that his fingers were only centimeters from my lips. It reminded me of our scene, the way he'd gently kissed the back of my hand.

"Okay, wow. Magic."

"Told you."

It was more than magic, though. I got to feel normal.

My heart was in a thousand pieces on the floor, but this casual hang-out session with a new friend was exactly what I needed to stitch those pieces up, if only for a few minutes. It felt like auditions, where I could be myself without worrying about anything. Just exist.

"So, are you doing okay with everything? I was surprised you came back to school," he said gently. "I mean, obviously, it's a hard time…"

"I'm… I mean, no," I said honestly. "I'm not okay. I'm terrified, but I have this feeling she isn't gone." I looked to my hands. Saying it out loud felt both ridiculous and right. "I know you probably think that's strange."

Above all else, I wanted to believe Mom's note. I wanted to believe she had a plan and that all of this would make sense later. But honestly? I was starting to worry that something else had happened.

"It's not strange," he said gently. His voice was soft, like caramel drizzled over ice cream. "Everyone processes these things differently."

"She can't be gone, Landon." I wasn't sure if I was trying to convince myself or him. "There's so many reasons, so many theories out there. You heard Miles the other day. I can't give up."

Trust me, the note said.

I was trying.

"Okay." He hesitantly put his hand on my shoulder. "I-I'm really bad at talking about these things. But I can listen."

"Thank you." I placed my head on his hand.

He scooted closer to me. I felt subtle heat radiating off his body. On this crisp September day, it was comforting, like sitting in front of a warm fireplace.

The TV in the McDonald's had caught my eye. It wasn't showing US133, but the tropical storm by Puerto Rico that was now named Hurricane Molly. Agent Rosenfield had been right. This large, threatening cloud was swelling off the coast of Florida, and people were evacuating by the thousands. The white swirl they showed made Hurricane Maria look pint-sized. I pictured gigantic storm surges and got a chill down my back.

Landon followed my eye. "That's one hell of a hurricane."

"I hope everyone gets out in time," I said, but honestly, that wasn't what I was thinking. I was wondering how the hell a missing Boeing 747 was now "old news" and how Mom could be right in the center of that wicked storm.

"Me too," Landon said. "It's scary. A lot of people die in these kind of hurricanes. Category Three is no joke."

The last thing I wanted to do was cry right now. I blinked back hot tears. I hoped Landon didn't notice.

"I feel terrible for all those people, and I know this sounds selfish, but I'm even more freaked out about my mom now. If Miles is right, what happens? Islands might not have the resources or the safe places or…anything to withstand a storm like that."

"It's not selfish," he said quietly.

"It is, because I keep thinking about how the news keeps talking about this, when they should really be talking about the plane. It's like no one cares anymore."

"A lot of people still care," he said. "I care, and I'm so sorry all this is happening to you, Violet."

"No." I shook my head. "I'm sorry. I didn't mean to

drag you to McDonald's, of all places, and then start complaining that the TV isn't talking about my mom anymore when I've been complaining that all they do is talk about my mom for the past few days. I can't have it both ways."

"I think you're being really hard on yourself," he said. "Grief…sucks."

I nodded. I didn't want to believe I was grieving because Mom wasn't gone. But I didn't know what else to call this bizarre period I was in, so… Yeah. It sucked. That was the best way to put it.

I quickly dabbed at my eyes with my sleeve.

"I feel bad that you only let me take you to McDonald's," Landon said. "You sure you don't want to go anywhere else? Somewhere special?"

"This is special." I took a sip of my shake. "I haven't been here in years. I know this isn't, like, romantic or anything, but it's—" I paused. Why had I said that? Why did my brain insist on sabotaging me at every possible instance? "Not that this is like… I mean… You don't have to…"

"Right now, I think McDonald's is the most romantic place in the world," he said. "Because you're here."

I blinked. What did this mean? Did Landon…*like* me, like me? Or was he just being nice because my life was a big Jenga tower at the moment?

Obviously, McDonald's was not romantic, in any sense. The place smelled like old plastic and the bathrooms probably hadn't been cleaned since I was two. But… I felt the same way. We might as well have been in a five-star restaurant. I was having fun, and I was able to be completely myself. I hadn't felt that way in a long, long time.

"Umm." He stared at me, his deep brown eyes wide.

"Sorry. That was weird, wasn't it?"

Laughter bubbled up in my stomach and burst from my mouth. It felt incredible to laugh. I wasn't sure if I had since Mom hadn't come home.

"Not at all," I said. "Wanna take a selfie?"

"Sure!" Landon sat up straighter, and I reached into my bag to get my phone.

Four missed calls. All from Savannah.

My stomach dropped. Did this mean what I thought? Or had Mom come home?

I called her back frantically as I explained the situation to Landon.

"Vi?" she groaned.

"What's wrong? What happened?"

"I need you to come home... Now," she said. "I passed out."

CHAPTER TWELVE

Day Four – Late Afternoon

This was why I couldn't have nice things.

Life wasn't meant to be perfect for me. I lived in this perpetual balance—I had an awesome time with Landon, Savannah got sick. It wasn't fair.

We raced back to the house. Both of us were nearly silent in the car. Landon's knuckles were white as he turned corners and pulled up in front of my house.

When we got inside, Savannah was on the living-room floor, her back leaning against the couch. As she saw us, she sat up, her hands limp in her lap. Her eyes fluttered open when I wrapped my arms around her.

"What's wrong?" I whispered.

My sister did not look like my sister. Pale, with blotchy cheeks, like she'd been stunned. "I don't know. I threw up a few times." Her voice sounded far away. "I might've fainted in the bathroom."

"I think we should go to the Emergency Room if you

fainted," Landon said.

"I *might've* fainted. I'm not sure," she mumbled. "No ER."

"We're going to the ER," Landon and I said together. We sounded like pissed-off parents. Carefully, Landon and I linked our arms around Savannah and ushered her inside his car. I sat in the back with her.

"Did you call Dad?" I asked. "Where is he?"

"I don't know," she mumbled. "I called Mom, then you. I don't know why I called her. It was…automatic, I guess."

My heart squeezed. It should've been Mom taking care of her. Not me.

I cupped my hands on her cheeks. If she were to puke in them, I wouldn't even care. This was a whole new terror than when I'd heard about Mom. I thought that had been the worst day of my life. So far, I'd been right. But now I had this aching fear that I'd lose Savannah, too.

My family had partied when her cancer had finally gone into remission. But it was always this brick in our backpacks, this lingering fear that maybe, one day, it would return.

"Are you still nauseous?" I held my hand under her chin, just in case.

"Mm. No."

Landon let me and Savannah out in the front of the hospital while he parked. I slipped my arm around her shoulders and walked. Her steps were small, but steady.

"His car is clean," Savannah said. "That's a good sign."

Was that what people put in their Tinder profiles these days? *Great kisser, clean car.*

"Okay, weirdo. I think you're dehydrated." I quickly gave a call to Dad. "Uh, Dad, something happened."

"What happened? Is everything okay? Is it Mom?" Dad's voice was full of anxious urgency.

"Savannah fainted," I said.

"Might've fainted," she mumbled.

As I explained the situation, Dad set off a string of curse words and promised to meet us there in a few minutes. Knowing him, he'd run every red light to get there.

I made sure Savannah sat upright as I checked her in. I knew it was wild, and it didn't make any sense, but as I filled out that paperwork, I kept glancing up at the patients walking by. Like maybe one of them would be Mom with amnesia, or a doctor who'd say they'd found her and she'd be fine.

Hope was odd.

Landon joined us a few minutes later. He looked pale himself, and I started to wonder if some bug was going around.

"Thanks," I whispered to him. "You okay?"

Landon tucked his hands into his sweatshirt and chewed his lower lip. "I'm not, like, a huge fan of hospitals."

"You don't say?" Savannah gave a quiet chuckle. "You can go home. Violet's got me from here."

"Yeah," I said. "Thank you, though."

"No, no." Landon's eyes flickered onto every door, like he expected disaster in human form to pop out. "I don't want to leave you guys alone."

I flashed a grin.

He returned it.

Luckily, it was a slow day in the emergency room. The only person ahead of Savannah was a six-year-old with a broken arm who genuinely looked pleased with the lollipop he received for the ordeal.

When the triage nurse called Savannah's name, I stood up. "She's my sister. I'm going with her."

"Where are your parents?" the nurse asked.

Good freaking question, lady. "My dad is on his way."

"You can join your sister when your dad gets here. I'm taking her to be checked now," the nurse said.

Savannah walked toward the nurse like a drunk desperate to keep on the sobriety line. "I'll be okay, Vi."

"But—"

The nurse took Savannah by the arm. "We'll take good care of her, promise." She shut the door behind Savannah, and panic rose to my throat.

What if I never saw her again? It was a catastrophic thought, but after everything happening to me this week, could anyone blame me?

I clutched the flight wings, still in my pocket. The edges were sharp against my fingertips. My instinct was to cut, the only way I could ever slow down and find control, but no. *No. Not now.*

Deep breaths.

"She'll be okay, Violet," Landon said.

What if she wouldn't be? The past few days, all I had been thinking was that Mom should've been there. To imagine Savannah gone too was... I rubbed my eyes to erase those awful thoughts. "I'm glad you were with me."

"It was a coincidence, but I'm glad I was," he said. "What an up-and-down day, huh? Auditions, McDonald's, now this..."

I shrugged. All that seemed so far away right now. "Your audition was awesome," I said. "I like your voice."

"Tell my band that." He chuckled. "They don't usually let me sing. I play guitar only."

"You're in a band?"

That explained the guitar photos on his Instagram.

"Yeah," he said sheepishly. "It sounds boring, but..." Landon reached inside his back pocket to slip me a flyer for his band. It was him and two other guys from our school, trying to look tough with their arms crossed, lips in a scowl.

"Thong Bong?" I asked.

"Yeah…" Landon ran a hand through his scruffy, pecan-colored hair. "We need a new name, but for now, we're Thong Bong."

"I love it." Actually, I hated it. But I loved the ridiculousness.

"For real?" He grinned.

His smile totally made me want to smile, too. "For real." I nodded.

I could relax around him, be totally myself. Landon was the one part of my life in the After that had nothing to do with Mom. But it still felt wrong, like my happiness was a betrayal to her.

E tu, Violet?

"Where the hell is my daughter?" Dad burst through the emergency room doors like Thanos. "All right, there's one." He pointed at me. "Where's the other?"

I face-palmed. Leave it to Dad to absolutely embarrass me. Not just in front of other patients, but in front of the one boy in my entire school who was both cute and kind—rarer than a four-leaf clover. My damn adenylyl cyclase was going wild.

"Mr. Ashby?" A nurse came out of wooden double doors. "Your daughter finished her medical exam." I held my breath and braced. "We're going to admit her. It seems like she's severely dehydrated and may be suffering from a kidney infection."

Kidney infection? Didn't people with diabetes get that, like, if they needed dialysis? Nothing made sense. "Is she going to be okay?" My hands trembled.

Landon tensed up beside me.

"A kidney infection is serious, but with some antibiotics and proper hydration and rest, she should be back to normal in no time," the nurse said.

My entire body felt numb. How bizarre to be relieved and terrified at the same time. Not to mention that a kidney infection was *not* cancer.

"Room 255," she said.

"Thanks so much," Dad said.

"I think this is my cue," Landon said.

"I can't thank you enough." I was tempted to take his hands, but instead, I slid my hands into my own pockets. I wasn't allowed to be happy. Happiness couldn't belong to me right now, and neither could Landon.

It felt like the universe was punishing me for those minutes of pure fun. I wouldn't make the same mistake twice.

"You would've done the same for me." He shrugged. Under the harsh lights of the hospital wing, his brown eyes were deep and solemn. "Tell Savannah I hope she feels better."

"Right."

He took a few steps toward the sliding doors, then turned to face me. "Take care of yourself too, Violet."

If taking care of myself meant binging on gummy worms and wanting to slice my arms up, sure. I gave a half-hearted wave. "I'll do what I can. Thanks for the Thong Bong flyer!"

I watched him walk away with this annoying thump in my heart.

Dad wrapped his arm around my shoulders and led me away. "What did you say? Thong Bong?"

"It's Landon's band. He drove Savannah here."

"That's the best band name I ever heard."

...

Savannah's room looked like a terrible Renaissance painting.

She was lying peacefully in the middle of the room while Dad tugged at his hair and spat an endless chain of questions at the doctor.

"She's only seventeen, how can her kidneys be bad? I don't understand."

"Oh, boy." I sighed and took a few steps closer to Savannah.

"Mr. Ashby, a kidney infection in this case is caused from an untreated UTI that went through the urethra and to the kidneys," the doctor said. "It isn't usually associated with fainting or vomiting, but your daughter was extremely dehydrated."

"Are you on a water protest these days?" I whispered to Savannah.

She opened her eyes wide enough to side-eye me. "This place is miserable. Buy me a Kit Kat from the vending machine." Her voice was whispery, and her skin was near translucent, but she seemed way more alert than before. A long tube pressed into her arm led to a bag of clear liquid hanging from a pole.

"Besides the dehydration, stress can exacerbate these symptoms," the doctor said. "High school is a tough time for many young women."

"Oh yeah, it's the cliques and math tests freaking her out. I am aware my daughters are stressed, thanks." Dad then shifted his position. "Wait, have you read *The Parent's Guide to Grief*? There's a fantastic passage out of…"

"Save me," Savannah whispered. "Kit. Kat."

"Fine," I said. "But you have to drink water then, since you're dehydrated."

"I think that's what this tube in my arm is for. Annoying."

The moment hung between us, not even interrupted by Dad's shrill, squirrel-like squeaks. "There are other avenues for a UTI besides sex. Bacteria is bacteria, right? Not that I am being some sort of Puritan, I am aware of what teens do these days, I'm simply asking how…"

"You all right, Sav?" I whispered.

"I think so." Her voice sounded firm with truth.

"Why didn't you tell me you had a UTI?" I asked.

"I-I told Mom. She knew." Savannah looked away. "She told me to take some cranberry pills and go to Urgent Care if it didn't get better after a day. And…"

It felt like the Twilight Zone that Savannah was here in front of me, fighting an infection Mom had known about, yet Mom felt millions of galaxies away from me. It had only been four days.

"Then with the stress of everything, it…became less important," Savannah said. "The UTI pain went away for a few days, so I thought I was fine. Then, yesterday, my whole torso felt like it was on fire."

I remembered Savannah clutching her side and groaning the other day. *Ugh*. Why hadn't I asked what hurt? I'd been so wrapped up in finding Mom, I hadn't seen what was in front of me.

"I wish I could've helped you," I said.

"You kidding? I'm so glad you're here, Vi. You have no idea. Dad is going to get on my nerves."

Dad and Savannah were usually perfect for each other: a pair of aloof cats who left each other alone and preferred it that way.

My whole life had been Mom and I coming home to

find Dad and Savannah in the same room, not talking but sitting together. He must've been really pissing her off for her to complain about him.

I took her hand. "I'm glad I'm here too."

Our hands stayed together for a solid ten seconds; a record.

"I'm serious about the Kit Kat," she said. "I'm dying."

"Shh! Dad will have a conniption if he hears that," I said.

"Then someone will have to get me candy." Savannah closed her eyes.

Manipulation was so ugly.

For once, I was glad for Dad's lack of attention. I ducked out into the hall.

A lot of people hated hospitals, but I thought they were cool. The buzzing EKG machines, the codes the nurses screamed out, the patients you walked by. So many stories happening all at once, so many people's lives I'd never know but could only wonder about. Besides, a hospital had saved my sister's life back when she'd beaten the hell out of cancer.

My phone peeped. I leapt for it, but disappointment prodded me again. Four days later, I couldn't believe I still thought Mom would call.

I felt so naive.

ALEX: Hey, is Savannah okay?

ME: Yeah, think so. A minor infection.

ME: Wait, how did you know?

Alex responded in less than a minute: She texted me. Long story. Well, please send my love to her. And to you too, bro. I'm sorry this has been the week from Satan himself for you both.

Even if it hadn't been Mom texting, I reminded myself

how lucky I was to have friends that felt like family.

I took a right toward the vending machine and tried to ignore the TVs in the hallway, but I couldn't. One of them was playing footage of a search-and-rescue operation flying over the Atlantic.

The caption read: *Teams have been searching a huge area to find the missing airliner, US133, but so far, no wreckage or survivors have been found.*

At least they were doing something. Proof that someone else besides me was trying to figure all this out.

I got the Kit Kat and took a different route toward the room to avoid the TVs.

I didn't want to see the blank, bleak ocean if nothing was going to come from it.

Instead, I found something super cool. It was a state-of-the-art globe planetarium that sat in the center of the wing—perks of the children's hospital, I supposed.

It had the circumference of a black bear and came up to my waist in height. The constellations were mapped out in white against a navy-blue background. Someone must've been disinfecting it daily, because it shone like the moon itself.

I traced my finger against the Pleiades, a collection of seven stars located by Orion, the hunter. They weren't tough to find, and they could be seen by anyone at any location on this world. These seven things connected us all, every one of Earth's inhabitants.

This must've been new. It certainly hadn't been here when Savannah had been a patient ten years back. If it had been, we would've been all over it. I wanted to run into her room and grab her to show her now.

"Are you a patient?" I looked up to find a tall doctor standing beside me. He held a chart in his hands and had a concerned look on his face. His salt-and-pepper hair was elegant, in a totally Anderson Cooper way.

"Oh, no." I brought my hands to my sides as if I'd touched hot water. "I'm just looking."

"At the Pleiades?" he asked.

I quirked an eyebrow. I thought the only random people on this Earth who knew about the Pleiades were me, Savannah, and Mom, since she had given us astronomy lessons on the roof. It wasn't a group of stars you knew about unless you were a real nerd like us.

"Yeah. They show all seven here. I like that." I recounted to be sure, but most people only saw six stars in the cluster. The seventh, the brightest, disappeared and reappeared. Finding it was supposed to be good luck.

"You know a lot. Going to be a future astronomer?" he asked.

"No. Just a hobby. It's a…family thing." Why wasn't this guy rushing off to some sick kid or something? I was sure he had more important things to do.

"I see." He nodded. "Well, take care." The man swept past me and I got a whiff of cologne. His scent must've knocked my neurons, *ping ping ping*, because everything hit me all at once.

I'd seen him before.

Only once, but it had stuck with me. I'd never forget the face in that photo now.

I pressed the tips of my fingers against the wings in my pocket and turned around.

"Wait!" I called.

But he was gone.

CHAPTER THIRTEEN

DAY FOUR – NIGHT

Savannah got to go home with us that afternoon, but she was under strict instructions that if her fever got above 104, or if she even felt faint, she had to come back.

I tucked her into bed, careful to smooth the blanket over her shoulders. The fight we had had the other night was no longer at the forefront of my mind. It was hardly even in the back. My brain had straight up rejected all memories of it. The only thing I could think of was whether that guy was Matthew Bryant or not. Of course, I hadn't confirmed that he was because that would've made my life easier, and we simply couldn't seem to do that lately.

"You want a snack or anything?" I asked. "More Kit Kats?"

Savannah glanced at the collection of full water bottles and Gatorades by her nightstand. "I'm good."

Dad smoothed her blond hair back. "Call out if you need anything. Don't even think of hesitating."

"Thanks, Dad," she said.

In that moment, they looked identical. Savannah had his ice-blue eyes and thick eyebrows, and I tried to focus on how sweet that was, instead of how it made me think of Mom, and how she wasn't here.

Dad planted a kiss on her cheek, then headed downstairs. He didn't shut the door behind him, which let Onion burst in. He sniffed around Savannah's feet, probably picking up on all the chemical smells from the hospital.

"He missed you," I said.

Savannah patted the area beside her, and Onion happily plopped himself against her torso. "I missed him too. Need him more than ever these days."

She gave him a gentle kiss on his forehead.

"So, now that we're alone…" she said. "What's up with you and Landon?"

"Me? Nothing." It was suddenly a thousand degrees hotter in her bedroom. Like the Sahara, honestly.

Her eyes were heavy with sleep. Or sadness. With Savannah, it was hard to tell. "I can't believe he saw me like that. It's embarrassing."

I shouldn't have been surprised that Savannah, who wore collared shirts and pressed jeans to school every day, was thrown off that someone had caught her being vulnerable. The horror.

"You don't think when you go into space, you're going to have embarrassing moments?" I asked. "Hey, what happens if you throw up in space? It flies everywhere?"

"Oh, gross."

"Get used to it." I put my hands on her arm, shook it gently, and leaned closer. "BLEGHH!"

She rolled over and swatted my hands away, but laughter buzzed under the blankets. "You're so annoying."

I felt a burst of pride for my sister. Vomit in space or not, she'd known she was going to be an astronaut since she'd been a kid. The plan was laid out in front of her, and she was perfectly in step. No one actually achieved their childhood dreams, but Savannah would. When I was a kid, I wanted to be a pilot like Mom, but the call of the arts lured me in.

"Okay, I'll leave you alone," I said. "By the way, Alex says to send her love."

I would've gone on, but Savannah's eyes were closed. She needed sleep like I needed to get to the bottom of who the hell that doctor in the hallway had been.

Onion followed me into my bedroom and leapt onto the bed with me as I grabbed my laptop.

First, I checked my email to see if Agent Rosenfield had sent me anything, but nothing. Sometimes it was easy to forget she was a real person with a real, high-profile job and probably a family, and I was…sitting on my bed with my five-pounds-overweight pug.

I dove into Google. It was much easier to search for Matthew Bryant now that I knew he was a doctor at a hospital a few miles from here. It took me only a few minutes to find him this time. The first hit was from the hospital's website.

I looked at the photo on my phone to double-check. It was definitely the same guy—older, for sure. But him. He'd cut his hair since and shaved his beard, but he had the same nose and piercing brown eyes.

I emailed Agent Rosenfield: *How's it going with the subpoena? By the way, did you find Matthew Bryant? Cause I did.*

The next page of Google told me he had a medical degree from NYU and his medical specialty was in pediatric oncology. He didn't seem to have any social media profiles.

So who was this dude?

Miles had known who he was right away when I mentioned he'd been Mom's boyfriend. But then why had Mom never mentioned him to me? The glaring thought that maybe they were dating *now* rather than earlier crept into my brain, but I pushed it away. That couldn't be.

I tried to imagine their last conversation. It felt so ridiculously, cruelly unfair that she had talked to him last, not me. I wondered if he'd tell me what it was about. If he knew what she was going to do—or not do.

I searched Flight US133. It was a compulsion by now. I couldn't open my phone or use my laptop without obsessively scanning the latest news articles. Even if every website, every news article said the same frustrating thing—no new info, no conclusive evidence. No one knew what had happened in that crucial moment between the transponder shutting off and losing signal by Puerto Rico.

And no one knew what had happened After. I was so sick of this, so sick of being helpless.

"Dammit." I smacked my fist against the bed.

Onion jumped as if I'd insulted his entire ancestry.

"Sorry, sweetie." I reached over to pet the dark wrinkles on his face. "I just miss Mom, that's all. Do you?"

He snorted, then lay back down.

There were three knocks on my door.

"Violet?" Dad opened the door and came inside. He ducked under the hanging solar system, which always used to make me laugh as a kid, and sat by my desk chair. "Whatcha doing? Instagrant? Faceplace? Twitter?"

"Yeah," I lied. "What's up?"

"Nothing, just wanted to check on you. I can't imagine

things have been easy for you the past few days," he said. "Especially with everything going on today. You cool, cucumber?"

"Very cool." I reached out my fist to bump his.

Dad pushed his glasses up his nose. His pert nose he'd passed down to Savannah. "You don't have some secret urinary tract infection? Anything I should know? I'd like to get all urinary or other issues out of the way now."

"Nope."

"Okay, good," Dad said. "Hey, I got an interesting phone call today."

A pit opened in my stomach. "Oh? What about?"

Please don't say they found Boeing 747 debris…

"From the flower shop. They want to send over some donations for your mom." He poked Mercury on the solar system. "Isn't that nice?"

"Oh. Flowers, yeah." I was so relieved it wasn't related to plane crashes that I'd nearly missed what he'd said. "Wait, what?"

"For the memorial," he said. "I'm thinking of putting something together. Family only, close friends. To celebrate her."

"What do you mean?" I hugged my legs. This couldn't be happening. This was something that happened to other people. Not me.

Onion licked my hands in sympathy.

"I thought in the park would be nice. Under the cherry blossoms? She loved it there." Dad put his hands on his hips. "We used to take you and Savannah all the time as babies. I even put in for a plaque, but I want you and Savannah to do some thinking on what you want on there."

"Dad—"

"I want your input on this. It's important that you feel

in control," he said.

In control? I was spinning like a planet kicked off its axis. It felt like I'd never control anything ever again.

"Mom isn't dead!" I spat. I didn't want to wake Savannah, but I was losing it.

Dad's face didn't change. "Honey... I want her to be alive just as much as you do."

"Then listen to me. The plane could've been cyber-hijacked. It's extremely possible that the government is covering it up—"

"Violet, that didn't happen," Dad said.

I clenched my fists. I was so furious I could hear my own heartbeat in my ears. "Then why can't the most complex government in the world find a huge Boeing 747?"

Dad shook his head. His face was still stoic. "I wish I knew, but it doesn't matter. Even if someone did cyberhijack the plane, it's still..." He sighed. "It's still not going to bring your mom back."

A jolt of pain spread through me like I'd gotten a shot at the doctor's. "How could you say that?"

He tried to put his hand on my shoulder, but I squirmed back. "I miss her too, but—"

"If you miss her, you'd be trying to find her! Not scattering some flowers." Logically, I knew grief was different for everyone, but this wasn't just anyone we were talking about. All logic and sense had evaporated the minute I'd seen that news report about the crash.

"I do miss her!" Dad shouted. "But it's been four days with no word! We can't keep..." A catch in his throat made him stop. "We can't keep pretending, honey. She would want you to move on."

I pressed my hands so hard against my eyes that I saw stars.

Onion leapt from the bed and settled on the floor. Arguing made him nervous. It had been quite a nervous year for him.

Dad wrapped his arms around me. "Look, we can have the memorial, and she can still turn up. We're not burying anything."

"If we have the memorial, we're giving up."

"No, we're moving on," he said. "And I really, really think that's what your mother would want."

It *was* giving up. The government investigation wasn't even closed yet. They were still sending out search parties and rescue boats. What if she came back and saw that we'd given up so easily? She would be so disappointed. Mom had never given up on me. Ever.

When I'd failed a test, or when I'd told her about cutting myself. She'd known I could get past it.

She was the one who'd made me push through it all.

Now it was my turn to do the same for her.

She'd asked me to trust her.

"It's not fair," I croaked.

I was too broken to argue about this. My bones ached with pain. My brain was fuzzy from exhaustion.

Even though I was fuming with Dad for letting her go so easily, I leaned against him. My dad. My protector. Savannah had always been his favorite, but I was the baby. Tears leaked from my eyes, wetting his shirt.

"It's not," he said. "It's so goddamn not." He reached over to take a tissue from the box and dabbed it against my cheeks. "Listen, Violet. This is why you need to see a therapist. I know you're not happy with the idea—"

"Correct."

"I get the apprehension, trust me," he said.

"I'll think about it." Not that I was interested in

blabbing all my secrets to anyone, but still. Sometimes my cutting scared me, whether I admitted it or not.

The fog that took over when I did it was an autopilot I couldn't control. I was practically counting down the minutes until Dad left the room so I could hurt myself right now.

"Well, here's the thing, buddy," Dad said. "You're going. You don't get a choice in this."

"What do you mean?"

"I mean I've made you an appointment."

"What? With who?" I blinked. It felt like someone had opened the bathroom stall while I was peeing. It was a deliberate breach of trust.

He handed me his open phone with a photo of a man who looked vaguely like Ed Sheeran if he were a serial killer. Wide, wide eyes like he'd stare into my soul.

"What the hell?" I asked, for *so* many reasons. I scooted away from him.

"He specializes in teenagers! And he's available for an emergency appointment tomorrow."

"No. No." I crossed my arms and stuck my back against the headboard. The more time I spent in front of some weirdo who was going to take notes on the way I spoke or breathed or whatever, the less time I had to find the truth and help Mom. Especially now that I was racing against this absurd memorial.

"I don't need therapy," I said. "I do theater. That helps."

"Sure, theater helps," Dad said. "But it isn't therapy. It's an outlet, sure. But you're not working through any real issues."

"That's not true." I thought about how incredible I'd felt doing that scene with Landon. That had been better than an hour with Dr. Serial Killer or any therapist would be. It had been time when I could forget everything else except me.

"It's not therapy. It's an escape. That's different," Dad said. "And someone with a PhD can explain that to you way better than I can. So, you're going to the appointment after school tomorrow."

"We can't go tomorrow," I said smugly. Aha. Foiled. "Savannah has SAT prep."

"She's not going to therapy with you."

I clenched my jaw. "What?"

"I'm not worried about her," Dad said. "I'm worried about you."

"That is such a cop-out!"

"Shh, you'll wake your sister."

Every time. This happened every *single* time.

Savannah could do nothing wrong. She was gorgeous, got the perfect grades, knew exactly which career she wanted, didn't fight with Mom or Dad. But me? I couldn't even handle stress properly.

"You're playing favorites," I said.

"I'm not," Dad said. "Savannah didn't fight me when I suggested it. Not like this. You have to admit the way you're acting... It's not healthy. Mentally or physically. You need someone who can actually help you. Yelling at me is a blast, I'm sure, but it won't fix anything."

"I'm not going," I repeated.

"Look, Savannah will see one eventually, but she's not feeling well right now," Dad said. "Plus, I'm still finding the right person for her."

"Why can't Dr. Madison do it?" I asked. "If I'm going to see a therapist, might as well be her."

Dad paused. "How do you know about Dr. Madison?"

Damn it. My big mouth. "I... I saw the business card

on Mom's dresser."

I conveniently left out the part about me sneaking off to visit her office in the city without anyone knowing.

"I see." Dad crossed his arms. "You'd want to see the same therapist as your mother? I mean, if that's what it takes, I'll ask her."

"She won't do it." I dug my nail into the soft part of my palm. The relief wasn't enough, but it was something. "But yeah. I want to see her."

It wasn't that I wanted to see her, really. It was that I wanted to use my time effectively. If I was going to have to sit in a shrink's chair, I might as well sit in one that could move my investigation along.

"Look," Dad said. "If Dr. Madison will see you, can we stop fighting about this? It's important to me that you stay safe."

"Everyone keeps saying that." I pounded my fist against the pillow a bit harder than I intended to. Onion cowered behind Dad's ankles.

"You're scaring my son." Dad picked Onion up into his arms. "What do you mean, who's saying that to you?"

"No one." Dr. Madison's words rang out in my head.

If I had a task to do, and it required a bit of secret-agenting or manipulation, so be it. If the subpoena was going to take a long time, I could at least try and squeeze information out of her. Anything to help prove Mom wouldn't hurt anyone—and that she was still with me.

If I had to do it, might as well get what I wanted.

"Do you promise that if I can get Dr. Madison to see you, you'll go?" Dad asked.

"Yeah," I mumbled.

Dad squeezed my shoulder and kissed the top of my

head. "That's my girl." He left my room and took Onion with him.

I rolled up my sleeve and looked at the faded scars along my wrists. There were far too many of them to count.

Stay safe, Violet.

I wondered if people around me knew more than I wanted them to.

When my tears dried on my cheeks and Dad was securely in the guest room, I turned to my wrists. So, so close to my streak, but the need to cut threatened to undermine it all. I tried snapping my hair band against myself, but this time, it didn't work. It wasn't strong enough.

I took a deep breath.

You're at day forty-seven. Make it to fifty.

Instead, I dug my nails into myself.

Hard.

Not like I normally did when I was distracted, or the type of digging I could do in public and get away with. I dug in deep enough to make myself bleed.

Only a little, though.

Not enough.

It was almost midnight, but I wasn't able to sleep. The embarrassment of scratching myself so deeply filled me with shame, even if it wouldn't leave a mark. Not a physical one, at least.

I tried painting, but the creative flow felt like a solid dam. I even watched a few minutes of other high schools' productions of *Beauty and the Beast* to get an idea, but nothing came. The prospect of letting Mr. Tariq and everyone else down made me feel even worse.

Four days and twelve hours since Mom had gone missing.

I wasn't sure this would ever get easier. I didn't think my brain would ever stop racing, stop hoping for a cyber-hijacking and a hostage situation.

Deep down, I knew it was pointless. I knew it wouldn't work and that I was in denial. Denying my denial: a new chapter of my mental health.

But it was the only thing I could cling on to.

Besides the family I had left.

So I knocked on the door to Savannah's bedroom.

I hadn't been in Savannah's room in at least a few weeks before today. A month, maybe. It had been neat as long as I could remember. She had matching folders for everything, even a filing cabinet to hold up the printer. Definitely the only person under forty-five years old to own one of those.

She only had two posters: one, a map of the solar system. The other, a poster of New York City that Mom had bought her when we'd visited Central Park years and years ago. In the darkness, it all looked somehow even more foreign.

Savannah was wrapped in her blanket, facing the wall. Her face conveyed pure peace.

"You scared me today," I whispered.

I felt safe talking to her the most when she couldn't hear me.

I curled up next to her, spooning her, and wrapped my arms tightly around her. Her hair smelled like vanilla and roses. Kind of like Mom.

"Don't ever do that again. No more fainting," I said.

To my surprise, she whispered, "I promise."

CHAPTER FOURTEEN

DAY FIVE – AFTERNOON

To: DianaRosenfield@fbi.gov
From: VioletMAshby02@gmail.com
10/5/21, 7:02 a.m.
Hi Agent Rosenfield,
Any new info? What about the subpoena?

To: VioletMAshby02@gmail.com
From: DianaRosenfield@fbi.gov
10/5/21, 7:35 a.m.
I'm coming by your house later today to speak with you all. –D.R.

To: VioletMAshby02@gmail.com
From: DianaRosenfield@fbi.gov
10/5/21, 7:35 a.m.
And no, we haven't found the plane yet. So don't get your hopes up. It's about something else.

It was the first time in history where I, Violet McKenna Ashby, went to school and Savannah Grace Ashby did not. Sixteen years, and all it took was an out-of-control UTI and a missing Mom. Agent Rosenfield's email distracted the hell out of me all day, so I tried to make up for it by paying extra attention in class. My last mission of the day was to pick up Savannah's work, and Alex followed along with me.

"Has Savannah texted you today? Is she alright?" Alex asked.

I neatly stacked the English work on top of the physics homework sheets. "She's been sleeping all day, but I think she's alright."

"Poor thing." Alex took a deep breath. "I'm so worried about her. You think it's okay if I visit?"

I raised an eyebrow. Alex had been to my house a thousand times, most of the time without an invitation. "Uh, sure. Are you and Sav, like, friends now?"

The three of us had never been an item. When we'd been kids, maybe we'd eat snacks and do arts and crafts together. But now, Savannah went upstairs if we were playing video games downstairs.

"I...don't know. Your family has been dealing with so much, you know?"

The receptionist in the main office took her glasses off and smiled at us. "Hi, Violet. I'm so sorry to hear about your mother. Planes don't work like they used to, huh?"

I forced a smile and tossed Savannah's AP Lit homework into my bag. I would've corrected her, but at least she hadn't blamed Mom. "Wait, don't you have callbacks later, though?" I asked Alex.

"I'd stop by after callbacks," she said. "They have me reading for all the girl leads, but that doesn't mean anything. I mean, I'm also reading for Cogsworth. The clock. Can you imagine? I'd leave the country, I swear."

"You'll do fine. Nothing to worry about," I said. "I want to take a look at the list before I go. Come with?"

"Sure. You alright? You're kind of jumpy."

"I asked Agent Rosenfield for an update and she said she'd come by the house later to talk. That sounds bad." I knew it was serious if she was offering to travel to me but she wouldn't tell me what it was over email. It was making me feel like I'd been electrocuted. The end of the day couldn't come fast enough.

"Oh, shoot. Hope everything's okay," Alex said. "The news hasn't reported anything."

"That's good, I guess."

We headed into the music and theater wing. I stood on my tiptoes to read the list. Fairly predictable. Landon got called for Lumière, Gaston, and Beast. Impressive.

"I want to do my own tarot reading, but that might not be the best idea," Alex said. "I'm afraid I'll give myself a self-fulfilling prophecy."

"Wow, someone's been listening during psych class," I said.

As we turned the corner, something caught my eye in one of the practice rooms. Landon sat on the floor, his face eerily green and his hand on his heart like he was signaling a heart attack.

"I'll see you tomorrow," I told Alex, and headed for the room. This clearly wasn't his own version of pre-game pump up. Something was wrong.

"You okay?" I asked.

"Shut the door...behind you, please." Landon's words were short, like he had trouble getting them out. For a second, I thought he might be choking, and my knowledge of the Heimlich was lacking.

I did as I was told and bit my lower lip.

"I'm having…a panic attack." He brought his knees up and buried his head between them. His lips moved, but no more words came out.

Crap. Crap. This had never happened to me before. I had no idea what a panic attack felt like, but I knew what it felt like to be so scared that you thought the world was ending. Or your world, at least. "Should I call a doctor? Do you need medical help?" I asked.

He shook his head.

"Do you want me to call Dr. Madison?"

Landon hesitated, but shook his head again.

I didn't know what else to do, so I plopped down next to him. He looked truly terrified, and I felt more useless than the external fuel tank on a space shuttle after it got into space.

"Is it okay if I touch your shoulder?"

He nodded.

Gently, I placed my hand flat on him. He was trembling. I thought about what I would want someone to say to me if I were in his place.

"It's okay. This is only temporary. You're safe here," I said.

He exhaled loudly and let his hand go from his chest. "I'm sorry." He avoided my eyes.

"No need to apologize. I just want you to be okay."

"I'm…fine." He squeezed his fist hard, then let loose, and repeated the process twice. "It's called muscle relaxation. It…controls the body's response to…the attack."

I did the same with my own fist and inhaled as I squeezed. Not a bad idea. I really felt the calm in my fingers after the muscles had been tightened.

"Talking helps too," he said. "I'm sorry. I know I-I… shouldn't be embarrassed, but I am. I hate…that you're seeing me like this."

I frowned. I wouldn't want someone to see the hardest parts of me either, like when I cut. But I didn't like Landon any less seeing him like this, so I wondered what he'd think if he knew I harmed myself. "It doesn't change how I feel about you at all," I said.

"Really?" Finally, he met my eyes. His own looked wounded, afraid. Sort of like Onion's when he's done something wrong like chomp on his favorite snack, my sandals.

"Really." I placed my hand on his. He stroked my thumb.

We sat in silence for at least another five minutes.

Landon took deep breaths in and out, and the color finally returned to his face. His lips, those beautiful lips, were finally pink again. "Panic attacks are terrible." He wiped his brow. "I'd never…wish them on anybody."

"It seems really rough. You're brave for facing them."

"Me?" He raised his eyebrows.

"Hell yeah! I knew you were nervous at auditions, but you still powered on. That's what bravery is. Moving forward when everything tells you not to." I felt like Dad, rambling, but my mouth didn't close. "You worked through it because deep down you knew it was the right thing to do, even if it scared you."

I expected Landon to smile, maybe give a shy laugh. But instead, he smirked.

"What?" I asked.

"Nothing." That annoyingly charming smirk, like he knew something I didn't. "But it's tough talk coming from a girl who refuses to audition."

"Wowwwwww." Absolutely brutal. "You went there."

"Yeah, I did," he said. "You killed it up there. We had

chemistry! I mean, er, our characters did."

"I'll admit it, yeah."

Landon gently took my hand. A more serious look crossed his dark eyes. Their beautiful brown reminded me so much of earth and soil. "So why won't you audition?"

I looked to our hands. I'd never told this to anyone before. "Sometimes, I get really…sad, I guess. And not like ordinary sad. Lately, I've been feeling that way a lot. Like it's an incredible effort to even open my sketchbook for the set," I said. "And things with my family are so serious right now. Trying out for a high school musical is ridiculous when my mom is…who knows where. My dad wants to have a memorial, but it hasn't even been that long."

I expected myself to blush or want to curl up, but actually? Getting it off my chest made me feel lighter.

"That sounds tough," Landon said. "You're a beautiful actress and artist. I-I mean. Your art is beautiful. Er, and you are too. But I meant —"

I chuckled. "I know what you meant." Suddenly, I was acutely aware that it was only the two of us, sitting knee to knee in this very tiny room. The same room lots of students took advantage of to make out in.

I thought back to our McDonald's date — if you wanted to call it that. It seemed like anytime something good happened to me, something awful followed. I had to be more careful.

"I felt comfortable up on stage with you," he said. "I don't think I can do that with anyone else."

I hesitated. Did Landon want me to be in the show because he thought I was talented, or because we read well together? "You can," I said. "You have to be comfortable with the person. That's all."

He shook his head. "There's no one else in theater club

I feel that way with."

Ugh. I loved that Landon saw me as different. As special—because he was right. On stage together, we stood out from the crowd. But I couldn't. Not now. "I'm sorry, but I can't handle auditions right now."

"I get it. I don't mean to pressure you," he said quickly. "I'm sorry. That wasn't fair."

"It's okay."

He took another deep breath. "I feel better now. I'm glad you were here, even if I still don't want you to ever see me like that again."

"I promise, I don't mind," I said.

"I know, but it's embarrassing."

"Land-o." I smirked. "It's not. It's okay."

"Thank you, Violet." Landon took my hand and brought it to his chest. "Feel my heart. Beating super hard."

Funny thing was, so was mine.

The same fuzzy feeling I'd had at Agent Rosenfield's office came over me. It felt light as a butterfly's wings.

Hope.

We left the room together, and I nearly jumped out of my skin to see Alex still there. It wasn't like her to wait around. Not on callback days, at least.

Her mouth hung open, her face arranged in disbelief, as she scrolled through her phone at a rapid pace.

"Everything okay?" I asked her.

"I was about to ask you the same thing." She sounded out of breath. "Have you seen the news?"

I reached for my phone and pulled up CNN, ignoring four texts from family members asking some variation of "Is it true?"

The headline on CNN: *Missing pilot Jennifer Ashby confirmed to have been involved in affair.*

CHAPTER FIFTEEN

DAY FIVE – AFTERNOON

'd never been more grateful that Dad and Savannah weren't home yet.

It was like the plane had gone missing all over again. I was glued to the television, a helpless victim to whatever slander the media wanted to broadcast.

Could ending things with her lover have caused pilot Jennifer Ashby to turn the plane on herself?

Exactly who is the man missing pilot Jennifer Ashby was seeing?

What if she was distracted by a phone call from the mystery man?

I squeezed my eyes shut. Mom having an affair didn't make her a murderer. But it did mean she wasn't the person I knew. And I wasn't sure what that person might be capable of.

My fingers dialed Agent Rosenfield before my brain caught up.

"I take it you've seen the news," she said. Her voice was quieter than usual.

"Is this true?"

"This is what I wanted to come over and discuss," she said. "But no need for that anymore, I suppose."

"Tell me everything you know." I didn't mean to snap at a federal agent, but whatever. It was going to be in a tabloid. Might as well hear it from a real source. "You're, like, the one connection I have to the truth. Please?"

She sighed. "I suppose you'll hear it anyway. Yes, she was likely having an affair with Dr. Matthew Bryant."

In all the times I'd searched him online, I'd still found nothing related to Mom. He wasn't even in a single one of her social media photos.

"I-I don't get it. I've never heard of this guy. They met in the military, but then did they stay in touch?"

"Yes, they served together," she said. "Briefly. Then they took flying lessons together."

"I guess that's why I found the picture with the flight wings," I said.

"Flight wings?" Agent Rosenfield asked.

It was the very first time since Mom was gone that I wasn't sure if I wanted more information or not. Learning about Dr. Bryant felt like I was on the edge of a precipice. It was like putting together a puzzle without knowing what image I was building.

At first, putting the pieces together had been an exciting discovery, but this one? It felt significant in a way that unsettled my stomach.

"I think... I think I might know something."

"Yes?" Agent Rosenfield asked.

But I couldn't give up now. I wasn't doing this just for me. I was doing it for Savannah, for Dad, for Mom.

I braced myself and told her about the necklace, Miles, and my own research.

"I strongly suggest not meeting strangers you meet online. At least you did it in public. Kids, my God." She sighed. "But that is interesting. Why was that photo with the wings, and not in a regular photo album? It doesn't make sense, unless…" Something changed in Agent Rosenfield's voice. "The last time she'd worn the sweater where you found the picture, when was that?"

I opened my mouth to explain about the driving test, how we'd celebrated with rich chocolate ice cream, but then I remembered I was wrong.

The black car. She'd worn the brown sweater the night before her final flight. It must've been the same day she'd gone to the jewelry store. She'd told Savannah and me that she was going out to buy paper towels at CVS.

We'd seen a black car pull up at the end of the street, and Mom had gotten in the front. The car had sat still for almost an hour.

Neither of us had asked why she hadn't come home with any bags.

I told Agent Rosenfield all of this. I had to. There had to be one person who could hear this story and still give Mom the benefit of the doubt. Someone besides me.

"I knew something was weird about it, but… I thought the store ran out of paper towels, something like that." Mom had told me to be honest, always, no matter what the situation. Cheating on my dad meant she was the one who'd risked their relationship, her family, and I knew she wouldn't do that. But what other possibility was there with this new puzzle piece?

"Violet, I'm sorry this is happening to you," she said. "But all this means nothing, really. Having an affair does not make your mother a villain. It does not mean she crashed a commercial jet intentionally."

"I know," I whispered. And I did. I knew that. But it was impossible to wrap my head around this. All of it.

This whole time I'd been trying to stop the world from seeing her as a villain, but now, I'd found evidence that she might have been one all along. If not to the rest of the world, at least to us. Her own family.

"We've spoken several times with Dr. Bryant, and we will do so again."

"You have to tell me what he said about that phone call." Acid spattered in the back of my throat. Last moments. I hated to think of it like that, but I was furious. She'd been the only person to keep me from drowning. An irrational kind of envy filled me to know that in her last moments, she'd reached out to someone other than me to be the same for her. "Please. No matter what he said."

"You know I can't do that."

"Why not!" I yelled. "I tell you everything, and you can't tell me a single helpful piece of information?"

I hung up and raced for the garbage pail in the kitchen. I upchucked—violently, like my guts didn't want to believe this bullshit either.

The choice was mine: I could find more truth, though every piece of truth I'd found so far had had a way of slapping me in the face. But if I ignored it all and gave up, then what? I'd be in the same position as I was now. Stuck.

I couldn't wait for Agent Rosenfield. I needed to find out about that phone call now.

. . .

I took an Uber to the hospital and headed up to the oncology unit. The very same place where Savannah had spent six awful months as a child.

Thankfully, I didn't remember it much, but something about the bright pastel walls and brightly colored cork boards seemed familiar. And the smell. That septic, sterile smell.

It was two floors up from where Savannah was hospitalized with her UTI. I wondered why Dr. Bryant had been milling about a different floor that day—had he known we were there?

It didn't take long to find him. He wasn't alone. Dr. Bryant halted when he caught my eye, and the other doctors walked ahead of him.

It was like he'd expected me.

"Pleiades girl," he said. "What are you doing back here?"

"Do you know me? Do you know who I am?" My hands trembled. After finding out apocalyptic news and subsequently puking, I didn't feel like the most confident girl on Earth.

His face softened. "I...think so."

His hesitation said it all. He knew why I was here, so there was no point in playing games.

"How long did it go on?" I asked.

"This isn't the place, Violet."

My knees threatened to give out, and I pressed my hand against the wall. I'd never told him my name. His inexplicable knowledge cut through me like an axe. I was right, and for once, I didn't want to be. "Tell me how long this went on."

His eyes flickered around the hall. A few nurses pushed patients in wheelchairs.

A bald child stood in front of the wall of stickers, intrigued by the butterflies. He pulled one off and held it protectively in his small hands.

"I'm sorry, but I truly can't discuss this. You shouldn't be here," he said.

"My dad doesn't know, does he?"

"Savannah said he might have an idea," Dr. Bryant said. "Perhaps you should speak to him instead. I'm sorry."

"Savannah?" I blinked.

She knew? She'd talked to him?

It felt like a tsunami was forming in my brain, pulling me under faster and faster.

A few doctors started down the hall and eyed us, probably wondering why Dr. Bryant was talking to a clearly annoyed teenager in street clothes and not a child in a hospital gown.

"You should really leave," he said.

"I'm not going." I crossed my arms. "You talked to Savannah?"

"You're an extremely stubborn kid, aren't you?" He curved his lips into a smirk. I hated that he seemed amused by that fact. His smile looked familiar, but I couldn't place it. Maybe from the photo. Since the photo was taken, his short, neat hair had grayed a bit, his brown eyes had become softer.

"I'm not a kid. But I am stubborn." I leaned in and spoke at plain volume. "And you're an adulterer."

"Can you keep it quiet?" he whispered. He glanced worriedly toward the hallway, as if making sure no one was walking by.

"No."

He took a long breath that at least gave him time to weigh his options and acknowledge that, like it or not, I wasn't going anywhere until he talked to me. "Fine. Follow me."

He turned to the left, then another left. I stuck a close three feet behind him as we approached a small but neat office.

His desk barely had any papers on it. Everything was filed into cabinets. His computer background was the Milky Way, and he had a signed baseball on the top shelf. Mets, I thought. We Ashby women had something in common, I guessed.

He dropped into his leather chair. "I assumed you would eventually find me and ask me these questions. I just didn't think it would happen this way." He gestured for me to take a seat, too.

I didn't. I remained standing and crossed my arms. "Tell me the truth. How long did this go on?"

He sighed. "This is very hard for me to talk about."

"Weeks? Months?" I asked.

He said nothing, his mouth a firm line. *Longer*. It had to be longer, even though my parents had separated only two months ago. The divorce papers hadn't become official yet.

"A very long time," he said. "Off and on. I don't know exactly how long."

Either the lights flickered in the hospital, or I was so stunned I was blacking out.

I wanted to hiss, *How could you?* But how could he not? He didn't know me, or my family. It had been Mom. She'd been the one.

How could *she*?

"You don't remember me at all, do you?" he asked. "From when you were younger?"

"What are you talking about?"

"N-Never mind." He waved his hand.

The way he stared so intently at my face made me wonder if he thought I was lying to him. Regardless, he could search my eyes all day long and find nothing but the desire to find my mom and put all this to rest.

"Did I meet you before?" I asked.

He shook his head quickly, as though he were done with the question. "I wish I could help you, but I don't think I can do anything except apologize. And please know that I cared about Jenn so much."

"Just tell me one thing," I said. "You were the last person to talk to her before takeoff. What did she talk about?"

"I can't say."

"What do you mean?"

"It's not fair to her," he said. "I'm sorry."

Bullshit. If I clenched my teeth any harder, they'd crack. "Will you at least tell the media or the FBI that she's innocent?"

"I can't. I have the right not to say anything." He squeezed his eyes shut, as if he were in pain. "This is very hard for me right now."

"Oh, it's hard for you? For *you*? That's really nice, Dr. Bryant," I hissed.

My mom was missing, vanished from the face of the Earth, but yeah, I was sure this was all *real* hard for him.

"Violet, you seem like a great girl, but I think you should go home and get some rest. This isn't where you should be," he said.

"Don't tell me where I should be," I spat. "You ruined my life."

It was unfair, I knew. But it came fuming out of me.

"You don't understand." He stood and placed his hand

on the doorknob. "Please don't make me call security."

"That would be nice, huh? Right now, you're still anonymous. The mystery dude on the news. But not if I open my mouth."

"Please don't," he said quickly. He dug his short fingernails into his arm, fidgeting. "I have a daughter, Phoebe. She's five. My ex-wife is not letting me see her because of all this. She's the reason I can't say anything to the media. I don't want any cameras around my house—"

"It's so nice you have the luxury to choose. You can decide if you want cameras. You get to be with my mom, then suddenly pretend it never happened when you actually have a chance to defend—"

The door burst open. Dr. Bryant's hand moved backward like he'd touched a hot stove.

"FBI, Agent Diana Rosenfield." She held up her badge, then placed it into her pocket. Her mouth was pressed into a firm line, her green eyes cold. "Violet, we're leaving now."

I was panting like a dog on a hot August day. When the hell did she get here? "But I—"

She placed her hand on my shoulder and led me out of the room. "We're going. Dr. Bryant, I will be coming by to speak with you in approximately one hour. If you're not here, I will go to your home. I will find you."

"Yes, ma'am," he said. He glanced to the gold Rolex on his wrist, then back at us.

Agent Rosenfield shut the door behind her. "Let's get out of here. I hate hospitals."

CHAPTER SIXTEEN

DAY FIVE – LATE AFTERNOON

Every inch of me wanted to plow into Savannah's room and shake her down for questions. But I couldn't do that, because I could picture the headline: *Deranged local girl arrested for screaming at sick sister, risking kidney explosion.*

So Agent Rosenfield took me for a drive.

"Can I get you some water? Food?" she asked. "Did you eat anything today?"

The mere idea of food made me want to upchuck. Again. "I did. Not hungry." *Won't be. Ever.*

She drummed her fingernails against the steering wheel of her car. It was immaculately clean. No surprise. "Okay," she said. "Where would you like to go?"

Home. Not home. Nowhere. Anywhere.

I shrugged.

"I have an idea." She turned left.

I didn't ask, and stayed quiet on the ride.

Mom is a liar. Mom is a liar. Mom is a liar.

Repeating the phrase in my mind was like a form of medieval torture. The truth was smacking me in the face, but I couldn't even talk to the one person who I truly wanted answers from.

Alex texted me: **Callbacks were fine. Brittany Thompson sang for Belle more than anyone OF COURSE. I swear, if I don't get that part...**

I tossed my phone back into my purse. With the world crumbling in front of me, some high school play was like a tiny crumb that had fallen under the couch. I didn't care enough for it to sap my mental energy. Not now.

"Cool phone case," she said. "Is that a Kate Spade?"

"No, it's a Violet Ashby," I said. "I made it myself. No big deal, mostly some hot glue and rhinestones."

"Oh, wow. You're talented." There was surprise in her voice. Somehow, that made me like her more.

"I'm sorry I yelled at you and hung up on you," I mumbled.

"I'd yell and hang up on me too, if I were you."

Agent Rosenfield pulled into Hollow's Creek. It was a stretch of grassy land overlooking the sparkling Hudson and the pointed trees that lined it. The orange sun cast a glow onto the water. I wanted to paint it, except that I didn't want to do anything anymore.

"I'm not going to say I know how you feel, because I don't." She looked over the steering wheel, onto the scenery. The sunset brought out the amber tones in her hair. "But I will say picking up teenage girls in my personal car is weirdly not in my job description, nor is it something I've ever done before."

"Good to know." Normally, I would've been embarrassed about my behavior, but now I wished I'd been louder.

That I'd screamed in Dr. Bryant's face and demanded he tell me everything he knew—every word in that final conversation. "This whole time, I blamed my dad for the divorce," I said. "I thought he was too much of a dreamer or too hippie or whatever. Now I realize it was her. It was all her."

"Well, divorce is usually two-sided," Agent Rosenfield said nonchalantly. "It's complicated."

Understatement of the year.

A plane passed by, twinkling its green and blue lights.

"I wish she was here, but at the same time…" I couldn't finish. It felt like yet another betrayal of the person I'd thought I knew.

But who was that person, really?

"You want her here, but you're angry with her," she said.

"Yes," I whispered. "Exactly."

Mom had dropped the mask and was now a stranger to me.

For who knew how long, she'd been hiding her happiness from me, lying to my father's face. How? This was the woman who'd sat through Pokemon movies and had made a "Happy Coming Out" cake for me when I'd told her I was bi.

She was supposed to be here. Either I'd make it to fifty days with no self-harm, and I'd see a way out, or I'd fail, and she'd be there to help.

To be my person.

Maybe you could never really know someone.

And if I didn't know Mom, then who was I to say she hadn't killed herself and 155 people?

Maybe I had it all wrong. I hadn't dared to let a negative thought about Mom enter my brain, but maybe I'd been too naive. If Dr. Bryant had broken up with her in that phone call, and she'd already been depressed… What would it have taken to push her over the edge?

I hated to think that when I was at my worst, cutting myself to get through the day, Mom had been there for me, but maybe she'd been struggling in her own way.

I was standing at the cliff's edge, thinking I was all alone, but really, Mom was there with me.

Deep down, though, I knew. She wouldn't do this. Not on purpose. And accepting that she'd crashed on purpose would mean accepting she was gone.

I thought of the note she'd left me. Whatever plan she'd claimed to have, it was gone now. This couldn't have possibly been her intention. But then, what had she been talking about?

"I want to know everything you know about the plane," I said. "Promise me you're not hiding anything. Even if you think it's going to make me upset."

Those two minutes and three seconds between the transponder shutting off and losing signal by Puerto Rico were going to haunt me until I knew every last detail of flight US133.

If I could reconstruct my mother, then I could reconstruct the flight. But I needed the truth, and I wasn't going to get that alone.

"I can't tell you everything," she said. "Even if I wanted to."

"Please."

"Violet, I know what you're getting at. An affair does not mean your mother is a murderer," she said. "People have affairs every day. People who wear nice suits that their wives pressed for them lie and say they're going to happy hour when they're really at a motel. It's life. It's not okay, but it doesn't make them murderers."

"Do you think she did it on purpose?" My voice was

meek. Unrecognizable as my own. "I-I can't believe I'm even considering this." I was absolutely mortified to even let the thought cross my consciousness, but it had to be said. *Trust me*, Mom had asked.

I was so pathetic, so broken, I couldn't even do that. Not anymore.

"I don't know. I'm as frustrated as you are." A beat passed between us. Agent Rosenfield gripped the steering wheel tighter. "We've cleared thirty-five passengers now, but they won't clear Ayesha. I presented enormous documentation that she had no intentions of harming herself or others. RSVPs to conferences, to baby showers, a doctor's appointment scheduled for next month," she said. "Homeland Security wants to investigate her 'connections to possible radical Islamic terrorists,' AKA her elderly mother and grandmother back in Iran. Give me a break."

The raw honesty in her eyes reminded me that I wasn't alone in this. Other people had lost spouses, friends, family. Moms.

"I'm sorry," she said.

"I'm sorry too," I whispered.

Agent Rosenfield glanced at her watch. "It's getting late. Let's get you home."

She drove toward my house and parked adjacent to the driveway, like that black car had the other night. She turned to look at me, and in the dashboard light, I saw her as Diana, the person. Not the federal agent, but the woman with tired eyes who was missing her friend just like I was missing my mom.

"Thanks, Agent Rosenfield," I said.

"You can call me Diana," she said like she'd read my mind. "Since, you know, we're in this together. But not in front of other people."

"That sounds fair." I hopped out of the car. "Thanks, Diana."

I arrived home right before seven thirty.

Dad was already on the phone. "I don't know what you want me to do, man. I'm getting enough royalties to live on for now, and we've got savings, but I need to access her account." His slippers flopped against the tile floor, the only sound in the kitchen.

I wanted to sit beside Savannah, but my legs refused to move.

Money. How had I been so ignorant not to think of how we'd live?

Everything had been always taken care of, and now— it wasn't.

"Where have you been?" Savannah asked.

I opened my mouth to answer, but stopped. I was sick of lying. And of people lying to me. Instead, I said, "What's Dad fuming about?"

"The bank is giving him a hard time," she said. "He tried to cover my hospital bills and, uh… We need Mom's bank account."

"I have some savings," I said.

She half smiled. "That's nice of you Vi, but hospital bills are expensive. We don't have nearly enough. Dad's been on the phone back and forth with them and her insurance."

"Insurance?" I felt like a useless parrot, but I didn't know what else to say. To do.

"Can I declare that she's legally dead without a body?"

Dad's voice was quiet. "I-I don't want to, no, but I've got to provide for my daughters now."

"Legally dead?" I croaked.

No, no. That wasn't right. A scream began to well in my throat, but I masked it as a cough. This was wrong.

It was too soon. It was only five days out. Mom could easily come in that door any minute now. Be found on a remote island. Something—anything.

Desperation took over me like a fog.

Dad glanced at me and did a double take. "I've got to think about this. I'll call tomorrow morning." He hung up and took a bottle of Sierra Nevada IPA from the fridge. "Well, I'm going to go out on a limb and say this is the worst week of my life."

"I take it you've seen the news?" I mumbled.

"Oh, the news that my wife was with another man for a large part of our marriage? Yes, I saw," he said. "I feel quite lucky. My other friends who got cheated on didn't get their stories on the evening news. Maybe the publicity will help my book sales."

I frowned. "I'm so sorry, Dad."

He waved his hand dismissively. "I don't want to talk about it right now. I'm sorry, I shouldn't have said that."

I looked to Savannah, but she looked to the ground.

"I don't want you girls thinking about that or thinking about me. It's not important," he said. "All I care about is making sure you girls are provided for."

"Everything is going to be okay," I said.

Clearly the wrong thing to say—Savannah stormed out of the room as if I'd offended all of our ancestors in one breath. A moment later, her bedroom door slammed.

Me, Violet McKenna Ashby, ruining one thing after another.

"You're right, honey. Everything will be okay. It's the insurance companies being difficult, that's all. They're designed to be agents of chaos." Dad took a sip of beer, and I wondered when he'd gotten the opportunity to go out and buy those bottles. Mom never drank.

"What if it's not okay?" I whispered.

"Then we'll burn the house down to get insurance money," Dad said.

"Dad!"

"It's all gonna be fine." He placed his hand on my shoulder. "The three of us are tight as ropes. Oh, hey, I'm gonna use that in my next book. Uh, anyway. I mean it. And besides, you're the daughter of a tough, amazing woman and a starving artist. You're built to be strong."

I looked into Dad's light eyes and felt sorry for him in a way I'd never had before. He still said Mom's name with respect, but she'd lacked so much love for him that she'd moved on a long, long time ago.

Life. Isn't. Fair.

"Right," I whispered. I couldn't even fathom the anger seeping through my veins at my mother. If rage was a superpower, I was a nuclear bomb waiting to go off.

Dad turned to me again. "I don't mean to make you more upset right now, but I got in touch with Dr. Madison. She agreed to see you as a crisis case. Okay?"

"Crisis case?" I said, playing clueless.

"Short term. It's an ethical violation, so she can't take you on as a full client, but she wants to make sure you're safe. We both do," he said. "So I'm going to find another therapist after our insurance figures itself out, but for now, you've got what you asked for."

A pang of guilt hit me in the chest. Poor Dad had really gone out of his way for me, only so that I could dig up some more dirt on Mom.

"Thanks," I said.

"The appointment is tomorrow at noon."

If I kept thinking about it, I'd explode, so I browsed through my phone.

Instagram, Snapchat, none of it was working to pull me out of this. I opened my email, hoping for a homework assignment or something to focus on. Instead:

From: MTariq@SCSD.edu
To: VioletMAshby02@gmail.com
Hi Violet,
I wanted to tell you that the designer will be at school this Friday, so you can talk to her about your ideas. I know things have been tough for you—even if you don't attend classes that day, you can still attend the meeting.
More importantly, I was impressed with your reading the other day. If you want, I can put you in the cast. You do not have to audition with a song or monologue. There are plenty of non-singing roles I think you would be great for.
Let me know,
Mr. Tariq.

Dad's voice pulled me out of it. "What are you reading?"

It was the email I'd been dreaming of for years now. My chance to act on stage without the awkwardness of my terrible singing voice.

But I couldn't do it. Not with everything crumbling down around me.

I can't afford to get distracted.

"Nothing."

I deleted it.

CHAPTER SEVENTEEN

DAY FIVE – NIGHT

I woke up from a nap with a hangover.

My head was bursting with pain and I'd never been more tired—except I hadn't had a sip of alcohol. I guessed that was how you were supposed to feel when your life was falling apart.

I checked my phone and found a text.

ALEX: Haven't heard from you since yesterday. You okay?

ME: Yeah, sorry.

ME: Did the cast list go up?

I knew I'd said I didn't care about high school plays. And I didn't. I didn't have the headspace. But I cared about Alex.

ALEX: Tomorrow. I'm freaking out.

Me: You'll be all right <3

ALEX: Hope so. I'm coming over later. I know it's a bad time, but I have something for you and Savannah.

I thought back to Savannah's locker: I'd picked up

every piece of homework, every folder. Savannah would've told me by now if she was missing anything. Huh.

ME: Cool.

I rolled over on my bed and touched the flight wings on the side of my desk. Instead of being comforting, they felt too sharp.

There were two gentle knocks on my door.

Savannah hovered by the doorway. "Hey."

"Hi."

"You look upset. You okay?" she asked.

"Fine. It's nothing." It was hardly as painful as the infection that had landed her in the ER. "How are the kidneys?"

"Bad. But Kit Kats help." She twirled a piece of her blonde hair. That was another of her nervous tells; I always knew.

"What's wrong?"

"Everything." She cracked a grin and sat on the edge of my bed. "But specifically? I want to talk to you about something. Sister to sister."

"Uh oh." I squinted. "What?" I leaned forward quickly. "Wait, the blood test from the hospital came back, right? Did it say anything bad?"

"No! It's fine. White blood cell count is up, yeah, but it's the kidney infection. No cancer."

A wave of relief washed over me, but it was quickly replaced by frustration. I hated that she had to deal with this. Getting sick from eggs, having tests whenever her counts were off. Telling people she was a survivor and having them look at her with those pathetic puppy-dog eyes. Cancer was always there, stored in the back of her brain like a permanent cobweb.

I would've traded places with her in a heartbeat.

I wondered if she felt the same way about me.

"Besides," she said. "I have to feel better. I don't want to defer Stanford."

I understood. All of this happening with Mom, and I still kept thinking about the musical. It was the little things that kept us going. Or not so little.

I thought about Landon, and how when I was with him, I could laugh. Be myself. Not think about everything else for a change. I wondered if he was thinking of me, too, the weird girl who'd sat with him at McDonald's as her life had fallen into pieces.

"You won't. Stanford will be happy to have you," I said.

"If I get in," she said. "Remember when Mom drove us there?"

Of course I did.

Endless hours in the car, listening to her musical theater soundtracks that I adored, but that had made Savannah want to leap out the windows. When we'd pulled into the university parking lot, Mom and I had stayed in the car to finish our "Defying Gravity" duet, while Savannah had bolted out of the back seat and Dad had quickly followed.

"I wish you'd sing duets with me," I said.

"Please. You don't." Savannah twisted her hair tighter around her finger. "Look, I have to tell you something. It's about—"

"I know already."

She raised her dark eyebrows. "You do?"

"I confronted Dr. Bryant."

Savannah's face was puzzled; I expected her to be relieved or even angry with me. "What are you talking about?"

"When you were in the hospital, I ran into Dr. Bryant. I asked him about Mom."

Savannah's eyes widened. "You knew? Before the news said anything?"

"I should be asking you that. I just found out yesterday." It took everything in me not to scowl. It hadn't only been Mom hiding things from me, it had been Savannah too. I pictured a mini-me poking their prefrontal cortexes until they were finally honest.

"Why didn't you say anything?" I asked.

She shrugged. "He saved my life. What am I supposed to do?"

"What are you talking about?"

"You don't remember?" Savannah tilted her head. "Dr. Bryant was my oncologist as a kid. He helped me through all my treatment."

Oh my God.

The realization felt like a car slammed into me.

Maybe it was because I'd only been five or six, or because the memories of my sister being sick were too painful, but it all came back to me now.

He'd cut his hair now; it had been more of the Dawson's Creek style back then, and he'd had a beard. He'd shown us how to make balloon animals on a day when Savannah had felt particularly sick. She'd gone with a cat, I'd gone with a duck. I'd laughed for five minutes straight when he'd made the duck squeak.

"I can't believe I didn't realize," I whispered.

"It was a long time ago. We were little." Savannah looked to the ground. "But, yeah. So, I didn't say anything."

"You lied to me when you saw the photo, then," I said.

"No," she said quickly. "Honestly, I didn't recognize him. I hadn't thought about him in a while, and you flashed the picture to me so fast."

"How did you even know about the affair?" The word

sounded dirty in my mouth.

She took a deep breath. "Little things. Like, last winter, I came home from school during lunch because I forgot my flight exam manual, and I had to study. Mom and him were having lunch at the kitchen table like everything was fine, like it wasn't totally weird."

"Wow." Winter had been almost a full year ago. How could she have kept a secret like that for so long? "You really didn't think to say anything?"

"That's the thing. I didn't know exactly what was going on. Mom didn't admit anything, but I knew. The look on her face was…guilty, to say the least. She said she was just grateful for all he did for me and a friend, but then two seconds later asked me not to say anything to Dad." She moved hair from her face. "Or you."

I wrinkled my nose. I tried to picture Dr. Bryant sitting at our kitchen table, studying the pure white of our walls, peeking through our cabinets.

He better not have sat in Dad's chair.

"I wish you would've told me." At the same time, though, I didn't. There was no chance I'd have been able to look into Dad's face and not scream that his marriage was about to crash.

"Why? You got to think Mom was a hero for a whole eight months longer than I did," she said. "What kind of sister would I be to take that from you?"

"One who tells me the truth." I regretted it the instant I said it.

Savannah shrugged but held my eye contact. "Well, that's not me, then."

"Wow."

"See, I knew you'd react like this. That's why I didn't say anything."

"I'm reacting like this because you lied," I snapped.

"Um, no. Every time you find out something that doesn't fit in your perfect worldview, you flip," she said. "Like when you first found out I wanted to move to the west coast for college? Remember that meltdown?"

Did older sisters have a storage box full of embarrassing memories they kept on hand? *Jesus*. The west coast was far, okay?

I looked to my phone. Alex was texting me, but her words were blurred by tears forming in my eyes. "Forget it, okay? Let's focus on today instead."

"Okay," she said, surprisingly soft.

"I feel terrible for Dad," I whispered. "That can't possibly be the whole story."

She raised an eyebrow. "What do you mean?"

"Between Mom and Dad or Mom and Dr. Bryant. There's got to be more to it."

Savannah gave me that look where she narrowed her eyes at me, like there was an endless gap between our ages. Like I could never mature and be as wise as she was. "It's not our place to judge. Mom obviously wasn't happy with Dad. We can't fault her for moving on."

There is no way this girl and I are related. "We can fault her for cheating on Dad. For hiding things from us."

"Of course she hid things from us. You can't expect her to tell her children everything," she said. "Mom was her own person—"

"Mom *is* her own person."

"Mom *was* her own person," Savannah said softly. "Who kept secrets from us, and that's okay. Sometimes we aren't meant to know everything."

I wanted to punch down Savannah's "I'm so tough" facade, but something in her stare made me hold back.

Maybe being stone-cold kept her afloat when the tides of missing our mother and painful infections threatened to pull her under. It wasn't my place to judge her, even if I thought she'd lost it. The pain was ours to share.

Dad knocked twice on the door and poked his head through. "Girls? You have a visitor."

Dad's cheeks were swollen, like he might've been crying. The last time I'd seen my dad cry had been when the Sandy Hook shooting had been on the news.

Savannah and I exchanged glances, silently agreeing that we were not going to say that she'd known beforehand. Ever.

"It's me!" Alex barreled up the stairs and into my bedroom, holding a gift basket and panting like she'd run a full marathon. "I wanted to give you this," she said. "It's stuff you like! Kit Kats, those vegan granola bars I always see in your cabinets, and I even found some freeze-dried ice cream! Mint chocolate chip, right?"

Not just one freeze-dried ice cream, but three. She'd nailed all of Savannah's favorites. My gaze darted from Alex to Savannah.

We'd been best friends for over ten years, and Alex had never done this for me. Not when I'd gotten my tonsils out, not when Mom had initially gone missing. What the hell kind of fantasy world was I living in this week?

Savannah's jaw fell ajar. She didn't even reach for the basket. Her eyes were wide with an emotion I couldn't quite read. Gratitude, happiness—but I thought I saw the tiniest amount of fear.

I took it instead, and walked with it to Savannah's room next door. I placed it gently on her desk.

"That's nice of you, Alexandria," Dad said. "I have my eye on one of those ice-cream packets."

Finally, Savannah broke her statue pose and flung her arms around Alex. Again: I seemed to be living in a parallel universe. Savannah might as well be Elsa from *Frozen*—hugs were not her thing—but here she was, tightly enveloping my best friend. In *my* room.

"Thank you so much," Savannah whispered. "This was so sweet."

"She knows the kidney infection is basically healed now, right?" Dad whispered to me.

I nudged him in the ribs. My best friend and my sister were finally becoming more than just people who acknowledged each other. I wanted to bask in the warmth of it, no matter how bizarre. It was probably the only good thing to come out of this week.

"You're welcome. You deserve it." Alex still held Savannah, her hands tight around her lower back.

Savannah broke the hug. "We can share the Kit Kats." She caught my eye, and her cheeks were red as shrimp sauce.

"I should freeze that ice cream." Dad walked toward Savannah's room and nodded at me to follow. He plucked the packets from the bag, and handed me the third.

We descended the stairs together. Onion sat up on the couch—where he was definitely not supposed to sit—and wagged his tail. He followed us into the kitchen, where Dad and I stored the ice cream and the rest of the perishable snacks. We had three casseroles to go.

"Do we have to freeze these?" I asked. "I thought they just stay in the pack?"

"Yeah, I just said that to get us away from them," Dad said. The TV from the living room flashed out of the corner of my eye. "Violet, I have to tell you something, but I'm afraid it's going to upset you."

Uh oh. "Did something happen?"

"No, nothing with the plane. But in order for us to get the insurance money we need, or money in general, I have to declare Mom legally dead."

Legally dead. Even though we'd already talked about this, the words were still sharp.

Health insurance was something that I didn't want to even think about until I was twenty-six, but now what? Dad worked for himself and lived off Mom's insurance. We didn't have a ton of options.

"I don't understand. Why can't they accept that she's missing, not dead?"

"That's not how it works, I guess."

"What if she comes back?" And worse, what if she came back and found out that we'd declared her legally dead? She'd think we'd given up.

"It's reversible," Dad said. "I'm only doing it for money. The same reason I teach summer classes."

"But…"

"We really need the money, sweetie." He looked to the ground. "I can't support you both on my writing. I… I had to take money out of our savings to pay Savannah's hospital bill the other day. I can't keep doing that."

"I thought you had to wait to declare someone legally dead? You can't do that right away. Not without…" I swallowed.

He should know. In all his crime books, they said seven years was what it took to declare a missing person legally dead without a body. Even if Dad didn't know, I'd read his books. All of them.

"You can't," I whispered.

"There's exceptions for… circumstances like this," Dad said.

Like this. When the entire world was pointing at a

conclusion I couldn't begin to think about.

It was wrong. So incredibly wrong.

I could feel her everywhere. In this kitchen, in the living room. Every time I turned a corner, I was convinced I would run into her in the next room. Every time I got home, I'd find myself looking on the couch for her, or waiting for the door to open. But it never did.

The tiny remainder of hope I had was a frayed thread. I was scared of the thread becoming thinner and thinner.

"I'm really sorry, sweetie," he said. "This isn't my choice."

After everything Dad had been through, I couldn't fight something that would make his life easier.

"Okay." I gave him a quick hug. I knew nothing had changed, but knowing that ink would soon be on paper saying Mom was dead gave me a weird foreboding. Like we were writing something into existence.

Maybe I should go upstairs and ask Alex for a tarot.

As I hugged him, I faced the TV.

The reporters were showing footage of the search efforts. For the past few days, small planes and boats from several countries had gone to the area where the last ping from the plane was. They'd found nothing. Absolutely nothing.

Only the wide, vast blue ocean. On a map, the space between Brazil, where Mom had left, and Puerto Rico, where the plane had last pinged, looked so small. But on TV, it looked endless.

"With Air France 447, it was a full five days before they found the wreckage, and the recorders were not found until two years after," one reporter said.

Today was day five. My mouth felt dry.

It was inconceivable to think I had to wait any longer.

When I used to watch the news, I used to feel so sorry for those families, and think about how they felt. The pain. Now—I didn't want sympathy. I wanted truth. I wanted my mom home.

"Oh no." Dad stroked his gray-flecked beard. It had gotten longer and more untrimmed these past few days. Few months, really. "This isn't good."

The footage switched to show the aerial weather map. A huge white swirling cloud, Hurricane Molly, was hovering over the area.

"With this new threat coming in from Hurricane Molly, the search is unfortunately going to be stopped," another reporter said. "The extreme weather would make it unsafe for search vehicles to progress…"

I squeezed my eyes shut. I knew it wasn't anyone's fault, but it felt like no one in the world cared anymore. No one except for me. I felt like I was falling for miles and miles, with no one to catch me.

"We've got to hang in there, Violet," Dad said gently. "This sucks, but it's temporary. The storm will go away, and they'll look again."

I didn't know if I should believe him or not.

This was a Category Three now. Less than they'd predicted, but that was still a big storm. People's attention could only hang on to one topic for so long. I was afraid the plane would fade into obscurity again.

Even with the affair—which they were talking about now. I hated, *hated* that it was on TV, but at least it was being talked about. For now.

But worse, the thought of anyone from the plane surviving and then being faced with a Category Three… Acid spurred to the back of my throat.

It was daylight, but darkness was coming for me.

I looked to my hands. "Dad, I'm so sorry about all this."

"Don't apologize." His voice was quiet. I actually would've preferred if he was angry. Instead, he sounded defeated. Like the world had steamrolled him and he couldn't get any flatter.

Way, way worse.

"It's not the ideal way to find out your wife is cheating on you," he said. "I would've preferred being told dramatically, having a decent cry. Getting sympathy from our friends. An Emma Thompson *Love Actually* situation, that sort of thing." He shrugged. "Something I could use for a good scene in a book, at least."

I cringed at the thought.

How long had this gone on? How?

I thought of Savannah's story and tried to picture Dr. Bryant in our kitchen, right where we stood. As hard as I tried, that puzzle piece didn't fit. *He* didn't fit.

"They weren't... This was a recent thing, wasn't it?" The idea of an affair was enough. An affair that had gone on for over ten years was as unimaginable as the Death Star actually existing.

"I hope not, but I think only one person has the answer to that now, and we'll never know." Dad shrugged. "I used to think he was amazing, the way he helped Savannah. Ignorance is bliss, I guess."

"I'm not sure if that's true," I said.

"Who knows? When Savannah first got diagnosed, Mom researched good oncology doctors in the area and found him. She told me she knew him from the military. I thought we were lucky." He snorted. "And honestly? If your mom having an affair is the karmic price I pay for a terrific oncologist that saved Sav's life, then fine. That's peanuts."

I'd been thinking about karma a lot these days. None

of it felt real. And if it was, I didn't owe anyone anything for the rest of my life.

"I don't want you to think too much about the affair. It's my problem, not yours." Dad turned to me, but his eyes were so fraught with sadness that I had to look away.

"I'm so angry at her, but I feel like I'm not allowed to be," I whispered.

A list of things I was angry at Mom for:

Not bringing Savannah to the doctor

Hurting Dad with the affair

Not being who I thought she was

Leaving

Leaving

Leaving

"I understand," he whispered.

CHAPTER EIGHTEEN

DAY SIX – LATE MORNING

The next day, I sat in the front yard with Onion. My sketchpad sat next to me, empty. Whether I felt like creating or not, I had made Mr. Tariq a promise that I'd help.

Dad was busy writing on the couch, oblivious to the news of Hurricane Molly flashing on the screen. I doubt he noticed I was outside. Deadlines were deadlines, even when your wife—*ex*-wife—was missing. I'd texted Alex to come over and investigate with me, but she hadn't answered. Probably praying to her God, Idina Menzel, for good theater luck.

It was the type of crisp morning that could only exist in September—a tease of what summer was, a preview of what fall would be.

Last night, the moon had been a bright crescent. I'd refused to look at the stars, so I didn't know if they had been out. It had reminded me too much of being on the roof with Mom and Savannah when we'd been younger, gazing into the sky above.

It was Savannah who wanted to be the astronaut, not me, but Mom had still instilled a love of outer space in me too.

I'd developed a bad habit the past four days: research US133, read the comments, hate the world, then close my laptop in dismay with no new information.

Today was not one of those days.

Hurricane Molly sustains 165 mph winds—catastrophic damage to the Caribbean ahead

Basketball star's ex-wife pregnant, is it his?

Flight US133—pilot's affair unraveled

NFL faces another lawsuit

I clicked the third article and sat up straight. In short:

An FBI investigation has revealed that the pilot of missing flight US133, Jennifer Ashby, was having an affair. Details have not been released, but specialists are speculating that the affair could've been a driving force in a murder-suicide.

"Dammit." I sighed. I rubbed my fists into my eyes as if I could unread that.

I hated, *hated* seeing that s-word.

Onion whined in sympathy.

"Can this just be a nightmare?" I asked Onion. "Something I can wake up from?"

He sniffed my laptop in response.

I then made the mistake of reading the anonymous comments section.

Ashby clearly got dumped by this guy she was seeing and decided to take herself out, and take 155 people with her. It's not hard to conceive. This is why women should not control heavy machinery.

Dying is her punishment for having an affair. Corinthians 6.18: Flee from sexual immorality.

I can't wait until they find the wreckage and I never have to hear about this woman and her stupid affair ever again. Everyone shut up!!

"My god, the human race is abysmal," I told Onion. He was so lucky to be a dog.

But then, two comments made me stop breathing for a second:

Darlenejackson22: Former fighter pilot here – I'm wondering if this was intentional now that I've seen more of the news. How did this disappear from the radar for that long? The pilot must've known where in the airspace she could get away with turning the transponder off. I believe she is responsible. Perhaps she wanted to run away from her life and divorce.

ThunderRoad68: I hank you for your service, first of all. Second, I know the pilot personally. You must believe me that she didn't do this on purpose. She loves her family, and she had plans for the future.

Plans? I thought about the note she had left me.

I looked away from my laptop to process. Thunder-Road68 hadn't posted anything new since the initial comment flurry when the plane had first disappeared. Why now?

And *know*. They said I *know* the pilot. Not knew.

If I didn't know better, I'd think it was me.

I bit my lip, then commented:

Elphaba243: How do you know the pilot?

Might be a while until they responded, if they ever did. But it was something.

I looked to the wall that connected my room to Savannah's.

Dad was always online, but he'd know nothing about

transponders and airspace. Savannah, though…

Alex still hadn't responded, so I texted Landon instead.

ME: What do you do when you feel your anxiety revving up?

He responded instantly.

LANDON: I try to relax as much as I can. But it's hard. It's physical, even though it's mental. I know that sounds weird…

It didn't sound weird at all. I glanced toward my wrist.

LANDON: Having a tough day?

ME: Tough six days, really…

LANDON: I know. Hang in there. Do you want to talk about it? You can call me.

ME: I thought you hate talking on the phone

LANDON: Not with you.

This boy.

This sweet, adorable guy with eyes that could melt me. In a different world, in another time, I thought I could be the girl for him. But now? I was only going to drag him down. I was a mess. Landon deserved better.

"Sweetie?" Dad knocked on the door twice. "Ready to go?"

I closed my laptop and threw my shoes on. If I had to see Dr. Madison, maybe she'd at least help me prove ThunderRoad68 right.

"Nice to see you again, Violet." Dr. Madison sat across from me holding a cup of tea. She wore a long skirt to her ankles with tennis shoes. I liked the juxtaposition.

"You too." I looked around for more clues to

Mom's existence. The place was fairly barren of any personalization at all, but I still tried to picture Mom here. I focused on the Brownstones again, and pretended I was Enola Holmes. Taking in tiny details to put the picture together.

"I'm surprised you decided to see me. You seemed resistant last time," she said.

"I'm busy, that's all."

"With what?"

"I'm designing the set for the school musical, and I have to keep working on finding out what happened."

"To your mother?"

"Yeah."

Dr. Madison tilted her head. "What do you think happened?"

"She would never, ever hurt anyone on purpose. Ever. You know that."

She gave a slight nod. I couldn't tell if she was agreeing with me or telling me to go on.

"Everyone online says horrible things. They say she's a horrible person or that she did it intentionally. I hate reading that stuff," I said.

"Then why do you?"

I blinked. "Well, like I said, I have to figure it out."

"You think internet comments will help you understand what happened to the plane?" If someone else had said that to me, I would've snapped. Savannah and I would've started a fun argument, same with Dad. But there was something non-judgmental in her tone. Like she genuinely wanted to know and understand me.

"There's one person in there who keeps defending my mom. I don't know who it is. They say they know her, maybe they don't," I said. "So I keep looking for their comment."

"I see. Why do you think that is?"

I looked to my hands.

"Do you think maybe it's nice to know you're not alone?" she asked.

There's a boy, I almost said. Someone who made me feel...not so alone. But I held back.

I knew what she was trying to do. Fix my head, or whatever. Well, good luck, it's quite unfixable. But I wasn't here for that. I needed to stick to my mission.

"Did you hear about the subpoena?" I asked. "Agent Rosenfield said she requested one from you."

Dr. Madison didn't seem surprised by the change in topic. Her eyes stayed their passive, cool blue. I probably could've gone streaking in the office and she'd have the same look. "She did. I filled out the request," she said. "Happy to comply."

"I hope it doesn't take too long. We don't have much time."

"What do you mean?" she asked.

"People can't survive without water or food for too long. If Mom and the others are okay but stranded somewhere, they need resources. Fast. The government is wasting time by trying to make her look like the bad guy."

And there it was. Finally, a shift on her face.

It stung, like it did every time someone didn't believe me. This time hurt worse, though. Like she was maybe the last person in the world who could believe Mom was okay out there. Somewhere, trying to find her way back home.

"You think she's alive?" she asked.

"She's not dead. She's missing," I said.

She shifted in her seat, and her bracelets slid down her wrists. I wondered if she was covering something—I'd done that trick before.

"My dad wants to have a memorial, but I don't think that's fair. It's only been six days." As I spoke, I wasn't sure if I was trying to convince her or myself. "So it's possible."

"Okay," she said. "What are you doing besides the search for your mother? You're not going to school, are you?"

"Well, yeah," I said. "I still committed to making the set for my high school's musical. I can't audition, but I still want to be involved."

"Can't audition?" Dr. Madison asked. "Or won't?"

"What's the difference?" I shrugged. "More time away from finding the truth."

"You mention the truth a lot," she said. "But have you considered the truth of what your mother would really want? Or what you want?"

I winced. What did she know about my mother? Oh yeah, probably everything. Maybe even more than me—which was why I was here. "What do you think she'd want?"

"That's for you to decide," Dr. Madison said. "But it sounds like you really want to audition *and* do the artwork, and you've been given the opportunity to do both. So why not?"

"I just told you. I can't."

"Okay, but all you've told me are reasons why you won't," she said. "Give me one reason why you can't."

Yikes. Straight for the heart.

I looked to the clock—only twenty minutes left. Had a half hour really passed that quickly? I pictured Mom sitting here, wondering the same thing.

I swore—I felt her with me. Like she was there, actually sitting beside me.

A presence.

It was the same sensation as being completely alone

but then feeling someone was watching you, all of a sudden. I was terrified to know what that might mean, so I pushed the feeling away.

"You won't do theater, but you'll draw. That's a healthy coping mechanism," she said.

"So I've heard."

Dr. Madison leaned forward. Her bracelets slid down her wrists again. "Last time you were here, I asked if you were safe. Are you?"

"Why does everyone keep asking me that?" I stood up and went to the window. Anger welled inside of me in a way that fueled me to keep going. It was wrong, I knew. It hurt me, but it kept me going. If I found a way to tame that, I was afraid I'd have no drive left. "My dad said it, you said it. No one is trying to hurt me. I'm fine."

"Okay, no one else is trying to hurt you," she said. "Are you hurting yourself?"

I refused to look at her and focused on the neatly lined gray buildings across the street. How did she know? She couldn't possibly. No one knew except Mom. Why would Mom tell her?

"No," I half-lied. I'd kept up my streak. So, so close to fifty days. But the rubber band snapping and scratching had become more and more intense lately. I needed to make it to fifty days clean, but how was I supposed to do that when the only person who'd helped me climb out of the abyss was gone? "You know what hurts? She talked to him last, not me. I know who he is, but I don't know who he *really* is. He won't even tell me what she said to him last. I deserve to know."

"Certainly," she said.

"I just… I can't believe Mom would let that happen, or that she'd lie to me like that."

"Nobody is perfect, unfortunately. Your mother had faults. She was human. She knew that about herself, and knew that about you. If you acknowledge those faults and acknowledge when you need help, things are easier."

"What are you saying?"

"Your mother loved you very much. She didn't expect perfection from you. She wanted you to be happy," she said.

"That's how I feel about her," I said.

"Then I wonder if you could feel that way about yourself."

I desperately tried to blink back tears. They stung in an unusually painful way. I didn't dare make eye contact, so I looked to the floor. It was a woven gray rug that looked worn from years of use. I pictured Mom's flats pushing down on it.

"Time's up," Dr. Madison said.

Time felt like it had been up a long time ago.

When I got home that afternoon, I went straight to my paint set.

I needed to work this out in a way where I could think on it for a while. As I painted the red roses in the sketch for *Beauty and the Beast*, I thought about what Dr. Madison had said. What would Mom want me to do?

You have a gift. Promise me you'll use it.

I would've been breaking my promise to her if I ran from the very thing that made me happy.

I googled US133 again—nothing. No new hits. And ThunderRoad68 hadn't responded to my post. No one had.

It stood alone in the forum.

Footsteps crept up the stairs.

In that moment, everything aside from my thoughts felt so normal that I thought it was her. Not even finally coming home, but dropping her bag down and kicking off her shoes like nothing was wrong. The way things had always been.

It was Savannah, though. I recognized her footsteps as she came closer to my room.

"Sav!" I called. "Where were you?"

"Talking to Alex, actually." She stood halfway between the hallway and my bedroom. "She wanted to know if I could help her with physics."

Every time I heard they spoke, it made me feel like a recharged battery. "Awesome! Wait, she hasn't answered me all day, but she talks to *you*?"

She shrugged. "Needed physics help. How was the therapist?"

"Fine." I shrugged. "Listen, have you been reading the internet forums about the plane?"

Savannah shook her head. "What did I tell you? Don't read that stuff. It'll give you an aneurysm."

"I know, I know. I'm asking if *you* read them."

"No. Not even once."

"Did you post anything?"

Savannah blinked. "No. What are you talking about?"

I squinted. She was impossible to read. I wished I had more of those genes, not the constantly-blush-and-blurt-out-truth genes. "If you're lying to me, I'm going to find out."

Blond hair fell over her shoulder as she turned to go to her bedroom. "I bet you will."

I began to paint again, not completely convinced.

"Oh, by the way." Savannah tossed something onto my desk. A King-sized Reese's Pieces! "Landon dropped this off earlier."

The Post-it attached read: *It gets easier. Especially with Reese's.*

I clutched the orange Reese's bag and held it close to my heart. I didn't want to open it yet—I thought I'd be saving this one.

CHAPTER NINETEEN

Day Six – Late Afternoon

Before dinner, I took Onion for a walk.

I hated to admit that Dr. Madison had gotten into my head, but she had. I supposed that was why she had a doctorate and I was on the struggle bus in biology.

Alex had called, so I'd told her to meet me and Onion at the stop sign on this dead end a few blocks from my house. We didn't need to say it, but the cast list would be out any minute. We could both use the distraction.

"Hi guys." She wore her typical combat boots and a tight red flannel shirt. "Figured I'd check on you and Savannah."

I was surprised Alex asked. Not that her and Savannah never got along, but it was more like they simply existed in different worlds. If Alex and I played video games in the living room, Savannah worked out in the garage. Even as kids, Savannah had done her own thing. Them actually being friendly now made my life a lot easier. So, thanks to Mom for that one.

"We're okay." I told Alex about Dr. Madison and the visit as we walked through town. Onion stopped to pee by the Post Office, so we sat on the cold, concrete steps. It was still light out, but barely. A streak of orange crossed the blue sky. Darkness seemed to be eating the day up faster and faster.

"Are you seriously okay, though? I'm glad you're seeing someone," she said.

"I'm okay. Shaken up by everything, I guess." Or had everything shaken me up so much that I'd flatlined?

"Understandable. Hey, man, I'm…sorry about the news. I never thought your mom would be the type."

"Neither did I," I whispered.

Alex placed her hand on mine. It was warm and shea-butter soft. "I can't imagine hearing about it constantly is helping, either."

"See, that's the thing," I said. "All anyone is talking about is this hurricane. They were showing the news in the waiting room and no channels were even talking about the plane. It's almost like I want them to talk about it because then…"

"Then they still care."

"Exactly!" I said. "Wait, is your family in Cuba going to be okay? They're close to it, too, aren't they?"

"They're fine! Thanks for asking. They're predicting heavy rain, but that's it. The storm is apparently going to be directly over Puerto Rico."

I buried my face in my hands. I was glad Alex's family in Cuba was okay, but I felt awful for the people in Puerto Rico. Was this the apocalypse?

Part of me hoped so, because then Mom wouldn't miss as much. If I died at sixteen in some sort of catastrophic, globe-wiping way, then Mom wouldn't miss my graduation, which college I picked, any children I might have, my wedding. Perks of being bi: will I end up with a man? Woman? Someone else? Or no one, and have six dogs instead? It's a mystery!

I couldn't imagine those events without her, which meant she had to come back, right? She had to.

"I'm glad your family is okay," I managed.

"Me too," Alex said.

We sat in silence.

She has to come back. She has to.

My throat was tight. I wanted a way to remind people of Mom, to tell them she was still missing along with all those other people. But what?

We walked back to my house and headed into my backyard.

It was chilly out, but not cold enough that we couldn't be comfortable outside with our coats on.

"I'm going to give Onion some food. Be right back," I said.

"Sure thing."

I poured dog food into Onion's personalized bowl—blue ceramic with his name on it—and gave him more water. He dove headfirst into the food.

As I put the dog food bag back in the closet, I decided I might as well work on some sketches for the show while Alex and I talked.

I fetched my sketchbook and pencils from my room, then felt a vibration in my pocket as I walked down the stairs. I checked my phone, eager for any US133 news, but instead I saw the cast list.

I should've waited for Alex, but I couldn't. There was a part of me that hoped my name would be on it, even though I knew it was impossible.

BELLE: Brittany Thompson
BEAST: John Nyugen
GASTON: Noah Bryne
LUMIÈRE: Landon Davis
BABETTE: Ashley Golden

I clenched my teeth. After all that, she still got the part? She still got *a* part? What the hell was Mr. Tariq thinking?! It wasn't fair; she didn't deserve to be up there with Landon. Not after Ashley had acted like she was too good to have any role but Belle. Landon and I had been the ones who'd rocked the scene. Together.

I pictured his strong arms in half-rolled sleeves sliding around her waist during a scene. His perfect lips kissing her hand. *Ugh.*

I was happy for him, but furious at the same time.

That was supposed to be *our* moment.

But I'd given it up. There was no one to blame except myself.

Alone, on the steps, I snapped my rubber band into my wrist. It felt like an insect bite—small, but insistent. It didn't feel like enough, so I dug my nails in instead. Their sharpness brought me slight relief.

I scanned the list again, hoping it was all a mistake. Then I realized I hadn't seen Alex's name. I read it a third time, and there it was:

ENSEMBLE

Utensils/Wolf: Alex Marquez

Oh no. This wasn't going to be good.

I headed to the yard, and Onion followed quickly behind.

Though someone beat me to it.

Alex was curled around Savannah like a cat, her

face buried in Savannah's shoulder. A little too close to the breasts for my liking. That was my sister, after all. Savannah, Ms. I-hate-human-contact, had her arms tightly around Alex.

I swore I was living in a parallel universe.

When they noticed me, they splintered apart like they'd done something wrong.

"I'm a fork," Alex said. "A useless, pointless fork."

"And a wolf," Savannah added. "Wolves are so cool!"

"But you did such a good job at auditions. You can sing better than anyone." My voice shook because I knew how unfair it felt. It was exactly the kind of outcome that kept me from auditioning. I could never be brave like Alex. To want something so bad, do everything you can, and not know if you'll get it? Torture.

"I thought so, too, but apparently not. Mr. Tariq sent a separate email asking me to be dance captain." She showed her phone to me.

I grinned and sat beside them. "Dance captain! That's really cool!"

"It's not cool! No one gives a monkey's butt who the dance captain is!" Her face was streaked red. "Dance captain is like getting 'best smile' at the awards at summer camp. It means you're a loser and no one cares!"

"It's because you're dependable and a good teacher," Savannah said. "He can count on you to help everyone else. That's what he said, and it's true."

Alex looked up into Savannah's face, and it was then that I knew. It was the way Alex looked into Savannah's light-blue eyes like they could solve her problems, like everything might be okay after all. It was full of raw honesty.

We'd been friends for years, and she'd never looked at

me like that. What would her girlfriend think? She's dating someone else, but still has a crush on Savannah?

My heart ached for her, because I knew Savannah wouldn't feel the same.

"I'm sorry." Alex grabbed a nearby leaf and blew her nose on it. Gross, but okay. "None of this is important to you, I know."

I frowned. "It is important to me. You're important to me."

"No, I know," she said. "But I mean… Your mom is missing and I'm complaining about wearing a wolf outfit."

I wanted to chuckle, but I knew it wasn't the time.

So instead, I drew.

I felt selfish for wanting to draw right now, but it happened automatically. The sketchpad was in my lap, and I traced the outline of a wolf.

A gorgeous wolf. A beautiful wolf who could sing and dance, even if it wasn't appreciated like it should be.

"I can't believe Brittany Thompson got Belle. She's not even brunette! We don't even have a wig budget! Imagine, a BLOND Belle!? That goes against nature," Alex said. "And Ashley got Babette, after the stunt she pulled? Seriously? Violet, you must be livid."

"I am," I mumbled. "But… There's nothing I can do."

"None of this matters anyway," Savannah said. "High school is this, like, tiny microcosm of life. There's so much to see out there that we don't know about. In college, theater is totally different. You'll see."

"Because you're a theater expert?" Alex laughed lightly.

"No, I just know you're awesome, and this little town is nothing compared to the real world." Savannah placed her hand over Alex's. Thin blades of grass poked between their laced fingers.

666

"Don't go away to college," Alex said. "Stay here."

"I can't."

"Please?"

"I wish I could," Savannah said gently. "But when you graduate, you can come with me. I think you'd like California. The sun, the water, the weather…"

They stared into each other's faces so deeply that I should've looked away, but I couldn't. It felt like I was intruding on a private moment, but here we were, in my yard.

In a way, I was jealous. It made me miss Landon, since he was the only person who'd look at me like that and—

Oh shit. Oh holy monkey shit.

"You're the hot girlfriend," I blurted out.

"What?" Savannah asked.

"You're HOT GF in her phone. The get-well basket, how she asked to come over when she'd never done that before." I ground my teeth. How on earth had I missed this?

"I-I…" Alex stammered.

"Yeah." Savannah met my eyes. Fearlessly so. "I am."

"How long has this been going on?" It felt like an affair. I loved them both more than my own breath could say, so why couldn't they tell me to my face?

I didn't know how to feel. This was squirmier than the usual "If they break up, will I lose one of them" sort of gig. This was a constant lie to my face. Repeatedly. Every single day.

Why couldn't anyone be honest with me lately? Mom, Savannah, Alex, Dad.

My faith in humanity wavered like a lit candle.

"About two months," Savannah whispered.

"Two months?!" I tried to temper my reaction. When

I'd come out of the closet, I'd been nervous, even though everyone had been cool about it and not surprised. I assumed the half-naked pictures of Mila Kunis in my bedroom had been a giveaway. So I knew how she was feeling—I just couldn't get past this idea that everyone had known something I didn't.

This is how Dad must feel.

I swallowed and scratched Onion's ear. Arguing made his little legs shake, so I tried not to scare him, but it was hard not to frighten my dog when I wanted to chokeslam my sister.

"Why didn't you tell me you're into girls?" I asked. Did Savannah not realize I was gayer than glitter? That her being gay was more than fine with me?

I didn't care that she was queer. I cared that she'd *lied*.

"I-I didn't know what to say." This was a Savannah I hadn't seen before. This wasn't the time she'd gotten caught cheating on her Spanish test because she'd been up all night studying for AP Chem. No. She was withdrawn, quiet, like her volume button had been pressed all the way down.

"Are you…gay?" I tilted my head, and Onion did the same. "Bi? Pan?"

"I… I don't know." She bit her lip.

I sat straighter. "What do you mean you don't know?"

"I mean that I don't know." She crossed her arms.

You would think my bisexuality would've come with a nice button I could press to tell me how to make other people feel better about these things, but apparently not.

I'd essentially gone through the same thing before admitting that yes, I had been making out with a lady or two my freshman year. No one had known what to say to me then, and I didn't know what to say to Savannah now.

This stuff shouldn't be so isolating. But it was.

"Whatever," I said. "I just wish you would've told me you were having sex with my best friend. That's some HBO plotline stuff."

Alex's face got redder than a blood moon. "We're not having sex!" She turned to Savannah. "I mean, totally open to the possibility, by the way, but yeah…"

What the hell was going on? This couldn't be real. None of this was real.

"I can't believe this is happening." I clenched my teeth. "The two people I think I can trust most were lying to me behind my back for two months!"

Poor Onion didn't like this one bit. He backed up and gave a small whimper.

"See? This is exactly why I didn't say anything." Savannah sighed. "Alex, do you mind if we catch up later? I don't want to fight in front of you."

"I should be here. I'm guilty too." Alex looked at me with a trembling lower lip, and I knew she was genuinely sorry, but that didn't make it better. "I really am sorry, Violet."

"Please go," Savannah said quietly. "I'll call you later."

Alex gave her a quick hug, and stepped up to me like she was going to give me one, but stopped short. "You're still my best friend," she said over her shoulder.

"I know. Sorry about the musical," I said. "I hope Brittany Thompson moves to another state and they throw you in."

Then it was just Savannah and me, alone in our backyard.

We sized each other up like two lions about to pounce. The air between us became heavier, as if thunderstorm clouds had rolled in.

"You didn't need to make her leave," I said.

"No, I did. You make everything about you. I knew you were going to do this," she said. "You're so self-centered."

I pressed my index fingernail into my thumb. Pain radiated in small circles. "I am not self-centered."

"Really?" She gave a brisk laugh. "You're exactly like Mom. Completely selfish."

She might as well have thrown acid on me. Searing tears burned in my eyes. Through clenched teeth, I hissed, "Take that back."

"No. I meant it. You need to accept it, like you need to accept she's gone."

"Screw you, Savannah." I gave her shoulder a push that was a bit harder than I'd anticipated.

She immediately hit me back, square in the chest. "She's my mother too, Violet! Did you forget that? She's my mom too!"

"Then start acting like it!"

The neighbors must've had their noses pressed to their windows to hear us, but I didn't give a rat's behind what they thought. My pent-up anger had finally found a leaky valve to push through, pumping like a heart.

I pushed her again, too hard this time. I hadn't meant to. On her way down, she clung to my arm and we landed on top of each other in the grass. Her body cushioned my fall. I was on top for only a second—but in that second, I was powerful.

It didn't last long.

She rolled over and pinned me down. "Did you ever stop to think for one second that your denial makes it harder for me? For Dad?" Savannah's hair fell in my face as her hands kept my shoulders flat on the ground. I squirmed, but she was too strong for me. I was too focused on the moment to be scared. "I found someone who makes me happy! I'm trying to move on with my life, and you should too. Instead, you're making it harder for me."

"How the hell am I supposed to just move on?" They hadn't found one piece of debris, and Savannah was ready to throw the dirt on Mom's empty coffin. "You don't understand how hard this is for me!"

"Why, because you were Mom's favorite?" A cold look came into Savannah's eyes. Ice. She applied more pressure to my shoulders, pinning me down even more. I couldn't move if I'd wanted to. Still, I wasn't scared. Maybe because, deep down, I knew my sister would never hurt me. "I couldn't possibly understand how it feels to lose my mother because I wasn't her favorite, right? Right?"

We'd never said it out loud, but we both knew Dad was hers the way Mom was mine. With Mom gone, I'd lost part of me. Savannah got to remain whole.

"No," I whispered. "That isn't true at all. That's not what I meant."

She got off me and stood up. I followed suit.

We eyed each other warily. There was a three-foot distance between us.

"It is true." Her voice broke, but her eyes stayed dry. "I wish I could be like you, the way you support her and talk about her. But I can't."

"Sav." I wanted to touch her shoulder, but I hesitated. "No one expects you to do anything."

"I feel terrible. Everything is happening all at once. Like the walls are closing in on me. Do you know what it's like to fall for someone when your mom is missing? It's weird and wrong, and I feel totally guilty for being in love."

I knew more than she thought; but she was right, this wasn't about me.

Wait.

"Love?" I asked.

"Well, okay, maybe not quite love yet, but… I've never felt like this about anyone before."

"It's Alex. She's perfect." Even if I was going to kill her for lying to me about her new girlfriend, I had to admit that I couldn't have picked anyone better for her.

My stomach soured again.

I wanted to be happy for them, but I only had to look at Mom and Dad to see that the higher your love made you feel sometimes meant you had farther to fall.

What if Savannah and Alex had a nasty breakup? Savannah was my sister, but choosing between them would be like splitting my body in half.

"How did this even start?" I asked.

" A few months ago when Alex slept over, I couldn't sleep, so I watched TV in the living room. She couldn't sleep either, and we ended up talking all night. When she would come over, she was always…"

"With me."

"Right. We started texting all the time after that, and then, when Mom disappeared…"

"You didn't have anyone," I said.

I'd been so absorbed in my quest to prove Mom innocent that I'd shut out my own sister. Arguing on internet forums and researching hostage theories had taken up so much of my time that I'd forgotten it wasn't only my time of need.

"I didn't mean to take your friend," Savannah whispered. "And I really didn't mean to lie to you."

It still gnawed at me. Why couldn't they have told me? After the plane had disappeared, I got it. Not convenient timing. But before? What had been the excuse?

Or what about me made them feel like they had to lie?

A jolt of pain in my arm snapped me back to reality. My fingernails had been digging into my soft flesh. I had to stop this self-harm thing. That it had happened without me knowing it was odd. Big time.

"Stop doing that with your nails," Savannah said. "I hate when you do that."

I was surprised she'd noticed. "Sorry. It's…hard not to. Everyone has been lying to me. You, Alex. Mom. Ever since I learned about the affair, I've felt like there's so much about Mom I don't know. Like she had multiple lives and was only showing us one."

"I felt the same way. I hate that only Dr. Bryant knows what they talked about before they took off."

I raised my eyebrows. Why hadn't we talked about this? "I asked him to tell me. He wouldn't. He said it wasn't the time or place," I said. "Wait." An idea hit me like a comet—specifically like Hyakutake's Comet. Strong, bright, but maybe dangerous. "What if we go to his house?"

"Okay, *that's* ridiculous." She crossed her arms.

"Why is it ridiculous? He wouldn't talk to me at the hospital because he didn't want anyone to overhear. At his house, it's not a problem. He won't hurt me. He loved Mom."

"We don't know if he loved Mom." Savannah jutted her chin out. "We know they were having an affair. That's it. Going to his house is weird."

"Oh, please. He saved your life."

"I saved my own life. He helped, though…I guess," she said. "Look, Vi. Are you sure you want to do this? Sometimes, the truth is better left buried. Know what I mean? The more you find out about things, the more it can hurt."

"Yes. I'm sure." I should've known Savannah was going to give me a lecture. "You owe me. If you want to make it up to me, come with me."

"You are so manipulative," she said. "See? Exactly what I said before."

I didn't know why I bothered with her sometimes. Every time we got close, we pulled apart like bumper cars. "You're the one who knocked me to the ground."

"No, you pushed first, then I took you down with me," she said.

"Forget it. I'll go myself. You don't have to come."

Savannah sighed and looked down at the spot in the grass we'd just been wrestling in. "Why is this so important to you?"

"You said it yourself. I want to know about those last few minutes. I want to know what her frame of mind was. If I don't know her, how can I know for sure she didn't hurt herself?" I whispered. "And all those people?"

"Because our mother would never do that," she said.

"Yeah, and a week ago, I would've told you our mother would've never had an affair."

Savannah dug her foot into the soil and didn't look at me for a solid ten seconds.

I sat up and stared at her until she made eye contact with me.

"I wish she were here," she whispered. "And we could ask."

"Me too. So much." I picked at my bloody cuticles.

"I miss her," she said. "I still can't believe she isn't here. It's like none of this is real. My heart...like, physically hurts."

"It squeezes, right?" I took my fist and held it over my heart. I knew that pain well. It throbbed with hurt—

usually in the quiet, unexpected moments. "Like this?"

"Exactly."

"I need to know who she was," I said. "I thought I did, but I guess that wasn't true. I don't want to feel like a liar when I say she's innocent. And…the note…"

Savannah raised an eyebrow. "The note?"

Now felt right. No matter how much I denied it, Mom's note had felt off. If she'd had a plan, this couldn't possibly be it.

I explained everything to Savannah. Speaking it out loud felt like a betrayal, but at the same time, I was dying to tell someone. All this time, no one would listen to me, even though I'd had proof.

Or…what I'd thought was proof.

"Wow." She looked to the ground again. "I didn't get anything."

"Savannah…"

"Whatever. That's not important, I guess." She shook her head. "What does it all mean? Did you tell the cops? Or Dad?"

"She told me not to," I said. "I had to listen to her. You've got to understand. That's why I want to track down this guy. Maybe… Maybe he knows."

A long stretch of silence descended on us. Savannah pushed harder and harder against the ground with her shoe. "He doesn't work Sundays. I know because I peeked at his hospital schedule when I was there."

"I found his address online."

"If you're serious about this, I'm not letting you go alone." She reached over to try and rub a grass stain from my shirt. No use.

"Okay."

"We'll leave tomorrow morning before eight," she said.

"Oh my God, that's so early," I whined.

"Fine. Nine, sharp."

"Great. But from now on, no lies between us." I extended my hand for a shake. "And... Let's not throw each other to the ground anymore?"

Hesitantly, Savannah took it. "Yeah. Let's not."

Gravity pushed my sister and me toward one another again, like a star igniting.

CHAPTER TWENTY

DAY SIX – EVENING

I couldn't wait for the weekend.
I'd finally be able to sink my teeth into the information I'd wanted. With Savannah by my side, Dr. Bryant might remember her as the little girl with cancer he'd helped and be more willing to help out.

But for now, I had a responsibility. As much as I wanted to avoid the play, I couldn't. They needed a set.

While the cast worked on a few songs in the music room, I spent the morning with the set designer. She was one of those cool, chic types, and she thought my notes were helpful. I tried to imagine how that could be my future: designing different sets, visiting different schools.

I loved meeting new people and bringing visions to life. That night, I was in charge of painting a backdrop.

It was weird to think of the future without having Mom here, but it was refreshing to focus on something else. Even for a little while.

The cast came back into the auditorium.

I spotted Landon first. He waved to me, and I waved back. Alex was all the way in the back of the group, alone. I tried to catch her eye, but she was too focused on the lyric sheets.

"Try the song among your vocal parts," Mr. Tariq said. "I'll check on you in five minutes."

The cast broke apart into smaller groups, and I focused back on my painting. The roses were coming along well, since I'd had practice.

Mr. Tariq walked over to me and crouched down. "Looks good."

"Thanks."

"Listen, can you do me a favor?" he asked. "Ashley quit the play. I need someone to fill in for Babette. Can you read for her part at rehearsal today?"

"She quit? Why?" I had to suppress a grin.

Mr. Tariq shook his head. "For some, the ego is a hot-air balloon. So, can you help us out and read today? It's the same piece you did at auditions with Landon."

"Sure." Why not? It was only reading.

A reading that reminded me of Landon.

I joined the rest of the group.

When the cast finished their song, Mr. Tariq stood in front of them. "Okay, guys. Violet is going to be reading for Babette today as we go through the script. That doesn't mean I've cast or recast anything. Okay? So, please, go on."

Landon made his way through the crowd and stood next to me. "Hi! This way we can read better together."

"Sure." I tried to ignore how broad his shoulders looked next to mine, or how good he smelled. Maybe it was his shampoo? I pictured him sudsing up his hair with foamy shampoo, the way water dripped down his—

"Eggs!" a castmate shouted. "Sorry, I forgot my line about the eggs?"

Woof. *Okay, focus.*

"How do you feel about the part?" I whispered. "Congrats, by the way."

"Thanks! I feel...excited? Nervous as hell?" He shrugged. "I was expecting to be a cup or something, honestly."

We got to our scene, and Landon and I faced each other.

For his first line, Landon cupped my chin. His hand was gentle and warm. I couldn't even hear the lines, I was so focused on his thumb being that close to the corner of my lips. I was tempted to bend my head to lean in even closer.

"Ah, Lumière," I improvised.

For his next line, Landon leaned forward and put his arms around me. The script called for me to giggle and push him away, but I didn't want to separate. The giggling part, though, I had down. Our first real hug. He felt strong and solid. And me? I felt safe.

I thought of our McDonald's "date", and how I hadn't had that much fun since. There was something about him that brought out a light in me that I was sure had been extinguished after Mom had disappeared.

"You're supposed to push him off you," someone whispered.

Oh yeah. Right.

I pushed Landon off like the script said, and our scene was done for now.

The rest of the cast chuckled or smiled along with us.

That was why I wanted to act—to make people happy. To make them laugh. I liked the idea that, maybe, even for a minute, I'd distracted them from their own real-life problems.

Finally, I caught Alex's eye. But not for long—she

looked back to her music instantly.

I couldn't tell if she was shy about earlier today or if she was irritated at me for playing Babette. It had only been for a few minutes. It wasn't like Mr. Tariq was going to give me the role.

As we finished the read, though, a part of me wished I'd emailed Mr. Tariq back about his offer for a non-singing role. I'd made no progress with Mom, unfortunately, so it wasn't like anything would've been different had I said yes. But I had to keep that to myself. Things didn't work like that.

The cast broke off into smaller groups to talk and pack up. The leads had to stay for extra practice, and I planned to stay to finish painting.

"That was fun," Landon said.

"It was!" I glanced toward Alex, who I could see watching us toward the corner of my eye. When I looked at her, she looked away. "Will you excuse me for a minute?"

"Sure," he said.

Alex had her purse slung over her shoulder. "Sorry. I can't stay. I'm not a lead." Venom dripped from her voice.

"Neither am I. I'm painting."

"Really? Doesn't seem like it, Babette," she snarled.

"Okay, seriously? If one of us deserves to be angry here, it's me."

Alex shook her head. "You're right. I'm sorry. Tough day."

"Tough day for both of us." I kept my voice down. I hoped I'd gotten all the grass stains out from my shirt, but yeah, tough day indeed.

"Why didn't you tell me about you and Savannah?" I whispered.

"I wanted to, but Savannah said not to," she said.

"Why did you side with her and not me?"

"See, this is what I was afraid of," she said. "It's all about sides with you two. I don't want to be in the middle or pick one of you over the other."

"You're supposed to be my best friend. You're supposed to tell me the truth."

"I knew you'd be upset, and I didn't want to lose you."

"This wouldn't be a big deal at all if you had told me upfront!"

She waved her arms. "How was I supposed to say that? Your mother is dead, you have way bigger things—"

"Missing! Not dead!" My voice echoed in the auditorium. I felt about twenty-five eyes on me. I wished I could've curled up into a hoodie and disappeared under it. Forever. I sighed. "Look, I told you I care about your life and what's going on in it too. Just because my mom is missing doesn't mean I have a monopoly on suffering. I care."

"Really? If you cared, then you'd understand I'm really pissed off about this cast list." She rubbed her right eye, which I knew meant she was trying not to cry. "Like, okay, I'm not Belle. But he couldn't have even asked me to be a Silly Girl, or Mrs. Potts?"

"You so, so deserve a lead." I meant it with all my fast-beating heart.

"Or Babette, especially now that Ashley left?"

"Why did she quit, anyway? Mr. Tariq said something about ego?" I asked.

"Yeah, she had a tantrum she's not Belle and doesn't want to do it anymore. Honestly? I judged her at first, but now I get it. I don't even want to be here." She adjusted the strap to her shoulder. "I feel like such a failure."

"You are not a failure!"

"No. I am."

"Alex." I reached forward to hug her, but she turned on her heel and walked toward the exit.

"Violet." Mr. Tariq approached me.

I turned to face him, ready to hand the script back. Instead, he shook his head.

"You keep it," he said. "You were fantastic up there. You have the heart and humor that I'm looking for in the role."

"Thanks." It felt surreal to hear, like I was in *High School Musical* or something. I'd always wanted someone to say that to me—to see something in me that I didn't see myself.

In the background, Landon gave a thumbs-up.

"One last chance," Mr. Tariq said. "Do you want to be Babette?"

My heart thudded. An email I could delete. But a second opportunity like this?

"What about Alex?" I mumbled. After our conversation, I would feel awful taking something she so desperately wanted. Our ten years of friendship was worth more than a role.

"I didn't ask Alex because I need her as Dance Captain. She needs to understand the ensemble is important as any lead," he said. "I'll talk to her about it. She'll have her moments to shine if she is able to see them."

It made sense. Alex was probably the best dancer in the cast—and, like Savannah had said, she was patient and would make a good teacher. It might not have been what she wanted, but it was what the cast needed.

"So, what do you say?" Mr. Tariq asked.

Dr. Madison's voice rang in my head. *Can't? Or Won't?*

Mom wouldn't back down. And, more to the point, she wouldn't want me to back down either.

"Okay!" I blurted out before I even realized what I'd said. "Let's do it!"

Mr. Tariq beamed. "Great. I'll make adjustments to the cast list. Congratulations."

He walked off, and Landon sped toward me with open arms.

"You did it!" He wrapped his arms around me, and I squeezed back. The ends of his curly light hair tickled my cheek. "I-I hope you didn't say yes because of what I said the other day. I didn't mean to pressure you."

"I know," I said. "You didn't. I chose this on my own."

He smiled that big goofy smile. Those crooked teeth really put a bolt of lightning in me. "Thank you!"

"Why are you thanking me?" I laughed.

"Because I'm not awesome without you," he said.

"You are." We slowly pulled apart from each other, but his eyes lingered on me. Like a piece of invisible thread was spooling us together.

Finally, things were looking up.

"I can't believe I said yes." I laughed.

"Why not? You deserve it." He placed his hand on my shoulder.

Did I?

The auditorium door squeaked open. From the corner of my eye, I caught a glimpse of Alex slamming it behind her.

CHAPTER TWENTY-ONE

DAY SEVEN – MORNING

I turned the volume down on the music so that it wouldn't distract Savannah, but more so that she could hear my singing. My awful, yet enthusiastic, Broadway belt.

"I'd make a fantastic Elphaba." I threw my hands up in the air as Savannah drove, to let the spirit of the Wicked Witch consume me as I sang. Mom and I used to sing in the car together all the time, so I pretended this was an homage to her.

Savannah gently pushed me away from her and made a left turn. "I love *Wicked*, but this is insufferable."

"Sorry we can't all have gorgeous voices like your girlfriend," I said.

"Yeah. Too bad she's stuck as a fork. It's a waste."

"I think she's angry at me," I said. "I accepted the part of Babette."

"What's a Babette?"

I didn't know how we could possibly be related. "The

feather duster. I have my first rehearsal tonight."

"Wow!" She turned to look at me quickly, then focused on the road again. "Congrats! I thought you weren't going to audition."

"I didn't. It's a long story. But yeah, I'm in the show now! I don't have to sing, though. Don't worry."

"I'm...proud of you." Savannah stopped at a red light and looked at me again. There was something different in her gaze, like she didn't recognize me. Or was trying to figure me out. "Wait, so why would Alex be angry? Because she's jealous?"

"I guess. I don't know. We had a fight."

"Hmm." Savannah bit her lip as she turned the corner. "That's not okay. I'll talk to her about it."

For the first time since we'd been kids, I felt that little sister protective bond thing. Like no one could get to me without crossing Savannah first. "What are you guys going to do when you go away next year?"

"We haven't talked about that yet," she said quietly. "I don't know if I want to go anymore. It's so expensive…"

I whipped my head toward her. "Is that the only reason?"

Savannah blinked those long lashes. "Yeah. I'm ready for a change. I want to take actual aero-engineering classes. But I could go to Syracuse instead. Maybe I'd get a better scholarship. Maybe I'd like the cold up there. I do love snow. Who knows if I'd even get accepted to Stanford."

"I've already bought a Stanford sweatshirt, and those are expensive, so you have to go there." I crossed my arms. "But in all seriousness, we'll figure it out. Mom, Dad and I, we all really want you to go."

Savannah twirled a piece of her hair and pulled onto Dr. Bryant's street.

It was in a suburban neighborhood, with tall trees poking out from a wood not too far from a small but shining lake. Each house reflected the colonial style in various blues and beiges and browns.

"I think Mom would want that, wouldn't she?" Savannah asked. "Same way she'd be proud that you're stepping on stage."

"Same way she wouldn't want us fighting in the grass," I said.

"Okay… You have to admit, in retrospect, it's kind of funny."

"Umm, you're saying that because you're all muscular, and I have the strength of a prawn."

"It's true." Savannah laughed like Dr. Finkelstein in *The Nightmare Before Christmas*—but all the laughter died down as we drove farther and farther down the street.

We were here.

As we pulled into Dr. Bryant's driveway, a chill crept up my back. I imagined Mom driving up the very same road in secret.

His house was smaller than I'd expected, but still stunning with its exquisite design and smooth architecture. The bricks were a dark chestnut color, with white trim on the windowsill. I'd expected a mansion from a doctor, though it wasn't like I'd ever been to a doctor's house before.

"You ready?" Savannah asked.

"Not really." I unlocked the car door. "But let's do this."

Savannah and I headed up his stone path to his front door. I knocked first.

We looked to each other; nothing happened.

I hadn't considered the possibility that he wasn't home. Suddenly, standing here with my feet planted on a stranger's doorstep felt foolish, like I was expecting so much from someone I didn't know and—

"Um. Hello?" Dr. Bryant stood at the threshold in a crewneck waffle shirt and sweatpants. He eyed me and Savannah like we were Girl Scouts—not exactly unwelcome, but not expected.

Savannah glanced at me as if to say, *Your idea, you do the talking.*

"Hi, Dr. Bryant." I took a deep breath. "Sorry to bombard you like this. But, um. As you know, the plane is still missing and… Well, honestly, I was hoping you could tell me a little about my mom. I think you knew her better than I did recently."

He tilted his head. A pause inflated like a balloon around the three of us. "Okay." He moved aside. "Come in."

When Mom would return from a long flight, sometimes she'd say, "It looks like a gaggle of men live here." That was what Dr. Bryant's house looked like.

Mismatched shoes were kicked by the door, and a long, barren hallway led to a sparse kitchen. One painting hung in the living room over a fireplace. Pink flowers. Cherry blossoms, maybe.

He cleared mugs and paper coffee cups from the table so we could sit. Then Dr. Bryant placed two glasses of water on the table. We didn't touch them. "You feeling okay, Savannah? Dr. Singh told me you had a kidney infection. You're taking your antibiotics?"

"Yes." She grinned, and I wanted to smack the smile off her face.

"Good." He sat across from us and clasped his big hands together. "I'm sorry to hear about your mother."

"It's your loss, too," Savannah said.

I side-eyed her. No, it wasn't. Mom was mine. Ours. Not his.

And she wasn't completely lost. Not to me.

I tried to picture her here, sitting on this wooden chair in the kitchen. Opening one of the cherrywood cabinets. Running her fingers across the army medals neatly lined up in a shadow box frame.

No matter how hard I squinted to make her lanky body, short, choppy blond hair and warm smile appear, I didn't see it. I was forcing a ghost of her to exist, but I saw nothing.

I didn't understand how sometimes I could picture her in a room, practically smell her vanilla perfume, but other times, she was completely...gone.

"Thank you." He nodded. "I don't know how I can help you. Your mother was a fantastic woman, and I cared about her a lot." He paused again, as if hoping that would be enough. His nails dug into his wrist.

This was more awkward than my first kiss in eighth grade, when lips and tongues had still confused the hell out of me.

"I really want to know about that last phone call," I said. "Please."

"I-I don't know," he said. "I feel like it isn't my place to tell you."

"Then who *is* going to tell us?" Savannah asked. "No one knows except you."

And Mom.

He sighed. "It started out as a fairly common conversation before takeoff. She said she was flying from Brazil and she loved doing that, and she said when she got home, she was going to come here."

My mouth tasted sour. "Come here, to *you*? She was

supposed to come to my play that night."

She was supposed to be in the audience.

She was supposed to be there for me.

"She mentioned that. She knew how important that was to you. Violet, she was *so* proud of you."

I hated how genuine he sounded. "So why wasn't she planning to be there?"

"Well… It's complicated," he said.

"We can handle complicated," Savannah said. "Trust me."

He sighed again. "Let me go get something she left here. That can explain it a lot better than I could." Dr. Bryant headed for the stairs, leaving us alone.

As Dr. Bryant zipped up the steps, I bundled my fingers into a fist, clenched, then let go. It wasn't working. Either I was too anxious, or I wasn't remembering Landon's instructions right.

"That must be his daughter," Savannah whispered and pointed to a photo of a young kid on the wall.

The kid had striking dark hair like Snow White, but she clearly had Dr. Bryant's dark eyes and smile. She looked familiar in a weird way, like I'd seen her before.

"He said that's why he didn't want to come forward about the affair," I said. "Guess it's too late for that now."

I walked toward the wall to get a better look at his other photos. Mostly his daughter, some photos of older people I assumed were his parents. Then I spotted a framed concert ticket. Bruce Springsteen, 1985, Oakland, California. Underneath the ticket was a listing of track songs from an album.

The song. "Thunder Road!" Like Landon said.

"Oh my gosh," I whispered. "He's ThunderRoad68."

It made perfect sense. It felt like the floor had opened underneath me.

I did the math—if '68 was a birth year, that would put him in his fifties, and that seemed to fit. He lived in the town, of course he'd be on a community page. Older people were into that stuff. I'd never been able to log into the anxiety and health forum because my account had to be accepted, but it promised answers from real doctors. Maybe he was *answering*, not asking.

Of course.

"What?" Savannah raised an eyebrow.

"For the record." Dr. Bryant came down the steps with a blue-and-white-checkered stationery box in his hands. "I believe I owe you girls an apology."

"Ya think?" I mumbled. Savannah elbowed me.

"I'm pretty sure it was my ex-wife who told the media about your mother and me. Sometimes Jenn was here when she had to drop off Phoebe. I was afraid she would've recognized Jenn on the news and called in to the hotline…"

"Why would she do that?" Savannah asked.

"To get back at me? Money?" Dr. Bryant shrugged. "I don't know. But I'm sorry. I would've kept it a secret forever if I could."

"Why?" I blurted out. "If you guys were so in love or whatever, why not just be together?"

"Well… We were going to."

I looked to Savannah, and she looked to me. From the stunned look in her eyes, I could tell she'd had no idea about this, either.

"We were in love," he said. "But she was afraid to leave you two."

A quiet fell on us like early morning snow. Hesitant, silent.

I'd thought this had been a simple affair. Sex, whatever (ew).

I hadn't imagined love was involved.

Love was a whole hell of a lot more complex.

Not that I knew anything about…either of those things.

"Was that the plan? To leave Dad and be with you?" I knew a divorce was coming, but was she going to move out too? Sell the house? Would I have lost her even if the plane hadn't vanished? "Were we supposed to travel back and forth between our house and…*this place*, or something?"

Dr. Bryant shook his head. "Not exactly–"

"Yes or no, was she going to be with you?" I spat. "It's not a hard question."

"Violet." Savannah placed her hand on mine.

I whipped it away. "No! Stop. It's a simple question. Was Mom going to leave us for you?"

He squirmed in his seat. "It's extremely complicated—"

"YES. OR. NO."

"Yes. That's why she wasn't planning to be at your show that night. She wanted to get a few of her things while none of you would be home, so she could move them in here." He pushed the box toward me. "Your mom wrote these for you, but she didn't want you to read them right now. They're letters. She wanted to wait until you were eighteen, Violet. She felt you weren't ready."

There it was again, this righteous insistence that no matter how much I wanted the truth, I couldn't handle it.

Savannah caught my eye again. My hand steadily inched toward hers.

"I'm almost eighteen," Savannah said. "Is there anything for me?"

"Um… I'm not sure. I think there are some addressed to both of you, but I really don't know. I've never looked," he said quietly. "She just told me to wait until Violet was eighteen. That was all."

My mother had been missing for six days now, and I was spending the afternoon with her lover. What wasn't I prepared for?

Then again, when Mom had written those letters, she'd assumed that that wouldn't be the case.

"Got it." Savannah's hand tensed in mine.

"She kept them here so you wouldn't find them but they'd be safe," he said. "I never read any of them except the ones she told me to. Promise. They are yours and yours alone.

"I don't feel comfortable hiding them from you anymore. I can't be responsible for your decisions. I can't speak for your mother, but…considering what's happened, I think these rightfully belong to you. You can choose to read them or not. I think she'd understand."

I clasped the box in my hands. It was cold.

I pictured it sitting by an open window, on a desk that maybe my mom used to write these letters. I fought simultaneous urges to burn them and devour every word.

"I'm assuming our father has no idea about these?" Savannah asked.

"Not sure. I would guess not," Dr. Bryant said.

Carefully, I peeled back the lid.

There were dozens of loose pages in a messy stack. I could make out Mom's neat print for sure, but each page got loopier as it descended. If I didn't know better, I'd assume they were from someone in a manic stage. Then again, did I really know Mom better?

"I-I think you should wait to read them at home." Dr. Bryant reached for the box, but I hugged it toward me. He didn't get to give and take.

Then I realized why.

The very first paper wasn't a letter at all:

Mother Child Alleged Father Paternity Index, Dated:
10/22/2007
    Mother: ASHBY, JENNIFER 08/01/1972
Child: ASHBY, VIOLET 06/07/2006
Alleged Father: ASHBY, MARK 01/27/1971
    Combined Paternity Index = 0
Probability of Paternity = 0%
    Conclusion: The results indicate that the alleged father
is not the biological father of the child.

The numbers and letters of the alleles presented before me blurred into nothing but shapes as my heartbeat slammed through my ears.

My entire genetic makeup, the person who I was, lay before me. The truth of my markers and genes, who I was and who I would become—and who I was not.

This couldn't be true. He had to have made this up.

I looked up at Dr. Bryant and only realized for the first time that his eyes were deep brown. Like mine. And that his nose was small and round, like mine. Eyebrows thick and long, like mine. The same shape, too.

"Is this real?" Savannah sounded thousands of miles away. I could barely hear her under the sound of my own internal screaming. "When was this taken? Did you know about this?"

"I-I…" Dr. Bryant looked between the two of us and stood. "I really shouldn't get into this. I think you girls should look at these at home."

"You knew about this, didn't you?" I ground my teeth. 2007? They'd been together for that long?

And if I was his child, then even longer? Sixteen years?

Nothing made sense. Nothing on this Earth was ever going to make sense again.

Savannah lunged toward the box and shuffled through. Besides the paternity test results, there were only handwritten letters in Mom's neat print.

He said, "Again, I think it's best if you girls look at these at home—"

"Did you take a paternity test?" My voice shook. I glanced at the water glasses, ridiculously thankful my lips hadn't touched the rim in case he had some plan to use my DNA.

"No, I didn't," he said. I loathed how I knew he was being honest from the sound of his voice. "Look, your mother didn't want me involved. It was only recently she decided to tell you when you were eighteen. We both wanted you to make your own choice. It doesn't matter when—"

"It does matter!" How could my DNA, my lineage, not matter? Zero, a zero percent chance the man who had changed my diapers when I was a baby and had taught me to drive was my biological father. But this man, this stranger, was?

"I promised her I would never intervene." His mouth was stoic, but his eyes softened. "I'm sorry. I should've never—"

"So you never took a test? There's no proof that you're my dad?" I asked.

"No. If you wanted to find out, I'm happy to oblige with a DNA sample. I… I'd like to know, too, to be honest with you." He scratched the back of his head.

"I don't care what you want," I snapped.

"That's fine! That's fine…" He waved his hands as if I were a burglar. "If it does turn out I'm your father, I can be in your life, or you can never speak to me again. Whatever you're comfortable with."

I was comfortable with nothing. The world was shrinking around me. My own skin felt too tight. The ends of my hair on my shoulders were tingling in all the wrong ways. I could barely exist.

"Let's go home, Violet." Savannah placed her hand on mine. "You can read it privately and digest it."

I pushed her hand off mine so I could grab the box and stomped out the door. I didn't want to digest it. I wanted to scream until my throat gave out.

You want the truth? You can't handle the truth.

It hurt to look at her because I finally saw it.

Savannah was all Dad. Their mannerisms, their connection. I'd always been so envious of it, but now it had become obvious why she and Dad were so connected and I'd always been on the outside.

The air had turned colder, but my face felt the heat of Venus. The box weighed me down, but my fingers clawed into the edges.

I was only beginning to accept that I'd lost Mom. I hadn't expected that I would lose my identity.

When we got home, I didn't look Dad in the eye. I couldn't.

"Where were you girls?" He sat on the couch with his sleeves rolled up and an IPA on the glass table.

"With Alex," Savannah lied effortlessly. The people we were becoming were eroded versions of us.

"Cool!" Dad said. "You girls want to watch some TV while I write? I have popcorn."

"Not right now," I mumbled.

I darted up the stairs with the box clutched tightly against my chest. I loved Savannah, but this was mine and mine alone.

I tossed off the top of the box and reached for the letters. My brain was so jumpy, I couldn't focus on any single letter. I scanned each of them for key words, begging for clues to why she was gone.

Dear Savannah,
Dear Violet,
my beautiful girls,
I'm sorry, I wish I could
I hope you don't mind
I want you to know

"Let me in!" Savannah pounded on my door. "They're mine too!"

Too many words. I would never be able to read these fast enough. And, honestly, I didn't want to. Not now. There were too many things I'd learned these past few days that I couldn't handle. I couldn't bear another.

I remembered the letter she'd written me, on my desk before she'd disappeared.

There was no other plan. This had been her plan. To leave Dad, leave us, be with that doctor. *This* was what she'd been talking about. Not the plane, not any of that.

How could I have been so naive?

I sank to my knees on the floor and buried my head in my hands. My heart quickened, and tunnel vision came over me. It was like a tsunami of anxiety engulfed me. I gripped my bedpost to keep steady.

I was desperate to reach for the razor I kept in my desk drawer and rip into myself, but instead, I scratched and scratched. The skin tore in angry red-and-white marks.

I wanted everything to stop. To leave me alone for one

minute. I couldn't deal with this. I wanted my mom, not some papers she'd left behind. Papers that told me my life was a complete lie.

The scratching wasn't enough. Only a tiny bit of blood trickled out. I needed something more. I opened my drawer and threw everything onto the floor until I found the razor—

Stop!

It sounded like Mom's voice, but I hated to admit that the sound of her voice was fading into nothingness for me. I wasn't sure I could even pick it out of a lineup.

What kind of daughter didn't remember her mother's voice?

Hot tears spilled down my cheeks, but I still suspended the razor above my delicate, blue vein.

She wouldn't want this for me. *I* didn't want this for me.

But I didn't know how to quit.

Fifty days, fifty days. You have to make it there.

I put the razor back in the desk and curled into a ball on my bed.

The gravity of all these painful, missing things weighed me down. Way, way down.

CHAPTER TWENTY-TWO

Day Seven – Night

As night fell, I didn't want to leave the house. It had gotten dark around six, and I wasn't even remotely hungry.

"Is Violet okay?" I heard Dad ask Savannah from the living room.

"She's fine. She had a fight with Alex," she responded.

I hated how good Savannah had become at lying. To me, to Dad.

I lay in bed and sketched a few drawings. Nothing *Beauty and the Beast*-related, nothing flight-related. Just people's faces. Blurry, not-totally-filled-in faces. All the while, I ignored texts:

ALEX: Rehearsal started 10 min ago. Where are you?
LANDON: You okay?
LANDON: ???
Missed Call (2): MR. TARIQ
ALEX: Did you quit because of me?? Don't do that.

ALEX: Get to rehearsal, we still have a few hours left.

None of them could ever understand.

I knew I'd made a commitment, but everything was off the table now. I didn't even know who I was. The only thing I wanted was for Mom to walk in the door, and I hated how I was starting to lose belief in that. In her.

And in me.

Savannah knocked on my door. "Landon's here to see you."

I curled deeper into my bed. The last thing I wanted to do was face him and explain why this high school play suddenly felt as important to me as dust under the rug. "Tell him I'm not here."

"No way," she said. "And don't screw it up with him. He's a nice guy. I'm telling him to come in."

"I've already screwed everything else up," I mumbled.

I headed downstairs, but Landon still hadn't come in. He was waiting on the porch outside.

"Hey!" He turned to face me. "Is everything okay?"

The last thing I wanted to do was crush Landon when he'd been so sweet to me. But he deserved someone who could be open with him. Someone who wasn't dealing with their universe closing in on them at every turn.

He was dressed in a flannel shirt and jeans with chucks. Usually, Landon's style was far neater and cleaner. Sweat lined his forehead, and he had a glow about him. I ignored the *bam bam kiss me bam bam* in my heart because, no. How dare I think that after everything today? How dare I be happy?

I'm the worst daughter. Mom deserved better.

Deserves.

"I'm fine," I mumbled. "I have a lot going on. I can't really talk. I'm sorry."

"Did something happen? I didn't see anything with the plane." Landon held up his phone. It was open to a Google page where nothing but Hurricane Molly was in the news.

"No. Look, I can't do the play anymore. I'm going to tell Mr. Tariq I quit tomorrow."

"What?" Landon blinked. "Why?"

"I said I have a lot going on." My tone was biting. I didn't want it to be, but my bones were exhausted and my self- control was out the window.

"Do you want to talk about it?" he asked.

I didn't deserve this. This kindness. This patient boy with soft brown eyes. Not when I was a horrible enough human to consider that my mother was a mass murderer. Not when I had no freaking clue what was happening with my life.

"No. I really don't." I crossed my arms. "I'm sorry I'm being such a bitch. But I really don't have time for high school stuff, okay? Thanks for everything you did, but I can't right now."

"I don't get it," he said. "Being in the play is what you wanted, and now you're giving it away?"

"You're just saying that because you don't want to act with anyone else," I said. "I told you I can't handle it right now. Stop being selfish."

"Fine, you know what? You're right. I am being selfish. I don't want to act with anyone but you," he said. "Yeah, I have anxiety, but I can find a way to work with someone else. You, though? You're wasting your talent and time."

"If anything, I wasted my time doing the show. I should've spent that time looking for Mom."

"Your mom is gone, Violet," he snapped. "I know you don't want to see that, but she's gone." He wasn't the first person to say it. He wouldn't be the last. But damn, it felt like a huge hornet had stung me in the heart. Landon was the last person I thought of as on my side.

But now I was alone.

I'd felt that way since Dad had told me the news on closing night, but now the darkness enveloped me even tighter. When all of this had started, I'd had my family. I'd had Alex, I'd had Landon.

Now I had no one.

"I'm sorry," he said quickly. "I shouldn't have said that. I'm so sorry."

"You should be." I crossed my arms.

"But it's true, Violet," he said gently.

"No, it's not." My throat felt like it was closing in as I tried not to cry. "I got too caught up in the show, in myself. I should've been spending that time looking for the truth."

"Looking for the truth? The truth is right in front of you," he said. "You want to do musicals. You want to act. That's the truth. And you're avoiding it. You pretend like you're hunting for the truth, but really, you're running from it."

It felt like he'd smacked me across the face. It was worse than what he'd said before. Whether he was wrong or right, I wasn't ready to hear it. Not now.

"I'm sorry it's harsh, but I can't stand to see you running in circles," he said. "Because I really, really like you."

"I'm done with this conversation. With this."

Landon took a few steps back. "I'm sorry. I shouldn't have come here." His eyes looked like a wounded deer's, shot for being too trusting.

He headed back to his car and I was so, so tempted to yell after him, but what did it matter? There was no such thing as true love. People cheated all the time. Even people you thought you knew ended up disappointing you anyway.

So what was the point?

I headed back inside and pressed my back against the

wall and took a deep breath. Wet, hot tears spilled down my face. There was no turning back from this. Any of this.

There was another pounding knock on my door.

Could he not take the hint?

"What!" I snapped.

But it wasn't Landon.

Diana looked surprised to see me open the door so quickly. She wore plain clothes, not her usual suit. "May I come inside?"

It was almost nine p.m. As far as I knew, the FBI kept fairly regular hours. This wasn't good.

The pit in my stomach told me something was wrong. Really, really wrong.

"She's gone, isn't she?" I whispered.

"Get your father and sister, please." Diana stepped into my living room and shut the door behind her.

"Dad!" I called for him, but on autopilot. I wasn't sure how much more of this I could take.

"What? Oh. Hi." The blood drained from Dad's face as he realized who had come knocking. Savannah trailed behind him, twirling hair around her finger with NASCAR speed.

"I think all of you should have a seat," she said.

Not that phrase again.

"What happened?" My legs refused to bend.

Dad and Diana exchanged glances.

She looked me in the eye and ruined my life in one sentence. Everything I knew and everything I was burst into a supernova of fire and destruction.

She said, "I've come to inform you that we've found pieces of US133 washed up on shore."

It was over.

CHAPTER TWENTY-THREE

DAY SEVEN – NIGHT

M y knees gave out and I sank into the couch. Dad wrapped his arms around me, but I felt nothing. I was only acutely aware of my own heart, beating aimlessly on.

"We've found a flaperon and we've confirmed that it is from US133," Diana said. "A flaperon is—"

"On the trailing edge of the wing." Savannah dropped to the couch on my left. "We know."

"We also found an engine cowling segment," she said.

Part of the wing. Part of the engine. When I'd forced myself to learn these terms over the past week, I hadn't been expecting to use them this way.

That meant the plane had crashed. That meant the plane had hit hard, choppy water with a velocity that had torn metal apart.

A delicate human body wouldn't stand a chance.

"How do you know it was US133?" I asked. "It seems

way too early to judge the age of what you found. It hasn't been tested yet, right?"

"It's in testing now," she said. "It is unfortunately definitely from US133, though. The piece itself isn't that large, only about fifty centimeters wide, but you can see it's part of a Boeing label."

"Part of the Boeing label," I said. "So not all of it. You can't absolutely determine anything."

The denial felt so pointless. I knew that. But I didn't have anything left to grasp on to.

"Violet, it's from US133," Dad said gently.

I frowned. It was almost like I needed someone else to say it so that it could be real. No way my brain would form the thought itself.

"Have you found any…anyone?" I asked.

"We haven't found any human remains, but these debris are a clear indication that the plane did crash," she said. "Given the time frame, it's unlikely that there will be any survivors."

Human remains. The person who'd made me, loved me, cherished me every day of my life was now a pile of decomposing flesh and bones somewhere at the bottom of the ocean. *Remains.*

I looked to Savannah. She sucked her lower lip in, but her eyes were clear, focused on Diana. Nothing had changed for her. She'd believed Mom was dead the minute they'd announced the plane was missing, and once again, she'd been right.

For her, this moment meant nothing, only a confirmation of known information.

But to me, it meant everything.

It had been seven days and nine hours.

How could I have been so naive? Deep down, I

thought I'd known she was gone the whole time. Denial had been my only way to get through it because I couldn't face it. Because that would mean my world would end, as it was now.

"We're going to get through this. We will." Dad's voice carried the gravity of the situation. It hit me with full force, with the velocity of a missing goddamn plane, that Dad was trying so hard. Even if he were the absolute perfect biological dad, it wouldn't be enough.

Because he wasn't Mom, and she wasn't coming back.

Savannah looked to me, then up to Diana, with dry, curious eyes. "Will the location of these parts give any idea as to where the"—she halted—"human remains will be?"

"That's the hard part," Diana said. "Hurricane Molly's path changed typical wave patterns. So, yes, it's possible that human remains will wash up in the Puerto Rico area where we found the flaperon and engine, but it's also possible that these were pushed in a different direction. It's impossible to tell."

"There'll be a search, though, right?" Dad rubbed my shoulder like he was encouraging me to speak. Why? I had nothing to say. I wasn't sure if I ever would again.

"Of course," Diana said. "The search is still being funded by five governments, including the US. We're using helicopters and search boats within two thousand square kilometers of both debris. It should be much easier to search once the hurricane completely clears."

I couldn't fathom a search that size. It seemed impossible.

I buried my face in my hands, hoping to vomit up the poison of this revelation, but I wasn't full of anything anymore. Only hollow.

It was almost like I'd expected this all along, but I had never expected my mother to disappoint me along the way.

I'd lost her, but I still didn't even know who she'd been.

And this didn't answer one big, glaring question.

"Was the flaperon extended?" I asked.

Diana quirked an eyebrow. "It's too early to say. The pieces were found last night and confirmed to be from US133 this morning."

The flaperon helped control the speed and position of the plane. People online had said that if the flaperon was extended, it meant the pilot had full control of the plane.

It meant Mom had gone down on purpose.

And it meant the Mom I knew wasn't this woman. This stranger I was coming to learn about.

This couldn't be happening. None of this.

My fingernails dug into my forearm. I knew they'd leave marks, but I didn't care.

"Tell me when you learn that information," I said. "I want to know."

"I know where your line of thinking is going," she said. "But it may not be that conclusive. The flaperon might be a helpful clue, but it might not tell us the whole story. I want to brace you for that."

Add another disappointing thing to the list. "Okay."

"I'll keep you all updated on the search," she said. "I'm sorry for your loss. Truly."

"I'm sorry for yours," I said. Ayesha Ahmad. I hadn't forgotten about her, even if the news had.

Diana's lips flickered upward, but the smile didn't reach her eyes. "Thank you, Violet."

She headed out the door, and an eerie stillness took over the house. None of us moved. We stayed, the three of us, in a neat line on the couch, our arms and hands linked.

Family—or what was left of it.

• • •

ONE DAY POST-LOSS

Unanswered texts; a collection:

ALEX: Hi girl. I'm so sorry, Savannah told me what happened. Are you okay?

LANDON: Hey Violet. I saw the news. I'm sorry. I'm here if you need anything.

LANDON: And again… I'm sorry for what I said. I don't know how to make it up to you.

ALEX: Thinking of you <3

ALEX: You alright?

SAVANNAH: Do you want to come downstairs for dinner?

SAVANNAH: Me and Dad are ordering Chinese.

ALEX: I love you

DAD: I KNOW YOU LIKE LO MEIN WANT SOME?? IF YOU SMELL IT, YOU'LL WANT IT

DAD: I DON'T KNOW HOW TO TURN CAPITALS OFF

ALEX: <3 <3 <3

SAVANNAH: Your door is locked. Please come downstairs.

SAVANNAH: Sorry Dad yelled, but you scared me. You weren't answering and your door was locked.

ALEX: Okay, I'll stop texting for a while, but please know I'm thinking of you and the fam. The Ashbys are my favorite people. Ever.

SAVANNAH: Please talk to me.

SAVANNAH: I left a Tupperware with dinner in it

outside your door

SAVANNAH: I'm sorry. I don't know how else to say this. Are you safe?

SAVANNAH: I'm really sad too. I don't know what to do...

DAD: ONION IS OUTSIDE YOUR DOOR WHINING, HE MISSES YU

DAD: I MEANT OU

DAD: DUCK

DAD: NOT DUCK, I MEANT DUCK

ALEX: Okay, I lied. Can't stop texting you. Love you.

SAVANNAH: I'm going to bed. I miss Mom.

SAVANNAH: Goodnight. I love you little sis.

• • •

The ultimate unanswered text:

ME: hey! Can you drive me and Sav and maybe Alex to the Trixie Mattel concert next week?

MOM: Sorry honey, I thought I could but I'm scheduled to work next weekend.

ME: Oh, I thought you could?

MOM: I'm sorry, I can't anymore. I love you.

• • •

I might've been asleep. Or lying here. I didn't know anymore.

The door whined open. Savannah crept through the door in jeans and a long-sleeved crew neck. Eyeliner too. Caring about her appearance felt intangible to me. Like how I knew the stars were long dead by the time I saw them.

"Please eat something." Her voice was quiet.

The Chinese food from last night was gone, replaced by the BLT in her hands on a Styrofoam plate. We never used real plates or silverware anymore. Everything was plastic, filling up the landfills one after another. I wanted to care—I used to care, until this week. But I couldn't wrap my brain around saving the Earth anymore. Lost cause.

I might've looked at her. I wasn't sure. Everything was blurry.

"It's good." I hadn't even heard Dad step into the room. I only saw him appear side by side with Savannah; that's how they always were. Together. Mom and I used to be like that. "Come on, Vi. Just a bite or two."

Part of me wanted to scream so loud I'd shred my throat. *Get out of my room! Leave me alone!* But it felt like too much energy. Everything was too much energy, everything was too much in general. I wanted to be nothing. I didn't want to be.

I rolled over to face the wall.

"We're going to leave this here," Dad said. "Love you. Okay?"

I imagined he put the sandwich down. I didn't know, but I heard the door shut. And they were gone.

"This isn't fair," I hissed.

My heart pumped, my breathing sped up.

Why did it have to be my mom? Couldn't it have been someone else?

She didn't deserve any of this.

None of us did.

I chucked my phone at the wall. The screen shattered, smooth to the touch on the outside. Cracked on the inside.

ALEX: Okay, please don't get angry at me. But you haven't answered in a long time and I'm worried.

ALEX: I've noticed sometimes you have like…scars on your arms

ALEX: I wanted to say something but I didn't know what to say. But now I do. Please don't hurt yourself and call me, okay?

That night, around midnight, I skimmed through the old pictures of Mom on my phone. The one of her cutting my birthday cake, the one of her holding a glass of champagne when Savannah had sent out her first college application, the one of her kissing Onion's head.

I had this weird sensation that I wanted to find out she'd killed herself on purpose. Because to take that person away from me for no reason at all seemed like the cruelest thing in the world.

I would've given anything, anything at all to have her back. Even art. Acting.

But none of that mattered.

I tried to pretend I was someone else—anyone else. But my brain refused to deny anymore. I was in reality, whether I wanted to be or not.

So I threw my phone. Again. I chucked the musical script in the garbage. And I snapped my brushes in half. All of them.

For the quickest second, I hesitated. This wasn't what I wanted to do, but I didn't have any other choice.

With the jagged edges of the brushes, I tore into myself. The tiny pieces of wood bit at me like leeches. The type of pain that radiated. But I kept digging and digging.

Blood poured out of me. Down my arms like Lady Macbeth. It dripped onto my rug and wove itself into the threads.

She's not coming back.

I'd been so close. A few more hours, and it would have been fifty days without cutting. But none of it mattered. Everything was trivial.

Worse than trivial. Futile.

I'd given up my chance with Landon, Alex and I had had our first fight in years, I had hurt Savannah. I had thrown away my one shot to do musical theater, and worst of all, Dad was…not my biological father.

Everything I knew had been erased in the white, sharp waves of the frigid ocean.

Weird thing was, I didn't feel any better. I'd cut, finally, but I was still miserable. Mom was still gone. The relieving effect seemed to have vanished right along with her.

I crept into the bathroom to run cold water on my wrist. I'd cut across the road on purpose, not down the street, but the blood kept running. I tried gauze—it became red in seconds.

Oh no. No, no.

"Violet?" Savannah knocked on the door gently. "Are you okay?"

Acid crept to the back of my throat.

"I need a second," I said.

More red. The water was colder than the Atlantic.

The Atlantic and its freezing, cruel waves that tore people and metal to bits.

I pictured the waves roaring, swallowing anything and anyone in their way.

"Violet, I'm coming in," she said.

"No!" I threw my body against the door. Red splattered on the white paint.

A tinkering sound came from the lock. Then Savannah's weight knocked me off balance, and I collapsed onto the bathroom tiles.

Savannah gasped and knelt beside me. "What happened?"

"It won't stop bleeding."

From the look on her face, I saw what it was like for someone else to see this.

I'd been so used to hurting myself that the shock didn't register anymore. But Savannah stared at my arm in horror, aghast at the crimson spread on me, in our bathroom.

She helped me up and brought my arm under the sink. With light strength, she squeezed on both sides of my arm. "You did this to yourself." She looked at me through the mirror.

I nodded.

Her face reflected the same despair I felt, and a flicker of hope rose in me that someone would care about me as deeply as I had cared about Mom. "Why?"

"I don't know," I answered honestly.

Her eyes were wide. Scared. "You have to stop doing this."

Wish I could. It made me feel even worse. "I don't know how. I'm trying."

"I can't lose you, too." She squeezed harder as she talked to me, like a girl on a sinking boat that knew every second counted. Blood ran over her fingers and nails. The water was painfully cold, but with all the pressure, the blood flow was finally slowing.

I finally felt like I could breathe again. Just a little bit.

My wrist was clean now.

"I wasn't trying to kill myself. Honest. I... I was..." I didn't know what I'd been doing, exactly.

Savannah didn't answer. Instead, she wrapped gauze around my arm, way tighter and more cleanly than I had. Only a little soaked through this time.

Relief spread through me. No stitches needed. I didn't want to think about what would've happened if she hadn't been there.

"We're still sisters, no matter what that test says." She refused to let go of my hands.

"Half," I said.

"No, full." She pulled me into a tight hug. My sister—half or not—was warm and strong. Hugging her felt like my favorite blanket. "I love you," she said.

"I know," I said. "I love you more."

"I don't think so."

She held my face against her shoulder, and I held her face against my hair, and we both wept for what we'd lost, but maybe also for what we'd found.

I finally got into bed an hour later, once my heart had resumed normal beating status. With my cracked phone, I looked at more pictures of Mom. The fractured screen made the pictures more real, sort of like my memories of her, now splintered by the force of unexpected truths.

I couldn't believe she'd only be in photos now. The smell of her perfume and hair seemed so far away. This was really all I had to live on, for the rest of my life? How long could these memories hold?

I was terrified of forgetting. The idea that someday this would be a simply painful memory that I looked back on occasionally felt impossible. This pain would always be raw, and real. I wanted to always remember her, with all the details that I did now.

There had to be something for me to hold on to.

The door whined open—I really needed a new lock, pronto. I'd left a chair in front of it, but its legs scraped the wooden floor every time Dad or Savannah came in, and it felt like a fork grazing my brain. Every sound was too loud lately.

I didn't turn, but I knew it was Savannah by her gait. Her gentle footsteps came to a halt at the edge of my bed. Her shadow sat down, and I felt a light pressure by my feet.

"I'm only sitting here." Her voice was raspy. "Just… being here."

I reached over and felt for her hand. When my fingers brushed hers, I laced them.

CHAPTER TWENTY-FOUR

Two Days Post-loss

I ate that morning. Like, an actual bagel, not just pieces like I'd been getting down lately.

It was the most I'd done in three days. Logically, I knew I couldn't sit in my room forever, but wow, did that sound appealing.

Savannah was still asleep in my beanbag chair, from the night before. Her arms were crossed and her long legs were tucked under her. We hadn't spoken all night, but knowing she was there, well… It felt like drinking a potion in a video game when your health was almost depleted.

I performed another first that morning: a shower. The hot water stung on my arms and when I looked down, I fought a gasp. It looked like I'd made my own version of railroad tracks. In the moment, the slashes I made always felt so necessary. But in the morning light, the shame nearly choked me.

Yeah… That habit needed to stop. Now.

When I got back from the shower, Savannah was rummaging through my closet. "You never wear this. Why not?" She held up a form-fitting purple tee with lace shoulders. "Purple looks really good on you."

"Violet wearing purple? The irony would be insufferable." Mom had always had me wearing purple as a baby. I'd looked like a plum in every photo.

"You should wear it." Savannah placed it carefully on my bed, along with some jeans. She held a gray cardigan in her other hand. "I'm borrowing this."

"All yours." Getting dressed felt like too much, so I sat on my bed in the towel.

Grieving is normal, I told myself. But this didn't feel normal.

Savannah shifted her weight by the door. "You want to talk about it?"

I didn't answer. When my mood fell like this, talking was really…hard. Exhausting, actually.

"How are the wrists?" she asked.

"Fine. Thanks to you. About that…"

"You don't need to thank me."

I nodded, but I did need to thank her, though. I really did. Even if that didn't mean saying those exact words right now.

She left, and I checked the internet and message boards for any new information.

JeanTouissant: If the flaperon was extended, then yes, the pilot had control over the plane at the time of descent. I'm sure they will inform us soon and we can finally solve this mystery.

HillaryClintonsEmails: The bitch pilot definitely did it. PROOF it crashed. PROOF she did it.

LiveFreeOrDie: The liberal media won't say the truth.

Click here to see what really happened

ThunderRoad68: There is no evidence about intent. Until we have that, please keep the victims and their families in your thoughts. This is a tragic loss for so many.

He hadn't answered my previous post. Maybe he hadn't seen it.

And their families.

Did that include him?

I retrieved the box of letters from the closet. I still wasn't sure if I was ready.

Though, if not now, when?

There were three knocks on my door.

I slipped a cardigan on. I wasn't ready to talk to Dad about this yet.

He took a step in, Onion in his arms. "I have to take a phone call from my editor. Can you walk the dog?"

The last thing I wanted to do was leave my room. After what I'd gone through, I felt entitled to lie in my bed for eternity.

"I don't know," I mumbled.

"Please? I took him yesterday, but he was being poop-shy," Dad said.

Onion was a little self-conscious, and he didn't like to poop in front of anyone but me.

I looked to Onion, with his big, clueless brown eyes.

"Okay, fine." I couldn't resist.

He snorted with glee.

"There's my girl." Dad placed Onion and his leash on the ground. "So! You showered this morning. And I saw a bagel is gone." Dad waved his arm around the room.

I'm trying, I wanted to whisper. But nothing came out.

"It's great you're taking steps! The book says even small steps toward a normal routine are good in times of grief." Dad grinned. It broke my heart that it was a genuine grin. Like I'd taken this so hard that I'd become a person who was only expected to do menial tasks.

He looked to the box sitting on my bed. "What's this?"

I thought about sharing the letters with him, but I wasn't sure what was in there. If he didn't know any of it, if he thought with certainty that I was his biological daughter, who was I to break that illusion for him? I knew way too well what it was like to have your world fall around you. I couldn't do that to him.

Someone had to help me process this, just not him. Dr. Madison might, but she couldn't verify the truth of it.

Dr. Bryant, though? He would know.

"School stuff," I lied.

"Gotcha." He nodded. "Well, thanks for taking care of Onion. And I'll be here if you need anything, okay?"

I kissed his cheek. I hoped it could express far more than I could with words. "I might take Onion on a longer walk than usual. We could use the stretches."

"Sure. Fresh air is great. Bring your sister."

Did he not trust me to be alone? Did he know?

Maybe he was right.

Actually, I knew he was right.

"Sure," I said. "Hey, Dad? Can you ask Dr. Madison for another appointment this week?"

Dad's face brightened. "You got it."

That night, I did something I'd never done before: I snuck out.

There had never been a reason to. Dad was so focused

on writing that he let me go anywhere, especially when Mom was away on a long flight. But now, Savannah and Alex had ruined one more thing for me. I couldn't say I was at Alex's without Savannah knowing, and her questions would lead to answers I didn't want her to know.

Around nine, I snuck out of my bedroom and grabbed Savannah's keys from her purse while I heard the shower going. I felt guilty, but hey, the car was meant for both of us. Eventually.

This time, I at least gave Dr. Bryant a heads-up with a text. I'd found his number on one of the papers Mom had given me. I parked the car and stood on his porch. This time, I felt weaker without my sister there.

He opened the door for me dressed in jeans and a black wool sweater that looked like it cost more than my laptop. "Good evening, Violet." He opened his mouth like he was waiting for someone else. He looked beyond me, to the car, then back at me. "You're alone?"

"Is that a problem?" I asked.

"No, of course not." He ushered me inside and shut the door behind me. "I didn't think you had your license yet. Sixteen, right?"

I took a few steps inside and crossed my arms. Of course he knew how old I was. Of course. "I'm allowed to drive before ten," I lied. It was nine p.m., but he was a doctor, not a cop.

"Okay. As long as you're being safe." He led me to his living room this time. The brown leather couches and glass coffee table stood out against white walls and an eggshell-colored rug. He might as well have had a sign: Children do not visit here. I wondered how often he got to see his daughter.

His… other daughter.

I hesitantly sat on the couch and crossed my ankles underneath me.

He sat across from me in a dark leather armchair. I pictured him and Mom curled up there by the fireplace. *Ugh.* "I'm so sorry about your mother," he said. "I saw the news."

"Me too."

An awkward silence fell between us. I tried to picture her again, but I couldn't. No matter how hard I tried, I couldn't picture her anywhere but places I'd already seen her.

It hit me that that there would be no new places for Mom. Everywhere I'd go from now on, I would have to see for the both of us. I'd have to carry her with me.

"So how can I help you today?" he asked.

"Well." I clasped my hands together. I didn't want to tell him, not yet. I was still deciding what to do while I held the power. "I have some more questions about my mom."

"Okay."

I took the box from my backpack and placed it carefully on the table. "I want to read these with you."

"With me?" he asked.

"Yeah. She left them with you for a reason," I said. "And... I know you're ThunderRoad68."

"What?" He blushed, the same way I did. Cheeks pink as peonies. "How'd you figure that out?"

"Long story. But the important thing is, I can tell you care about her. *Cared.* So, that means a lot to me." I opened the box and toyed with the lid. "You defended her when no one else would."

"It felt silly, talking out loud to no one on the internet. I never, never comment. But the way those people talked about her... I had no choice," he said.

I hated how much I agreed with him. Those comments had cut me each time. Speaking into the void under an anonymous name had somehow made it less terrible. "And you're the only one who can verify if these are true or not."

He hesitated. "I've never read them before. I don't know if it's my place."

"Then who else can I go to? I can't exactly ask my mom." I didn't want to pull the *dead mom* card, but seriously?

Dr. Bryant gave a deep sigh from his chest. "All right. If it's best to read them together, then okay. I trust your judgement."

Well, that made one of us. I nodded. "Here goes nothing."

Not all of the letters were addressed to me. Some were to Savannah. Some were to my father. Some were to Dr. Bryant, and some had no salutations at all.

The first answered all my old questions, and new ones blossomed like flowers in fast forward.

Dear Violet,

I'm sorry. I can't say that enough.

I'm going away. I don't know for how long. I'm an awful mother to abandon you when you need me right now. I know you do, because I've seen your scars. New ones.

I didn't say anything to Dad, promise, but he and I have talked about it in the past. He loves you, and we are both concerned. I wish you would listen to me when I try to talk to you about them. I've been where you've been, and without help, it gets worse. That's where I am now—in the worst of it.

I know you get it, but I owe you an explanation for being a bad mom right now. I'm working on myself so I can be the mom you and Sav deserve. And no, this is not because of Matthew Bryant.

I love Matthew. But I'm going to be on my own for a bit. I'm giving Dad full custody while I'm gone and after the divorce. Then, I'm moving in with Matthew. You will always be my world and my life, but this is something I need to do for myself. Dad is an amazing father to you and deserves everything I can't give him. Someday, I'll explain that too.

Thank you for reading. You're a better daughter than I am a mom. You deserve more.

Please forgive me. I love you.

Love,

Mom.

I expected hot tears to fall on the pages rattling between my shaking hands, but my eyes were dry and my hands were steady with the clarity I was finally craving. With that clarity, though, came an avalanche of new questions.

"Is that what you expected?" he asked.

I inhaled, exhaled. "I wasn't sure what I expected at all."

There was a sad irony in that if I had seen this letter only a few days ago, it would've filled me with hope. That Mom only had gone away for a little while. But washed-up engines did not lie.

"So she really was going to miss my show to go off by herself, then move in with you," I said. "You weren't lying."

"That's right."

"She wasn't going to kill herself." I blinked. "She didn't want to die."

The implication of all this struck me as I put the letter down.

Not only did my mom not want to die, but she hadn't

laid out any plans for murdering 155 people. I wasn't sure if it counted as proof to a jury or the media, but it was proof to me. I felt awful for ever questioning her.

Deep down I'd known she'd never do that, but after hearing about the affair, I couldn't help but feel like I didn't know her. At all.

She'd needed me, and I was a terrible daughter. The worst.

This was what Savannah had meant when she'd said the walls were closing in.

I'd let my mom down. I hadn't believed in her.

Trust me.

That was all she'd asked in the first note.

And I couldn't even do that.

I glanced to my wrists. I wanted nothing more than to take out a razor and slice it across my lower arm, or slash myself with keys until it burned so bad that I cried. I deserved it.

I balled my fists and clenched tight, like Landon had said to. When I let go, I didn't feel any better, but I also hadn't scratched or dug my nails into myself.

He said, "Before she left, she said she'd written you another one? A shorter letter?"

"That's right," I said.

"She wanted me to give this one to you eventually, once the dust settled," he said. "I told her she should've told you and Savannah in person, but she couldn't."

Couldn't, or wouldn't?

Dr. Madison's voice rang in my head.

Again, I was confronted with similarities between me and Mom. We both ran from things that made us happy; we both hurt ourselves to make the sadness go away, but it never really worked.

I dug through the box and scanned the other letters.

All versions of the same thing. It was weird, but I understood. There were many lives I wished I led, but you only got one, so I could see writing letters and letters but only wanting to give one, like a choose-your-own-ending story.

Well. Mom hadn't gotten to choose her own ending.

"This is what we discussed in that final phone call, how she was going to go off on her own for a bit. But we met up the night before—"

"You were driving that black car."

"Yeah. She wanted to be gone for a month, while her and your dad figured out things with making the divorce official." He picked at the cuticle on his index finger. "I didn't think it was right to leave you two."

"Or you didn't want her to leave you."

"That's true too." He lit the fireplace, and it roared to life. He placed the guard in front of it. "But she'd left me before. When we first met, we were young. Then I didn't see her again until, like, seven years later. She was already with your dad, pregnant with Savannah. I was with my ex-wife by then." He rubbed his chin, the tiny hairs prickling his fingers. "It wasn't supposed to happen. We went to an army reunion, started talking…We didn't plan on it."

Didn't plan on it, or didn't plan on me?

I tried to imagine what it must've been like for Mom to pretend I was Dad's. Whether every time she looked at my face, she saw a dark-eyed doctor's mistake, not the disheveled but loving writer she'd married.

I hoped she only saw her daughter.

"Then when Jenn came to me and told me about Savannah being sick, we…" He caught my eye. "Nothing happened, I swear. Not until recently. Back then, she was nervous as hell about Savannah, and there's no way to explain what it was like to see you. All grown up! I mean, not really grown up, but a fully formed child. I had so many questions. Do you remember me talking to you at all?"

I thought back, but it was hard to bring up memories from when I'd only been five or so. Most of what I remembered was the smell of antiseptic and how Savannah had retched over the toilet all night during chemo. "I remember being grateful for you. I thought you were a hero for saving my sister," I said. "And honestly? Still do."

A small smile played on his lips, but disappeared when he ran his hand over his face and dragged it down.

Savannah texted me: **Where are you?**

I ignored it for now.

"I wanted to get to know you so badly. You told me your favorite color was purple, but you hated that because your name is Violet. You told me you loved math and science. Especially earthquakes! You'd just learned about them, and I couldn't believe how much you knew. Oh, and you knew about the missing Pleiad!"

I blinked back tears. Everything he said was true. This man knew the important bits of me, but I knew nothing of him. The flames of the fire licked my right side. It was getting warm.

"I'm sorry." He bit at the ends of his cuticles. They were all bloody and torn. "I shouldn't have said all that."

"No! No. I'm glad you did."

"I think I made a mistake. I shouldn't have given you those letters." The fine lines on his face became etched with guilt. "I didn't want to overwhelm you. But they weren't my letters to keep. I… I haven't been thinking properly since all of this happened."

"No, no, I mean it," I said. "I'm glad."

And it was true. I didn't know it until I said it, but suddenly, DNA didn't matter to me. At all. My mom was my mom forever and always no matter what, and I didn't need letters to say that. My dad was my dad because of who he was and what he'd sacrificed for me all his life, regardless of alleles and genes.

And now it was time to prove that. To protect him.

I stood, surprised by how wobbly my legs felt. "I really am thankful for what you did."

If it hadn't been for him, I would've never found out any of this. I would've never known my mother was about to leave me anyway, or that my father would never leave me, despite it all.

"You're welcome," he said. "And if you give any thought to doing a DNA test…"

"I don't think I need that."

"Okay." He nodded.

And that was that.

Dad was my dad. He always would be. When I'd gone looking for the truth, I should've started with him all along.

As I got into the car, I checked my phone:

SAVANNAH: You need to come home. Now.

ME: Everything okay?

SAVANNAH: They found more of the plane. The FBI is going to release the results of the black box.

CHAPTER TWENTY-FIVE

Two Days Post-loss – Night

D ad sat us down on the living-room couch and explained how Hurricane Molly's waves had pushed even more pieces of US133 onto the coast of Puerto Rico.

They hadn't found any bodies or airline seats yet, but they'd found pieces of clothing. Little scraps washed up ashore. Even some luggage. Only problem was, it was hard to tell which pieces had come from the plane and which had been a result of the hurricane's wrath on San Juan. Wreckage on wreckage.

"The FBI said they've finished the report and will be releasing details to the public this evening," Dad said. "Which means the press is going to be all over it. So don't be surprised if there's news trucks outside again soon."

Funny how press trucks and bright lights outside didn't scare me anymore. I wasn't sure if I'd gotten used to it, or if I'd realized that far more awful things happened in this world.

We had the TV set to the news, but right now it was still showing the devastation from Hurricane Molly. Diana had told Dad it would be televised as breaking news any minute. It dawned on me that I had started this awful week watching the news at three a.m., and here we were again, staring at the television as the clock crept closer to midnight.

"What did the cockpit voice recorder say?" I asked.

"Yeah, do we know what happened to the plane yet?" Savannah asked.

"They haven't told me anything except that they were going to have a press conference tonight," Dad said.

I noticed Dad didn't say we were invited to it. I wasn't sure if families were typically invited to that sort of thing, or if we were excluded for a reason.

My palms were already sweating.

"We'll watch it together as a family," he said.

Savannah and I looked to each other, then to the ground.

I wasn't sure I could handle this. Any of this.

The TV switched rapidly, and *Breaking News* flashed across the screen.

Dad's hand took mine, then Savannah's, creating a chain.

Agent Rosenfield stood on a podium, peering out into the crowd with a pensive look on her serious face. I wondered if she had listened to the recording herself, or if that had been someone else's job. Had she heard her friend's voice? Did she want to?

"Good evening," she said. "This afternoon, the FBI closed the report on US133. In recent days, we've found debris, including the flight data recorder and cockpit voice recorder, and we were able to extract data from both items."

I glanced at Savannah. She toyed with the hem of her shirt, eyes down.

This was it. Here, my life would end. In one way or another, I wouldn't be the same person I'd been ten minutes ago. I'd be a new Violet. Wiser and jaded, or dismayed but relieved.

I hoped to be dismayed but relieved.

"The black box, along with the wreckage, was able to tell us that Flight US133 suffered a loss of cabin pressure that rendered the aircrew and passengers unconscious," she said.

My heart stalled. Unconscious?

Accident, it was an accident. Right?

"Findings from a cargo door indicate that it likely malfunctioned and flew open during flight. This led to debris causing fires in the engines and explosive decompression. The cockpit voice recorder indicated that the pilots were aware of these issues, and attempted to land at the nearest airport," she said.

I could've thrown up. I *wanted* to throw up. But I did nothing except stare in front of me at the blue TV screen light.

"Smoke and fire, as well as decompression, ultimately led to an electrical failure that turned off the transponders and prohibited the flight team from signaling a mayday." Agent Rosenfield looked beyond the camera, then directly into its eye. "I would like to reiterate that all passengers and crew are officially cleared by the FBI, and that this is in no way a terror-related activity. This is a sad day for US Modern Airlines and the friends and family of the 155 aboard. Our deepest sympathies go out to them," she said. "Many new tools and regulations will be put in place to make sure this type of accident doesn't happen again."

Accident. Accident.

Diana leaned into the microphone and began to thank a few people, like the New York City mayor and government officials from Puerto Rico who'd helped with the search. "I'd also like to thank Violet Ashby, daughter of the main pilot, for being so vocal about this incident and raising awareness. I wish her and her family the very best."

It was like hearing the teacher call your name when you weren't prepared. My name sounded so strange coming from the TV, it was like they were talking about someone else. Then again, this whole week and a half had felt like it had been someone else's life.

"Violet!" Dad half smiled. "See? Your hard work was recognized."

"Yeah." I swallowed. That heavy feeling in my stomach squeezed at me, like I might vomit. "So it was an accident?" I asked. "Mom didn't do anything wrong?"

"Right, honey." Dad kissed the side of my head. "She was innocent."

It seemed even more unfair. A door open, a fire, electrical failure. It had all been stacked against her. An image of her helplessly mashing buttons in the cockpit invaded my brain. She must've known she was going to die. All of the passengers had probably been terrified.

I tried to imagine the cockpit voice recorder. There would've been fire alarms, screaming. Mom's voice trying to stay steady.

"I knew she would've never tried to hurt anyone." Dad reached for a tissue, and it was only then I realized he had tears in his eyes. "I always believed in you, Jenn."

I winced at the use of my mother's first name. It made her more than Mom. It made her a real person; a real person who'd had a terrifying last few minutes of life. A person who'd suffered.

I almost wished she'd done it on purpose. At least then she wouldn't have been helpless.

Her hands. I couldn't stop picturing her hands trying to signal for a distress call, or gripping the gears so hard her knuckles turned white. And then…

Then?

There was no then, no next. It would be *over.* Over in one burning white light.

"I need some water." I headed into the kitchen and held a glass under the faucet. It wouldn't keep steady, so I needed to use both hands.

Savannah joined me a moment later and turned off the faucet for me when the glass was full.

"Thanks." I brought the glass to my parched lips but barely took a sip.

"They said awful things about her." Savannah's eyes were glazed over, like she was drunk. "They blamed her. Now they think they can apologize and that will be it."

I agreed, but words didn't come from my mouth.

"They don't understand." She pressed her lips tightly together. "This was a person. A human person who tried her best. They tore her apart in the media for a week, and now they're just going to forget about it? No real apology? I mean, what the hell? And a door malfunction? Our mom *died* because of a door malfunction?!"

I took another sip, but I was trembling too much. My fingers released the glass and it shattered onto the hard kitchen floor.

Savannah and I both leapt back like it was an explosion.

"Girls?" Dad ran into the room. "Back away, you're both barefoot!"

Savannah took a few steps backward, but I stayed still.

Tiny pieces sparkled by my feet. Water stretched out like a growing river.

"I'm so sorry. I didn't mean to," I whispered.

"It's okay, don't apologize." Dad dug for the dustpan under the sink. "Where the hell is that mini broom thing?"

"I'm sorry," I said louder this time. "I ruined it."

Savannah wedged herself between the wall and cabinets, and eyed me incredulously. "You didn't do anything."

"It's my fault." My knees couldn't hold me anymore. I collapsed into a ball on the floor. Glass pricked my feet, and a sharp bit nicked my knee. I backed up toward the sink.

"Violet, get away from there!" Dad roared.

"It's my fault!" I screamed. Tunnel vision, again. My heart pounded in my ears so loudly, I could've sworn it was a snare drum. My hands covered my face, and I trembled with the force of a small earthquake. Everything was happening so fast, I couldn't breathe.

"I'm so sorry!" I screamed. The world was moving so fast, it felt like it was leaving me behind.

Rough hands clasped over my shoulders. I peeked under my hands to see Dad's hairy feet, some dark blood staining them now.

"Listen to me, Violet." He tried to gently pull my wrists away to see my face, but I didn't want to look at him. I couldn't.

"This was no one's fault." Dad finally pried my hands from my face, and I was forced to stare into his light-blue eyes.

Eyes exactly like Savannah's.

Eyes so different from mine.

"I love you." Dad scooped me into his arms. I held him tighter than I ever had as a child. Like if I let go, he would vanish too.

Dad was still Dad, no matter what. I needed to tell him that soon. I just didn't know how. If I held him like this here, maybe that would be enough.

"It was an accident," he said quietly. "And we're going to be okay."

I went to lie down in my room for a while. No TV, no phones.
I needed to process all of this without distraction. One thing I noticed though – I didn't feel like cutting. Not even a little bit. After seeing Savannah's face and my blood on her hands, it was like the spell had been broken.

Maybe that fifty-day streak was the magic number after all.

Savannah knocked twice on my door before coming in. "You okay?"

"Yeah. Just needed a minute."

"Me too." She sat on the edge of my bed with a creak. "Hey... Do you think it's okay if we do that memorial now? I could use some closure."

I chewed the idea over in my head. This time, no denial. No resistance. "Okay. Sure. You can tell Dad."

Weird. Acceptance was weird.

Savannah crawled into my bed and slipped her arm around me. She smelled like vanilla, vaguely like Mom. We sat there, alone together.

"I dreamed about her last night," Savannah whispered.

"Really?" I raised my eyebrows. "What happened?"

"I know this sounds weird, but I was sitting in an airport,

by myself. I saw her come out of the gate. She was wearing her uniform, but I noticed the wings were missing. Even in the dream, I was surprised to see her."

I could see it easily. The navy-blue uniform, the hat, the gold accents. Her short hair, framing her deep eyes and kind smile. The person I missed every single minute. I was never going to be whole without her.

"I asked her where she was going, and she said she wasn't sure, but she couldn't wait." Savannah's eyes welled up with tears.

My mouth felt dry. It sounded more like a séance than a dream. I wasn't sure if I believed in any of that stuff, ghosts and whatnot, but this sounded eerily real. Like Mom was reaching out.

"I think it's her way of telling me she's okay," she said.

A selfish thought pierced my brain: why didn't I have any dreams? Why wouldn't Mom come to me? Was it because I couldn't totally trust her, like she had asked me to?

"That's really nice, Sav," I whispered.

She slung her arm around me. "You have your note, and I have my dreams."

I wanted more than a piece of paper with her handwriting, more than a dream that I couldn't touch or replay. But for now, that would have to do.

CHAPTER TWENTY-SIX

FOUR DAYS POST-LOSS

Dad had decided to have the memorial in the cemetery near us.

I'd told him I felt weird about going to a cemetery when there would be no real grave, but he'd insisted we needed a place to return to when we wanted to visit. He'd been right, I thought.

The cemetery was open, airy, and there were cherry-blossom trees that could shield us from potential rain. Beautiful cherry blossoms, like the ones in the park Mom used to take us to.

He'd gotten a small headstone with her name engraved, and it was put in that morning by the groundskeeper.

By the time Dad, Savannah, and I arrived, my entire family was there, standing in a circle. Aunts, uncles, Grandpa, my grandparents from California. A few people from school, some teachers. Miles Miller and some of their military group. A lot of our family had called, but they had mostly talked to Dad. I wasn't ready. My brain already felt too packed, like I couldn't handle another conversation about this or I'd burst.

Alex and Landon stood together in the back and shared an umbrella. Alex shivered in the cool September drizzle, and Landon hesitantly huddled closer to her so that she would be covered by the umbrella. I avoided eye contact with both of them.

It meant the world to me that they were here, but I still couldn't forgive myself for the way I'd treated Landon until I'd apologized. Grief was no excuse.

We broke through the circle and stood toward the front, facing the headstone. It was made of slate, maybe granite too. The rock itself wasn't shiny, but the dark brown slate on top was.

JENNIFER ASHBY

MOM, WIFE, FRIEND.

ALWAYS WITH US.

It didn't seem real. Surely there was another Jennifer Ashby who was a mom, wife, and friend? I stared at it, taking deep breaths.

No. This was real. And it was happening.

I had to face this, even if I wasn't sure I could.

Gentle rain fell on us. Cold, but light, the type you could walk through without being upset.

Dad spoke up first, talking about how cool he'd thought she was when they'd first started dating, and how they made each other laugh. I'd read every one of my dad's books, but as I heard him speak, it reminded me of why his books were so successful. He spoke with heart, but most of all, with raw honesty. Despite everything, his voice still held love and respect for her.

But this whole thing felt so wrong. She wasn't here. There was no body, no real proof. I mean, I had all the proof I needed, but...

My legs wouldn't stop shaking. Maybe it was the rain, or the words. I wasn't sure. I crossed my arms tightly around me, but I couldn't get rid of the chill. The black blazer and skirt I'd chosen to wear suddenly felt too light in the wind. It cut right through me. It felt like a frigid January day, even though it was barely fall.

"Cold?" Landon appeared beside me. "Take this." He wrapped a pink scarf around my shoulders. It was misshapen, a bit wonky, and looked like a few stitches were out of place.

But I loved it. Absolutely loved it for all its imperfections.

Imperfect things were somehow still perfect.

"Thank you," I whispered. "Thank you."

He smiled and took a few steps back, joining Alex again. I wrapped the scarf tighter around my neck, letting it hang over my shoulders. The softness made me feel safe, and knowing Landon had made it stitch by stitch only made it sweeter. It smelled like him, warm and sort of like the outdoors after rain.

I tried to imagine Landon sitting in his room on his bed, taking the care and concentration to make something for me. Only me.

This was not the kind of guy I wanted to let go.

But to be honest? I wasn't ready for a relationship. I knew that. Not right now.

I wished you could put boys on layaway.

Still, I was shaking. Not cold anymore, but I couldn't control my muscles.

I needed a minute.

"I'm going to the bathroom," I whispered to Savannah.

"What? We're in the middle of…" she whispered. "Are you alright? You want me to come with?"

"No thanks." I knew it was weird to leave during your own mom's memorial, but I felt like I couldn't breathe if I didn't scurry off for a second. Silence. I needed silence.

I went off toward the indoor mausoleum.

It was stunning. Marble everywhere, quiet, and a fountain in the middle. The only sound was the running water, a gentle, steady swish. I walked to it and peered into the collecting water. It was clean and clear.

"So, this is really happening, huh?" My own voice echoed. No one was around for at least a hundred feet. "I just need to know. Are you here?" I asked Mom. "I know you're not…*here*, here, on Earth anymore. I got it. I understand now. But are you…here?"

I peered into my reflection. Just me. Brown eyes blinking back at me, slightly wet hair falling into my face. I clutched the edges of the scarf so they wouldn't get wet.

"Up there, then?" I looked up instead. "Anywhere?"

Silence. I was waiting for a sign of some sort. A light to flicker. A bird to fly in. A plane to go by, even. Anything.

I'd read about other people seeing signs from their loved ones. Savannah even had dreams. Beautiful dreams that sounded like Mom was speaking right to her.

But not me.

"Are you here?" I asked. I stood completely still, waiting for a noise, a whisper. "With me?"

Nothing.

I took a deep breath from my diaphragm. Of course there was nothing. Because she wasn't here anymore.

I knew it, I really did, but I couldn't stop myself from asking one last time. I needed to know where she was. That she was okay, somewhere beyond time and space. Beyond all the beautiful stars she'd taught us to identify.

How was I supposed to go on without her?

"Okay then. I understand." I looked to my reflection one last time before heading out. As I held the edges of the scarf, I noticed Landon had sewn in a small brown patch on one side with black handwritten pen on it.

It read: *Keep going.*

After the memorial, we talked to my relatives for a bit. I'd been avoiding my aunts, uncles, cousins, and grandparents so long that I'd forgotten how nice it felt to be around them. But in a way, it hurt. Grandpa, Mom's father, looked so much like her. I hugged him tight so that I didn't need to look him in the face anymore and see her older, warped reflection staring back at me. I wondered if he did the same.

And my dad's family. If they knew the truth, would they want to see me anymore? Did my grandparents love me because he thought we shared blood, or did they love me for me? I barely spoke to any of them. I was afraid that if I did, I'd scream the truth.

"She's just upset," my dad's brother told my aunt. It was glaringly obvious they were talking about me. "We'll give her the space she needs. When she's ready, we'll be here."

"I know. I can't imagine how she feels. Poor kid," my aunt said. "I love her and Savannah so much."

I wanted my family to always be my family, but now I saw them through a different lens—I didn't love them any less, I just worried that they'd love *me* less. If they knew, of course.

Savannah was busy talking to Alex, but there was no sign of Landon anywhere. I looked in the crowd, toward the mausoleum. Nowhere.

"Looking for your boytoy?" Savannah waved me over.

"He is not my boytoy," I grumbled. "But, uh, yes."

"He left a few minutes ago to make it to rehearsal," Alex said. Her black combat boots were splattered with mud from the rain.

"Oh." Was it really because he'd had to go, or because of how cruel I'd been a few days ago? It felt like what I'd done was beyond repair. Landon was done with me now. I held one end of the soft scarf tightly in my hand. Had this been his way of saying goodbye?

"Are you going to rehearsal?" I asked Alex. "How come you're not on your way there?"

"This is slightly more important," she said. "I can be late."

"Well… Listen," I said. "I'm going to tell Mr. Tariq that I want to be involved. Even if I'm just painting the set or a spoon in the background with no lines. I want to come to be a part of it."

"Really?" Savannah grinned. "That's great!"

Alex's frown turned into a small, discreet smile. "You're sure? Positive?"

"Yes," I said quickly. "Not tonight, or this weekend. I need some time to…unwind and think. But Monday? On Monday, I am totally ready."

"Perfect," Alex said. "But if you're coming to rehearsal, you'll need a script."

"I'm sure I can get one," I said.

She shrugged her backpack off her shoulder and opened it. "You need this one, specifically." It was marked with blocking notes, and all of Babette's lines were highlighted. "This should be yours. If you want to be Babette, I'll step aside."

I blinked. The shock didn't even register. "What? You got Babette?"

"Yeah, but you're perfect for the part. It's a no-brainer." Alex finally met my gaze. Her dark eyes were red-rimmed. "I know how badly you wanted this all along. If I was a better friend, I would've encouraged you a long time ago, but... I was jealous. Honestly. You're talented. More than you think."

"Alex," I whispered. "I can't take this role from you."

"You're not taking it. I'm giving it."

"Why?" I asked. "Don't do this because of Savannah, or because of my mom. Seriously."

If I was going to have this part, I wanted to have earned it. Not because Alex felt guilty about lying to me.

"I didn't say anything!" Savannah raised her hands in innocence.

"It's not because of her." Alex shook her head. "It's because of you. This should've been yours from the start. I've been thinking about this ever since Mr. Tariq gave me the role. I already asked him, and it's okay."

Apparently, I still had tears left to cry. I thought everything was dried out. "Are you serious?" I whispered.

"Serious." Alex wrapped her arms around me. "I'm so sorry Vi, for everything. I miss your mom so much already."

I squeezed her tight, and years and years of our friendship radiated around us.

"I love you," I whispered. "You're my best friend."

"You're mine too. But I swear to God," she hissed in my ear. "There will be no photographic evidence of me in a fork costume."

CHAPTER TWENTY-SEVEN

FOUR DAYS POST-LOSS – EVENING

That night, I spent time with Dad, Savannah, and Onion. We cried a little, laughed a little, but mostly, we simply were together. I was numb and exhausted from the long day and couldn't wait to get into bed.

Of course, when I did get under my sheets and comforter, I couldn't sleep. My brain was jogging with memories of my mom, of what lay ahead. How I could focus on school, how to tell Dad that he wasn't really my father. Breaking his heart like the paternity test had broken mine seemed especially cruel after today.

And still, I kept thinking of Landon. He'd been there for me, this entire time, and I'd only used him for support and snapped at him. He deserved so much better.

I texted him: Are you awake?

He responded a few minutes later: Wow! My first "u up" text. I am honored. What's up?

I held the phone to my chest. I couldn't figure out his

tone. Was that sarcasm?

Since I'd gotten home, I hadn't taken off the scarf. It was soft and cozy and made me feel like things might actually be okay. The same way I felt around him.

My feet hit the ground. For the first time in a week, energy coursed through my veins. I had an idea. At one in the morning, but an idea was an idea.

Quietly, I scampered into Savannah's room, hoping she would be awake. The darkness coming from under the door said otherwise.

"Sav?" I whispered.

Asleep. Shoot.

Guess I'd have to drive to the McDonald's myself—not that I wanted to make breaking the driving laws a habit. I fished around for the car keys on her desk as quietly as one possibly could with the jingling chains, and snuck them into my purse.

A chocolate milkshake, he'd ordered. And I'd had vanilla. As I snuck down the stairs, I figured I should add fries too. If I could recreate that perfect moment, maybe I could hold it in my hands again.

"Watch the house while I'm gone," I told Mom.

I paused for a moment, and waited for a light to flicker, a dog to bark. Something.

Nothing.

But that was okay.

I opened the door and tiptoed out. I wanted fries so badly that I could practically smell them. The salty, savory—

I smelled fries because there were fries in front of my face.

Landon stood in my front yard, his curly hair tousled and peeking out from his hoodie. He wore a smile, but more importantly, he held two milkshakes—one chocolate, one vanilla.

And french fries.

"How'd you know?" I gasped.

"Know what?" He came closer.

"I was going—never mind. This is for me?" I touched my hand to my heart, blocked by the scarf.

"Of course!" Landon handed the vanilla one to me and sat on my front steps. "Is this okay? I'm sorry it's a little weird. I just felt bad that I had to leave today, and then you texted me that you were awake…"

"This is amazing." I sat next to him and instantly dipped a fry into the shake. I couldn't believe I had gone so many years without doing this. "Don't feel bad. I should feel bad. I texted you because I wanted to apologize."

"No. I should never have said that. I should be the one apologizing."

"Landon, don't worry about it." I shook my head.

"No. I was careless, talking to you about an unimportant musical while you have real, important things going on," he said. "And I'm so sorry about your mom, by the way. Today was a really nice ceremony. I can't imagine how you feel, though…"

"I know. That isn't the point, though." I sighed. Why was being a social human being so hard? You got one shot at all this. Only one. Might as well make it count.

"You were right about everything you said. I was obsessed with proving my mom innocent and fell into this rabbit hole of denial," I said. "I ignored what was really in front of me and what I actually want in my life. I guess I get a pass for this week, but I can't do that forever. So… I'm sorry. I am."

He wrapped his arm around me. He felt sturdy, secure. "The other day, you said something else happened. What's been going on? I was worried about you."

How could I even summarize the last few days? Nothing felt real. Actually, no. It felt way too real. I told him everything. About Dad, Dr. Bryant, even about Alex and Savannah.

I wiped a drop of drizzle from my forehead. Or maybe it was rain from the roof.

"I don't know what to do," I said. "Savannah and I are okay now, and me and Alex made up. But how the hell am I supposed to tell my dad he isn't my biological dad? How can I even do that? It'll break him."

Landon swirled a french fry into his shake, around and around. "That's…a lot."

"Tell me about it."

"I think you know the answer, though," he said. "You have to tell him."

"Do I? I mean, can't I let the guy live in ignorant bliss?"

"You just said it. You've been obsessed with finding the truth," he said. "That's who you are. Now you found the truth. You're not going to be happy unless you face it. All of it."

I thought about how it had felt when I'd found out that Alex and Savannah had lied to me. How they had both knowingly lied to me had made it hurt so much worse, like a bone breaking over and over again. That was what I'd be doing to Dad. Lying every single day would build and build up so that if he ever found out the truth, it would crush him.

Dad deserved better.

I crossed my arms and leaned my head against his shoulder. "I hate that you're right about everything."

"Am I right about this? Yes. Everything in general? Meh… Perhaps." He smirked.

I smirked back and toyed with the scarf. I wondered if, when he looked at it, he saw all its perfect stitches or only the frayed edges.

I only saw beauty.

I looked back at Landon. We held eye contact for a moment so intense I heard my heart thud in my ears. Electricity buzzed between us. I leaned forward and pressed my lips against his. I hadn't exactly pictured our first *real* kiss to involve McDonald's, or to be the night after my mom's memorial. Not perfect, but that was perfect for us non-perfect folks.

His lips came toward mine hesitantly, the same way his arms reached around my lower waist. I wanted to run my fingers through his curly blond hair or even place them on his arms, but I stayed still. I was pulsing in the moment, finally able to simply exist and not be me.

Or maybe it was that Landon's kiss made me *feel* like me. Not pretending to be strong or thinking about anybody else. Just me.

We pulled apart and both our eyes fell to the floor. Electricity lingered on my lips, and the magnetic pull I felt toward him set my body ablaze in the best way. It felt like the first time, only far more real.

"I hope that was okay," he said.

"More than okay."

He leaned in and pressed his forehead against mine. "I think I understand what Lumière feels like now. On fire."

I grinned. "Me too."

We stayed silent for a moment, but then I wrapped my arms around my legs.

"I just… I don't want to lead you on," I said. "I like you so much, but I don't know what I want, or what I need. I'm so confused and still dealing with everything…"

"Take all the time you need," he said. "I'm not going anywhere."

Not going anywhere.

It was exactly what I'd needed to hear.

Finally, I looked up, toward the sky. The stars were dim, but still there. Waving to me, from far, far away.

CHAPTER TWENTY-EIGHT

SIX DAYS POST-LOSS – AFTERNOON

I walked out of rehearsal with Landon on my left and Alex on my right.

I wondered if this was how Alex felt when she walked with Savannah and me. Best friend and crush all in one place. On top of the world.

"*Be our guest! Be our guest!* It's this song that I detest," Alex sang.

"'Be Our Guest' is a great song!" Landon said.

"Yeah, because you sing the whole thing," Alex said.

Around us, our castmates got into their cars. The seniors and juniors got into their own, while the sophomores and freshmen piled into their parents' cars.

"Would you like a ride home, both of you?" Landon offered.

"I have a car," Alex said. "Thanks, though. By the way, I heard about that whole kissy thing. If you break my friend's heart, I'll break your candlestick."

"Wow." I shook my head.

"Nice metaphor, Alex. I won't," he said. "But please don't break my candlestick. Or refer to it as such."

"Fine," she said. "Whose car are you riding in, Violet?"

A car honked in the distance. I ignored it at first, figuring it was someone else in the cast, but it honked again. As it came closer, I recognized the blue Accord.

Dad?

He waved to me from the driver's seat.

"Guess I found my ride," I said. "See you both tomorrow."

I climbed into the passenger seat. "Did I call you? I don't remember asking for a ride. Sorry. I could've gotten one."

"Nope," he said. "Your teacher called me the other day. I've been here waiting. Wanted to make sure you had a ride."

"You've been waiting this whole time?" Sunday rehearsals were always long. At least four hours to learn all the music and blocking. I'd gotten to join the cast in going over all the songs, and stayed behind to paint.

"Yep," he said. "I notice you're with that boy."

"You know who he is, Dad."

"Yes. A Mets fan."

I rolled my eyes.

"I have something for you." Dad nodded toward the space under the glove compartment. There was a white paper bag that I recognized instantly—the local art store. Greedily, I grabbed the bag and opened it.

Inside was a set of beautiful natural-bristle paintbrushes. The kind with the soft, light-brown tips and durable handles. The kind that would cost me about ten hours at the pickle store to save up for. Next to them, there was an array of five colors of acrylic paint.

"Dad," I whispered. "You didn't need to."

"I hope they're the right kind. The lady in the store helped me."

I turned to look at him. "How'd you know?"

He didn't look away from the road. "I know everything."

"Savannah told you, didn't she?"

At first, I flared with anger at my sister. That was supposed to be between us; our moment. How dare she? Then I realized, no. She hadn't betrayed me at all. She was doing exactly what she had to in order to protect me.

"I'd much rather you pick up one of these when you feel pissed, okay?" he said. "Paint me a picture of Onion or something."

I looked to my wrists with shame boiling on my cheeks. This whole time, I thought I'd hidden everything. That it was my secret. But apparently, nothing was mine and mine alone.

It was helpful and horrible all at the same time. All my secrets were exposed, but it also meant I had help. I didn't need to hide anymore.

"It's hard," I whispered. "I don't do it on purpose."

"I know, sweetheart." Dad pulled into our driveway. No vans, no cameras. The media had moved on once they had realized there was no villain in this story. "From now on, you tell me when you want to hurt yourself. Or tell Savannah. Or even tell that Mets fan. Okay?" He turned to look at me with absolute sincerity in his eyes.

"I promise." And I meant it, too.

Dad turned off the car and led me back into the house with his arm around me. We walked in step, left then right.

"Dad knows all," he said. "If you try to lie to me, I'll know about it."

He started for the stairs, but his words rang in me like the ticking of a clock.

"Wait," I whispered.

Dad turned to face me.

I brought him over to the couch. The TV was on but muted. It showed footage of workers cleaning up the wreckage of Puerto Rico. The houses hadn't been rebuilt yet, but slowly, the carnage was being restored to what it once had been.

"I... I love you," I told him. "But I might not be your actual daughter."

I braced. Braced for impact.

"Yeah." He placed his hands in his pockets. His face didn't change. "I know."

Our cuckoo clock chimed. Jack Skellington popped out once more in his black-and-white pinstriped suit. I hardly registered the sound. I was way too focused on Dad.

"You know?"

I mentally retraced my steps. I'd put the letters away in the far back of my closet, buried underneath clothes and shoes. He'd never look in there. I was positive I'd never let the paternity test letter see the light of day, either. When all this was over, I'd planned on using the fireplace in Alex's house to burn it. Savannah, maybe?

"I always had a feeling," he said, "I knew about the affair the first time. I let it go because she was pregnant and I wanted us to be a family. But as you grew up, I wondered... It's uncommon to get brown eyes from two blue-eyed parents."

"It happens," I offered.

"Certainly," he said. "But not often. You look a little like him, and to be honest... I just knew. It was a feeling."

I looked to the rug. He'd known the whole time. Yet

he'd still bought me paintbrushes. Expensive ones, when we didn't have the money. Through the years, I'd never had any idea. Not until that paper had told me so. But he'd known the entire time.

"You never asked her to be sure?"

"Why would I? It doesn't matter to me, Violet," he said. "You're still my daughter. I love you the same as if I'd birthed you myself."

I rolled my eyes. "Dad."

I threw my arms around him and clung tight. Through all the uncertainty, through everything, Dad was there.

"Genetics suck," I said.

"True." Dad held me close.

With him, I was happy. I felt it in my bones, in my DNA.

CHAPTER TWENTY-NINE

Two Months Later

Opening night started exactly the way it should have; me, Alex, and Savannah walking into the theater together.

I walked in front, sunglasses on, and Alex and Savannah trailed behind me like the stars of some eighties teen movie.

"Can someone pull a tarot for me?" Alex asked. "I'm curious how this night is going to go."

"It's going to be great." Savannah took her hand and laced their fingers.

"You promise you'll record my dance solo?" she asked.

"What about no evidence of you as a fork?" I asked.

"I need footage to show colleges, duh," Alex said. "I'll pull some nonsense about how being in the ensemble made me a stronger person in the end."

"Did it?" I asked.

"Fork no," Alex said. "I'm serious, though. Let's do a tarot."

"Okay, okay, fine," I said. "I'll pull one before we get in the dressing room."

"What, you don't want Laaaandon to see you yet?" Alex teased.

We were taking it slow. I wasn't ready for a full-on relationship, but he was pretty hard to resist. We went on dates, and we kissed—a lot. But yeah, slow.

"Shut up, no. I just want to get it over with," I said.

"Then get it over with." She took the deck of cards from her purse and held them out to me.

The three of us stopped walking. I studied the pretty tie-dye pattern on the back before I chose one. They all looked the same to me, but one felt right. I'd been trying to listen to the tiny voice in my head more. Be more connected with, well, me.

"The World," Alex said. "And you chose it upright!"

"And that means…"

"Fulfillment, harmony, completion." She smirked.

I crossed my arms. For such a long time, those three words had felt intangible to me. Now, though, I could maybe hold on to them.

"I like it," Savannah said. "Can I do one?"

"Anything for you, princess." Alex shuffled the cards and chose one. "Oh look! This one says you're dating a cool person and you have to bring me to California with you."

Savannah had been accepted to Stanford with a partial scholarship and a personal letter from the Admissions head. It had said they would be happy to have someone as strong and courageous as she was join their class of 2026.

Savannah laughed and took Alex's hand. Alex reached over and kissed her. They held it for a moment, like no one was in the hallway but them.

Cute, I hated to admit it.

"Uh…okay."

We all turned to find Dad standing there. He held a plastic bag of my stage makeup, which I'd apparently left in the car. The four of us stood there in silence for at least five, six full seconds.

"I came to return this." He handed me the baggie, then waved his hand toward Alex and Savannah. "Is this a thing now?"

Alex's shoulder slacked like she was about to let go of Savannah's hand, but Savannah tightened her grip.

"Yes," she responded quietly. She looked at him the same way she'd looked at me when I'd opened my letters from Mom; eyes wide with fear that her life was about to be shattered.

I held my breath. Even though I knew Dad was awesome, that he wouldn't care, I was tense. We all were. It probably wasn't the way she'd wanted to tell him.

"Is that cool, Mr. Ashby? I promise I'll treat her right, never make her sad, never leave her on read. I'll have her home by midnight when we go out," Alex said. "I even have a perfect driving record."

"A perfect driving record isn't impressive when you got your license two months ago, but okay." Dad rolled his eyes. "Have her home by eleven and you have yourself a deal."

Hence why my dad was the coolest.

"You have two gay daughters, yay!" I clapped.

"I always told your mother she watched too much Ellen DeGeneres when she was pregnant." Dad ruffled my hair. "Okay, see you guys on stage. I'm going to get M&Ms. Sav, I'll get you a Kit Kat."

"That went better than I thought." Savannah exhaled once he was out of earshot.

"Nah, that's Dad," I said. "He always has our back."

I truly believed it. I knew she did too.

. . .

Act One was fantastic so far.
The audience was laughing when they were supposed
to, and I knew they were absolutely in love with the
characters. Especially Lumière. Who wouldn't be?

I felt alive out there. When I spoke, people listened.
Telling the story and making them laugh made me feel
powerful. Made me feel like me. I couldn't believe I'd
denied myself this opportunity for years and years because
of something as ridiculous as fear.

Landon and I stood shoulder to shoulder in the dark
in the wings. Our big scene was coming up, and I knew
the audience would love him. Love us. I reached over
and laced our fingers. There was no one I'd rather do this
adventure with.

"Is your family here?" I whispered.

"Yeah," he said. "They really want to meet you after
the show. Is that cool?"

"I'd love that."

"Is your dad here?" Landon asked.

"He is," I whispered.

I knew I shouldn't have, but I peeked my head out. No
one was paying attention to me anyway. Belle was belting
her heart out and doing a damn fine job—despite what
Alex might have said.

Dad and Savannah sat front and center. Savannah had
magic in her eyes, appeared transfixed by the ensemble
beginning the steps of "Be Our Guest". It seemed like she
was focused on a particular utensil. Alex knew every step,
and every beat had grace and enthusiasm. Even Dad seemed
amused, bopping his foot and eating his packet of candy.

And in the back row — Dr. Bryant. I told him I was never going to take a DNA test, and he wasn't my father as far as I was concerned, but I still emailed him back and forth a few times. I even visited once. He was someone who loved my mom, who knew things and stories about her that I didn't, and I wasn't ready to lose that connection.

He seemed to be enjoying the show.

"Ready to go?" Landon whispered.

Right as I was about to turn back to him, something caught my eye.

I swore, in the seat next to Savannah, I saw Mom. While everyone else stared at the cast, she was looking right at me. She moved a piece of her short blond hair to get a better look at me. Her smile was wide, teeth perfectly straight, and she wore her red lipstick. She was in her uniform, the hat tucked neatly in place, and her golden wings fixed to her jacket.

"Mom?" I whispered.

But when I blinked, she was gone.

The seat was empty. Dust from the stage lights remained floating in the air where she was, like glitter.

"Violet? You ready?" Landon whispered again.

"I am."

I took his hand and stepped forward onto the stage. The warm lights welcomed me. Confidence soared within me.

Mom was going to see me shine after all.

END

ACKNOWLEDGMENTS

First, I'd like to thank you, the reader. It means so much that you've chosen to read this! In this book's journey, I could not have done it without these people below:

I don't have the words to properly thank my editor, Jen Bouvier. You made my dream come true when I was so close to giving up. You "got" this book in ways I dreamed a reader would, and you made it better in the way I dreamed an editor could. A million times, thank you. I am forever grateful.

Big thank you to my agent, Moe Ferrara. Thank you for believing in me and for your words of wisdom! I know I'm in good hands with you.

Thank you to all the crew at Entangled who brought this book into the world, including Stacy Abrams, Curtis Svelhak, Meredith Johnson, Amarilys Acosta, Heather Riccio, Bree Archer, Lydia Sharp, Elizabeth Turner Stokes for my gorgeous cover, Jeannie Knott, Rae Swain, and Hilary Shelby.

Thank you to Katie McCoach—you were the first publishing person to believe in me. You gave me confidence, and I will never forget that.

My Scribiophile/Ubergroup "Weeping Kiddies", especially Brenda Baker, Maggie Stough, and Laura Reynolds. You all helped me get started as a writer and form my craft.

My PitchWars family, the "Slackers"—I can't believe how lucky I am to have such a supportive group of writer friends. Your support has guided me through so many publishing and life challenges. I am so thankful for you all: Alexis Ames, Ruby Barrett, Chad Lucas, Elvin Bala, LL Montez, Jen Klug, Jessica Lewis, Rosie Danan, Leslie Gail, Lyssa Mia Smith, Mary Roach, Meg Long, Meryl Wilsner, Nanci Schwartz, Rachel Morris, Rochelle Hassan, and Susan Lee.

Thanks to FBI Agent Raymond Hall for helping me with details around Agent Rosenfield and the case investigation.

To the libraries that let me read voraciously and inspired me as a teenager—especially the Harrison Public Library in Harrison, NY, and the NYPL Midtown location.

Thanks to my family and friends for their support, and specifically to my Uncle Johnny for giving me laptops as a kid that allowed me to discover that I love writing.

Thank you to my amazing parents, who always support me and my creative pursuits. I hope reading this book was better than sitting through Faustus. Your excitement about and pride in this book means so so much. I'm lucky to have you both. Thanks for all you do.

To my cat, Zoe, who is always there for me. I know you won't see this, since you don't know how to read, but we will work on that.

Lastly, thank you to Kevin. Thank you for always knowing my books would be out there in the world, and for your constant love and encouragement. You are everything.

Don't miss the first book in the hottest new series of the year from #1 New York Times bestselling author Alyson Noël

Turn the page for a sneak peek...

1

A Southern California High School
Present day

"God, I hate this place."

Mason shakes his head and mashes a plastic fork into a clump of avocado, quinoa, sweet potato, and some silky white block I'm guessing is tofu. I recognize it as one of the more popular Buddha bowls from the vegan café where we work. But to me, it looks like the adult version of baby food.

"I mean, what messed-up twist of fate landed me here?" He sweeps an elegant brown arm past the row of vending machines and the hot-lunch station of our school's cafeteria, his collection of silver bangles clattering softly, before pausing on the tables reserved for the popular kids. The same tables where I used to sit, back when I was another girl, living another life. "I'm ninety-nine percent certain I was switched at birth, and now I'm trapped in someone else's dystopian nightmare."

I pick at my bag of vending machine chips, remembering how I used to play that game, too, until my mom unearthed my birth certificate and waved it proudly before me. *"See?"* she said, face flushed with triumph as she dragged a chipped nail across her name and my dad's just below it. *"Like it or not, we made you."*

I shut myself in my room and cried all afternoon.

"Just take me away. Anywhere but here." Mason abandons his lunch and stretches leisurely across the bench. With an arm draped over his face, I'm left with a view of perfectly drawn red lips, reminding me of an actress in a black-and-white movie badly in need of some smelling salts. "Draw me a picture with words," he pleads. "We're in Paris," I say, not missing a beat. It's one of our favorite games. "We have the very best table at the chicest sidewalk café, and we death stare anyone who dares to dress better than us. Which is basically no one, since I'm wearing a silk slip dress with a faux-fur stole and jeweled biker boots, and you're practically swimming in an elaborately embroidered tunic, vegan suede leggings, and five-inch blue velvet mules."

"And what are we eating?" he prompts, licking his lips.

Since I'm not exactly a foodie like him, I stick with the basics. "I'm idly picking at a chocolate croissant while you nurse a dairy-free but remarkably creamy café au lait that somehow never goes cold no matter how long we linger."

"Do you ever miss it?" He sits up so abruptly, it yanks me right out of Paris and back to our suburban hellscape of boring cinderblock buildings. "You know, being part of all that?" He sweeps a hand over his shaved head and nods toward the place where I used to sit—before I ended up next to the recycle bin.

"No," I say, quick to turn away so he won't see the lie on my face. While I don't miss the table or the people who sit there, I do miss the person I used to be—the one who cared about my grades, the one who dreamed of a brighter future beyond these beige hallways.

I'm about to add something more when Mason groans and starts gathering his things. "All hail the queen," he says, and I look up to see Elodie approaching. "I can't believe you're still hanging with her."

I watch as Elodie makes her way across the cafeteria. Like a celebrity on a red carpet, so many people clamor for her attention, the trip takes much longer than it should.

"She's fun." I shrug. "And she has access to some pretty amazing things. VIP guest lists, courtside seats to the—"

"To the Lakers?" Mason shoots me a razor-sharp look. "Since when do you give a shit about sports?"

"I'm just saying…maybe you should give her a chance."

Mason shakes his head. "Trust me, I know a bad vibe when I see it, and that girl is trouble." He slings his knock-off designer bag over his shoulder, wanting to be gone before she can reach us.

"Sometimes trouble is fun." I laugh, needing to lighten the mood. But the way Mason scowls, it clearly didn't work.

"Magic always comes with a price," he says.

"Are you seriously quoting Rumpelstiltskin?"

"Just stating the facts. Someday all this *fun* is going to catch up with you. If it hasn't already."

"And now you're quoting my mom," I grumble, but then I remember how he met my mom the one time he showed up at my house unannounced. "Well, someone's mom."

"It's not too late." His earnest brown eyes meet mine. "You can still turn it around, get your grades back on track. So why are you acting like the choice isn't yours, like you're not the one who writes your own story?"

He's right, of course. But what he doesn't understand is that I'm nothing like him.

Mason lives with his grandma, and what she lacks in money, she makes up for in her determination to help him succeed. His grades count toward his future—they'll pave the way to a brighter life in a much better place.

I could be valedictorian and it wouldn't change a thing. I can't go off to college because I can't leave my mom. She's completely dependent on me.

As Elodie closes in, she sings out my name— "*Natashaaaaaa.*"

I really need her to stop calling me that. Natasha is the before picture of my life. The name given by a mom who dreamed of her baby girl's shiny future.

Nat is who I became after my dad ran off and never came back, leaving my mom too depleted to bother with the extra syllables.

Mason mumbles something about texting me later, then bolts before I can try to convince him to stay. It's the deal we agreed on. He'll (mostly) stop talking trash about her if I stop bugging him to give her a chance.

I know I should follow him before it's too late, but I find myself turning toward Elodie instead. And when she waves, and I watch her face break into a grin, I secretly smile to myself, pretending not to notice all the envious looks directed my way as the coolest girl in school sings out my name.

2

"*Na—ta—sha!*" Elodie drags out each syllable. Her face flushed, eyes lit, she stands before me in all her teenage dream glory.

"*Elodie Blue,*" I reply, trying to match her tone, only I'm way off-key. Still, it sounds like a stage name, totally false. Her mom must have been an even bigger dreamer than mine.

Better at it, too, considering how her dream came true.

I lower my gaze past the prominent cheekbones and the sort of perfect pillowy lips people pay good money for, and onto what actually interests me—her clothes. One of the perks of hanging out with her: fashionable by association.

My mom used to joke (back when she still joked) that I went straight from reading Dr. Seuss to devouring *Vogue*. I love high fashion, design, art, artifice. Just because I can't afford it doesn't mean I don't fantasize about the day when a pair of thousand-dollar heels and the perfect shade of lipstick will transport me into a whole new existence.

Elodie catches me looking. "You can borrow it anytime. Say the word and it's yours."

The weird thing is, I know she means it. Elodie acquires as quickly as she discards. Though sometimes I wonder just how much longer before she grows bored of me and drops me as easily as the silk duster she's offering.

She starts to slip it from her shoulders, but I wave it away. On her tall, willowy, runway-ready frame, the slouchy piece she's paired with a white ribbed tank top and faded jeans looks breezy and effortless. On my five-foot-three inches (in heels), it would look like I went to school in my bathrobe.

She loops her arm through mine and leads me past the row of lockers sporting a fresh coat of paint that fails to hide the most recent graffiti scandal. "Check it out—" Elodie taps a ring-stacked finger against the locker. "If you look closely, you can still see the word 'dick.'"

I roll my eyes and start to speed up, until Elodie catches hold of my sleeve. "What's the hurry?" she says. "You're not actually going to class?"

At first glance, with her fairy-tale blond hair, creamy white skin, pert little nose, valentine of a mouth, and flashing blue eyes, Elodie resembles an earnest cartoon princess. But I know from experience that Mason is right— she's exactly the sort of "bad influence" your parents warn you about.

"If I ditch, I fail." Seconds after I've said it, the final bell trills, sending the rest of the stragglers dashing for their classrooms, leaving just Elodie, me, and a deserted school hallway.

"Correction." She grins. "You're already failing, and now you're getting a tardy as well. Also, we both know you're not working today, so come." Another tug on my sleeve. "I know a club where we're guaranteed free admission—probably even free drinks if you're willing to ditch that bulky hoodie."

"Seriously—a club?" I check the time. "At one thirty?" My voice pitches high, making me sound as outraged as my mom when the phone rings while she's watching TV.

"That's what makes it exclusive." Elodie laughs. "Maybe this will convince you?"

She hands me her cell so I can squint at a picture of a boy with features so perfectly sculpted, I'm sure it's thanks to some serious filter abuse. Still, there's a slight hitch in my breath as I linger on his sweep of dark hair and those navy-blue eyes. For some reason, he strikes me as familiar, but that's probably because he reminds me of the kind of boy I once knew in my former popular-table life.

"His name is Brax." She snatches the phone away and flings it into her bag. "He wants to meet you."

"Um, yeah. Super believable, El." I shake my head. "You're telling me that guy—that face-tuned pixel jaw—" I motion toward her bag as though he lives there with the tubes of lip gloss and breath mints. "Wants to meet *me*?"

"You up for it?" She smiles excitedly.

Even though I recognize the con, given the choice between the disapproving glare of my history teacher and some sketchy afternoon club with a boy whose face is too good to be true…there's really no contest.

Textbook history is basically the memorization of places, dates, and highly sanitized tales of old white men accomplishing heroic feats. It's an unrelatable bore of a class that's better used for napping.

Still, she doesn't even give me a chance to respond. She just bolts down the hall, yelling, "Race you!"

I remain fixed in place, watching Elodie sprint through the quad as she heads for the gate as though the usual school rules don't apply to her.

I wish I could explain my connection to her, or why I keep ignoring Mason's advice. All I know is that for the last few years, he's pretty much been my only true friend—

and up until she came along, it felt like enough.

But then one random Wednesday, Elodie Blue showed up at our school and from that moment on, everything changed.

I remember watching in awe as she made her way across campus. She was so confident, so effortlessly cool. In other words, the exact opposite of me. And I have to admit, I was totally starstruck.

Of course, Mason disliked her from the start, claiming he could see right through her shiny facade to the layers of moldering rot. I think he even referred to her as a future cult leader, junkie runway model, and crooked politician, all rolled into one.

But for me, Elodie was like the living, breathing embodiment of everything I aspired toward but could never manage to be.

Within days, the whole school was obsessed. And yet, despite the number of kids who'd be willing to risk their perfect GPAs to play hooky with her, she chose me.

Maybe it's because she knew I was already so far along on my own downward spiral that she couldn't be blamed for jeopardizing my future.

Maybe it really is like she's said, that I'm smarter than most, prettier than I think, and not afraid to take a few risks.

At the time, I brushed it off and mumbled some botched version of a Janis Joplin quote about freedom and having nothing to lose.

None of that was true, of course. When you have as little as I do, you can't afford to lose a single thing.

"C'mon!" Elodie cries, her voice competing with the one in my head warning me to go to class and get my life back on track.

If I don't follow that voice, I'll be solely to blame for whatever comes next.

With my heart about to explode in my chest, I ignore the voice and race to catch up.

A blast of thunder cracks overhead as a bank of clouds bursts open and unleashes a downpour.

Immediately, I duck my chin and yank my hood up.

Elodie, of course, does just the opposite.

Tossing her head back, she flings her arms wide as though she loves getting drenched. Next thing I know, the gate screeches open, and Elodie makes a run for her car.

With my feet splashing behind her, I race to catch up.

3

"I thought we were going to a club?" I glance between Elodie and the parking attendant who's simultaneously holding the passenger door and motioning toward the curb as though he doesn't think I can find it on my own. Elodie is the only person I know who will give it her all in spin class, only to valet park at the mall.

Without a word, she grabs me by the arm and drags me into some big, glitzy department store with gleaming white marble floors and the kind of aspirational price tags that are way out of my orbit.

"So I'm guessing the club is hidden in some sort of password-protected dressing room?" I release myself from her grip. "Or maybe a secret basement beneath the MAC counter?"

"Look—" Elodie turns on me so quickly, the toes of my Chucks bump against hers. "I don't know how to say this politely so I'm just going to say it." She places her hands on her hips and inhales a theatrical breath. "You need a new look."

I blink. She's right—that wasn't the least bit polite.

"I'm not trying to be mean, but for someone who's supposedly so into fashion, it's strange how you don't even try to look cute." Her finger traces a line from my ratty hoodie, to my baggy jeans, down to my worn Converse sneakers. "It's like you're purposely trying to sabotage yourself. And honestly, Natasha, I just want to help."

I breathe my own version of a theatrical sigh and shove right past her, pausing before a display of designer sunglasses that cost nearly a quarter of the monthly mortgage my dad stuck us with. But I try a pair anyway, just for kicks.

"Rumor has it you used to put in an effort. But I'm not sure I believe it."

"Understandable," I say. "I mean, why would you?" I switch the glasses for a pair with exaggerated square frames and lean toward the mirror. At first, I chose them as a joke, but now I'm thinking I like them. I slide them off and check the price.

Maybe in another life, with another bank account.

"But then I saw a yearbook from when you were a freshman."

I reach for another pair, mirrored and round. They don't fit my face, but they do hide my eyes, buying me enough time to prepare for what's next.

I know exactly where this is going. The one person who's never seen the Natasha version of me is now fully caught up with what the rest of the senior class has known all along: My freshman and senior years appear to belong to two different people.

"Not only were you smokin', but you were also voted ninth grade homecoming princess, class president, and you were rocking the honor roll."

I gape at her, fuming. It's not like my A-list past was a secret, but why the hell is Elodie checking up on me?

"I mean, it's a pretty dramatic shift, and I'm curious how it happened." She reaches for my wrist. There's genuine concern in her gaze, but the story of my downfall is not up for discussion.

"*Nothing* happened," I say.

Elodie's blue eyes fix on mine, searching for the truth she's sure I'm holding back. The smoking gun—the single, cataclysmic event that kick-started my descent. But the thing is, it was nothing like that.

I mean, it's not like anyone *died*.

It's not like my life imploded overnight.

It was more of a gradual decline. A small series of events that caused poverty, depression, and hopelessness to roll through my house like a virus, spreading first to my mom and then to me.

For a while, I tried to keep up appearances. But it wasn't long before the divide between me and pretty much everyone else at my school caused me to fall further and further behind until there was no point in trying.

What looks like failure is just self-preservation. I save my energy for my after-school job because we need the money. And since no one's paying me to take a history exam, it doesn't top my list of priorities.

Still, I'm disappointed in Elodie. She's supposed to be the one person who allows me to tune out from my regularly scheduled life so I can indulge in a little fantasy and fun. If she's looking to switch it up and act like my life coach, then maybe she should embrace her new role and take me back to school where I belong.

"Is this supposed to be an intervention?" I say. "Because I'd rather go clubbing." I peel her fingers away from my arm and return the sunglasses to the slot where I found them. "I mean, you can't have it both ways, El. You're either my partner in crime or my guidance counselor."

"Fine." She snatches the square frames and calls for a salesperson. "But like it or not, you're getting a makeover. Because this"—she shakes a disapproving finger at my hoodie— "is not going to fly where we're going."

4

We're outside. My long brown hair, stripped of its usual frizzy ponytail, has been coaxed into soft waves that fall around my newly made-up face, while my dress exposes way more thigh than the shorts I wear in PE.

"I feel like *Pretty Woman*," I say, referring to my mom's all-time favorite movie, which is basically some old-school story about an escort who gets a makeover from a rich client when he plucks her off a street corner.

When my mom decided I was finally old enough to watch it with her, she spent the entire movie either grinning giddily or anxiously clutching a damp tissue to her lips like the ending might change from the previous hundred or so viewings. By the time the final credits rolled, I guess she thought my own untouched box of tissues meant I didn't understand, because she tried to explain.

"But look!" she cried, rewinding to the part where the sex worker and the corporate raider ride away in a limo. "She saves him right back!"

Which I guess, in her mind, made up for the fact that this woman had to change literally everything about herself to be good enough for some dude. Yeah, no thanks.

"It's a seriously badass makeover." Elodie shakes me away from my thoughts and back to the present. "And the best part is, you don't even have to blow me in return."

I tug at the hem and frown. Makeover ethics aside, it's been a long time since I allowed myself to actually try to look pretty, and the effect is simultaneously aspirational and disturbing.

Like, one part of me is thinking: *Yes, this is who you are meant to be!*

While the other side insists: *You are never going to get away with this.*

"Honestly?" I say. "I feel…kinda weird."

My arms hang awkwardly by my sides, like I've forgotten how to use them. Between the dress, the shoes, the sunglasses, the makeup, and the new bra that makes my breasts appear way bigger than they actually are, Elodie has made a major investment, and she doesn't even seem to care that I can never repay her.

"Thanks," I say. "Really." I mean, it's the right thing to do when someone spends a bundle on you and asks nothing in return.

She waves at my reflection in the window before us. I wave back at hers. Elodie didn't get a makeover, mostly because she didn't need one. She just swapped her tank top for a silk cami and her sneakers for strappy heels.

Still, it's the first time I've ever stood beside her and felt like an equal.

So I decide to seize the moment and act like one, too.

I cock my hip, shake my hair, and adopt a vacant expression, like a girl in a misogynistic music video. Elodie responds with a raised brow and tilted grin that can only be described as mischievous, if I used words like that.

"Ready to venture into the vast unknown?" She hooks her arm through mine.

I run my gaze up the length of the building—a block of mirrored panes stretching from the sidewalk to the bank of gray clouds overhead. It's the kind of place filled with people who followed all the rules and did all the right things, only to end up slack-faced and numb, trudging through the calendar in pursuit of the weekend.

"I ditched my hoodie for this?"

Elodie throws her head back and laughs, then marches me toward the building next door, which is notably shorter, darker, and the few windows it has are painted all black.

"Oh, and one more thing." She presses something hard and rectangular into my palm. "It's members only. Just follow my lead."

The plastic card bears a picture of me that I know I never posed for, mostly because I'm wearing a top I don't own.

"Either magic or Photoshop." Elodic winks. "You be the judge."

I stare at the ID again. Apparently, I'm approaching my one-year anniversary since becoming a member.

"Arcana?" I glance between the name of the club and her. For some reason, the word feels like it's tugging at my brain. But Elodie's already approaching the bouncer and flashing her card, so I bury the thought and follow along, whispering to myself, "What the hell is this place?"

Although Violet is an eternal optimist and her story is full of hope, *The Gravity of Missing Things* contains some difficult themes and elements that might not be suitable for some readers. These include: divorce, leukemia, therapy, funerals, cheating, mention of suicide, hospitals, anxiety, panic attacks, racial profiling, potential aircraft crashes, and occasional self-harm. Readers who may be sensitive to these, please take note.

Discover the heartbreaking and wryly funny book
Publishers Weekly *called "refreshing" and "real"*

SICK KIDS in LOVE

HANNAH MOSKOWITZ

Isabel has one rule: no dating.

It's easier—

It's safer—

It's better—

—for the other person.

She's got issues. She's got secrets. She's got rheumatoid arthritis.

But then she meets another sick kid.

He's got a chronic illness Isabel's never heard of, something she can't even pronounce. He understands what it means to be sick. He understands her more than her healthy friends. He understands her more than her own father who's a doctor.

He's gorgeous, fun, and foul-mouthed. And totally into her.

Isabel has one rule: no dating.

It's complicated—

It's dangerous—

It's never felt better—

—to consider breaking that rule for him.

He has no idea what happened when Molly
disappeared…but that could be a lie…

we told six lies

VICTORIA SCOTT

Remember how many lies we told, Molly? It's enough to make my head spin. You were wild when I met you, and I was mad for you. But then something happened. And now you're gone.

But don't worry. I'll find you. I just need to sift through the story of us to get to where you might be. I've got places to look, and a list of names.

The police have a list of names, too. See now? There's another lie. There is only one person they're really looking at, Molly.

And that's yours truly.